"My daugh… doorstep this…

"Betsey is well?" Sandor inquired.

"Not Betsey. Victoria—Ria, as she asked to be called."

Ah. The demon child. Destroyer of families. Sandor had been told the story one night when he and Cleo were both working late after the shop had closed. He understood how much Victoria had devastated this woman who was his friend. "What does she want?"

"I'm not sure. Shelter, perhaps. Probably money, as well." Cleo cast him a glance. "She has a little boy. They were both filthy and hungry. They've been living in her car for God knows how long."

Then she studied the ground, her voice barely audible. "He looks like David."

Now Sandor understood why Cleo was upset.

Dear Reader,

This is the second of a two-book set written in an unusual format: the same flow of events mirrored in both books, but viewed from the very different vantage points of opposing sides. It began in January with *Coming Home*, the story of Cleo and Malcolm Channing, whose lives and family were shattered by the death of their youngest child, the responsibility for which rests squarely on the shoulders of their troubled daughter, Victoria. Now we hear Ria's side of the story—the prodigal who has returned home only for the sake of her beloved son. But the family she ran away from six years ago no longer exists, and she is devastated by the knowledge that she is the cause.

Sandor Wolfe is a man with dreams too long denied and plans under way to change that. Cleo has given him a new start, and there is nothing he wouldn't do for her, including defending her from the daughter who had caused her so much pain. But he doesn't expect Ria to be so vulnerable or to touch his heart so strongly. A man of great compassion, he treads a difficult course to honor his debt to Cleo while helping Ria find the path not only to her parents' forgiveness but to a means to forgive herself.

I was so in love with Cleo and Malcolm when writing their story that I didn't expect Ria to speak to me so deeply. I hope you, too, will find yourself admiring her courage and cheering her in her struggle as she seeks to prove that the child she once was is not the woman she wants to become.

As always, I love hearing from readers, via my Web site (www.jeanbrashear.com) or www.eHarlequin.com. For postal mail: P.O. Box 3000 #79, Georgetown, TX 78627.

All my best,

Jean Brashear

JEAN BRASHEAR

FORGIVENESS

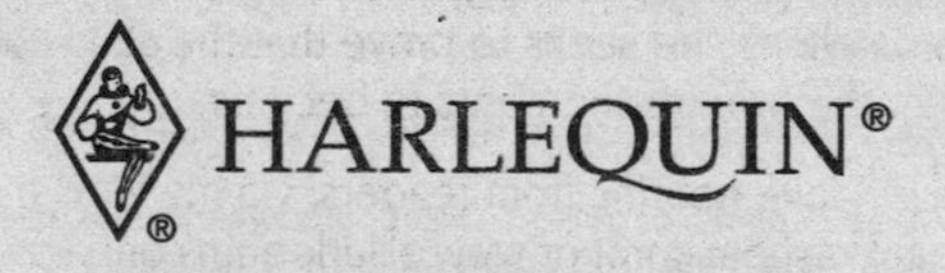

TORONTO • NEW YORK • LONDON
AMSTERDAM • PARIS • SYDNEY • HAMBURG
STOCKHOLM • ATHENS • TOKYO • MILAN • MADRID
PRAGUE • WARSAW • BUDAPEST • AUCKLAND

ISBN 0-373-71267-7

FORGIVENESS

This edition published by arrangement with Harlequin Books S.A.

www.eHarlequin.com

Printed in U.S.A.

To Marcie and Mike, with great admiration and wholehearted best wishes on the very happy occasion of your wedding. May your years together be many more in number, every one of them rich with abiding love, sparkling laughter, robust health and all manner of good fortune.

ACKNOWLEDGMENTS

My thanks to Debbie Dirckx-Norris, Lawrence Watt Evans and Ronn Kaiser for invaluable assistance in building Sandor's background in Hungary, and to Sarah Samson, reference librarian extraordinaire, for her help with researching past immigration matters. Any errors made or liberties taken are most definitely my own.

Books by Jean Brashear

HARLEQUIN SUPERROMANCE

1071—WHAT THE HEART WANTS
1105—THE HEALER
1142—THE GOOD DAUGHTER
1190—A REAL HERO
1219—MOST WANTED
1251—COMING HOME

CHAPTER ONE

September

THE FIRST THOUSAND MILES out of L.A., Ria Channing spun tales of thrilling adventures in store for her bright-eyed four-year-old son, Benjy.

The next five hundred, she tried to convince herself.

The last leg of the endless trip, head achy and light from denying herself food so her child could eat, Ria alternated between terror and fury.

It won't work, Dog Boy. You shouldn't have made me promise. My parents have never forgiven me, and that won't change. The wrong child had died six years ago, the golden one, David. The Son.

But her only friend was beyond hearing now.

Unfortunately, she could still hear him.

Go home. Make...your peace, he'd gasped. Carrot curls, dark with sweat. Pale eyes fever-shiny.

The mere thought of returning had her blood roaring in her ears. *I can't. They hate me.*

Your son has no father. Benjy needs...family. Safe... place. Go home, Ria, back to Austin. Promise.

You don't understand what you're asking. After a lifetime of mistakes, I committed the final, unpardonable one—I killed their favorite.

Try, Ria. Give them a chance. Grant yourself one.

She'd wanted so badly to ignore him. To run away. Again.

But she owed him everything. He'd saved her life. Preserved her son's.

On the long-ago night, she'd fled from home with no idea of her destination. At the Austin bus station, she'd met Dog Boy, who was headed to L.A. Though barely seventeen to her twenty-one, he was streetwise beyond his age; he'd been her mentor, teaching her how to maneuver through a world her protected existence had never even imagined. He'd been brother and friend and father when no one else cared.

At his bedside six weeks ago, she'd pleaded again, but his eyes had been merciless in those final moments; he knew the strength of her love for him. They'd never been physically intimate; their bond was far closer than that. The only person she cherished more was the boy now asleep in the backseat, surrounded by their pitiful few belongings.

Damn you. She'd smiled as tears rolled down her cheeks. *You couldn't ask for ice cream or a mariachi band?*

The fear was back now, full force, as she navigated the tree-shaded streets in the early-morning hours. Temptation grinned and lured...taunted and seduced, willing her to fail Dog Boy, as she'd let down everyone else.

Her breath was coming in pants, her heart beating too fast as she rolled up to the curb across from the house where she'd grown up.

Two-story, Victorian, exquisite. Wraparound porch, gingerbread trim, a gracious lady nestled in the embrace of live oaks, magnolias and azaleas. "There it is, Dog Boy," she murmured. "Home." The very picture that should be in the dictionary beside the word.

But not for her, never again.

"Where are we, Mom?" A small, sleepy voice spoke.

Ria glanced in the mirror at Benjy's precious face, his black hair—her hair, David's hair…her mother's hair—standing up in spikes.

Eyes the melted-chocolate brown of her father's blinked. "Mom?"

Please. Hate me, but help me save him, she begged the people inside. But because she had no idea if they would, she hedged on their identities. "We're going to visit the people who own this place."

"Do we know them?"

Had she ever? Once she'd been a part of them, but not for many more years than she'd been gone. "Yes." Then it hit her again, sheer terror. Could she even be sure that Mother and Daddy still resided here?

Of course they did. Their roots ran true and deep. They would only leave if carted out feet first. What her mother held, she never let go.

Except you, Victoria. She couldn't wait to see you depart.

I can't do this. Her fingers tightened on the key, and she began to turn it.

Nothing happened. The car, pushed to its limits just as she was, had caved. Ria barely contained the urge to drop her head to the steering wheel and give up. She was so tired she could barely see straight.

"Mom, I have to pee."

She smiled, bubbles of hysteria welling upward. *You stacked the deck, Dog Boy. What kind of guardian angel are you, anyway?*

Only the best friend she'd ever had.

Sweet mercy, she missed him.

Benjy's car-seat buckle clicked. "Hey, I did it, Mom! All by myself!"

Ah, children. When you thought you couldn't manage one more step, face one more day, they pulled you back into life, willing or not.

She unfastened her own seat belt and emerged. Dark dots danced before her eyes; she had to grab the doorframe to remain standing.

Not now. Please. Let me get him inside. Just a few more steps. A smattering of minutes.

"Come on, tiger. Can you make it a bit longer?"

He crawled across the seat and held up his arms.

She wanted him close but was terrified she'd drop him, so instead of picking him up, she held out her hand. "Ready for the next stop on our adventure?"

"Yeah!" His head bobbed with enthusiasm at first, but he fell silent as they crossed the street and moved along the sidewalk.

Just before they stepped up on the porch, he balked. "Mom."

She could barely hear his voice over the pounding of her heart. The buzzing in her head. "What, sweetie?"

Earnest dark eyes turned up to hers. "Will these people like me?"

"Oh, honey." She dropped to her knees, though she was afraid she wouldn't be able to get up. "They'll love you so much." *I hope.*

They'd better, Dog Boy, or I'm gone, you hear me?

"Okay," he said. "Want me to knock?"

She eyed the red front door her father had installed so many years ago, the brass knocker she'd never had to use, back when she'd belonged. "I'll do it this time." She smiled past her fear and rapped on the wood.

Please, oh, please...Mother, don't punish him for my sins.

The door opened. Ria gawked. "Aunt Cammie?" Why was she here?

"Victoria?" Stunned silence, then the tiny, gray-haired woman blinked. "Oh, Lordy. Just a minute. I'll go get—" Aunt Cammie vanished, leaving the door wide-open.

Ria clung to the frame. Wondered if she should enter, even as her head swum. Tried to think, to decide—

Chaos erupted. "My God in heaven, he looks just like David," said a voice that had to be the former B-movie actress grandmother who would only answer to Lola.

"Oh, dear me, child, please come in," she thought she heard Aunt Cammie say—

Hold on, hold on, she told herself, gripping Benjy's hand.

Then, at last, there she was.

Ria's nemesis.

Green eyes wide, camellia skin ashen. Statue still. Her gaze filled with horror.

Ria wanted to weep as the truth sank in. Just as she'd feared, nothing had changed between them.

Her mother still hated her.

But then Cleo Channing caught sight of Benjy, and everything about her was transformed. The initial horror mutated into confusion and hurt…then into longing so sharp it was painful to witness.

He's safe. Thank you, Dog Boy. Whatever her mother thought of her, she would cherish Ria's baby. Save him. Fight the world to protect him, just as Daddy would.

Relief broke past the inky veil stealing over her vision. "Mother—" Ria reached out—

But the darkness swallowed her.

CHAPTER TWO

THE MURMUR OF VOICES teased at her hearing, and Ria stirred. Exhaustion dragged at her bones and weighted her feet as she attempted the climb from amber shadows pressing her into blessed oblivion.

She could sleep for a week. A month.

Forever, but something—

"Is my mom okay?" The child's quavery tone penetrated the seductive embrace of slumber.

Benjy.

"Uhh…" *So tired…*

"I want my mom." Frightened now.

"Benjy," she whispered. Instinct propelled her to her feet. Dizzy and swaying, she bumped a chair. A table. Squinting against darkening vision, she staggered toward the sound.

"Hey, doll, what are you doing up?"

Ria barely spared her grandmother a glance, her whole being focused on one voice. One person.

"Benjy, what's wrong?" She propped herself against the doorframe of the kitchen she'd thought never to enter again.

She saw the woman kneeling, her arms around Ria's child, her green eyes filled with wonder.

"Mom!" Benjy raced from Cleo's embrace to her own. "Are you okay? I was scared."

She clasped him against her hip, fingers spread over the thick hair so badly in need of washing. "I'm just fine, sweetie."

Cleo rose and faced her slowly. "Victoria," she acknowledged carefully. "Should you be up?"

"My name is Ria."

She saw the shock reverberate through all of them. "Ria" had been David's special name for her. No doubt her mother believed she had no right to it.

Ria agreed. The name was her penance.

"Why—" Cleo battled for composure. "What brought you here, Victo—Ria? Is something—"

Wrong? Her mother might as well have finished her sentence. Anger battled with bitter disappointment. Bone-deep sorrow. Her mother would always be suspicious of her. "Never mind. We're out of here. Benjy—"

"No—" Cleo grabbed her daughter's arm. "Don't—"

Ria stiffened. "Let go of me."

Slowly, Cleo removed her hand, but in her expression Ria found something she'd never seen in her mother before. Something she'd almost call fear. Uncertainty.

"Please. Don't…leave."

But Cleo Channing was always sure. Unafraid.

"Don't hurt my mom." Benjy's voice trembled.

Cleo looked at him. "Oh, sweetheart, I'd never—" She halted, perhaps unwilling to complete the lie. She and Ria had damaged each other over and over for years. "I didn't mean—I want you both to stay, that's all."

Benjy glanced up at Ria, checking her reaction, his eyes big and sad and confused.

"It might be wise for you to see a doctor, sweetheart. I'd like to take you both, only to be sure—"

Of course. Suddenly Ria saw how they must appear, despite her attempts to clean them up. For Benjy's sake, she was furious. "Afraid we've got fleas, Mother? Just because we've been living in my car doesn't mean we have cooties or carry some dread disease. A bath will suffice." Her voice went sharper. "I'll clean your pristine tub afterward."

"Please don't, Vic—Ria. Not in front of—" Cleo compressed her lips and gestured toward Benjy. As Ria watched, she metamorphosed into the cool, neutral woman Ria remembered. "I was about to make Benjy some French toast. Perhaps you'd care for some, too?"

Ria couldn't stifle the harsh bark of laughter. "Always the perfect hostess."

Benjy's chin trembled as he darted glances between the two of them.

"Whatever you think of me, consider your child, at least. Let him eat his breakfast in peace. Aunt Cammie, would you mind—" Cleo turned away. "I—if you'll excuse me, I must open the shop." With quick steps, she headed for the doorway, giving her daughter wide berth.

"Where's Daddy?"

Cleo halted in mid-step. She and Lola exchanged glances.

Ria tensed.

Cleo took a deep breath. "He doesn't live here anymore." She paused. "We're divorced."

Dear God. Shock rooted Ria to the floor. "What?" Her parents were more in love than any couple Ria had ever seen. It was unimaginable. Crushing. She wanted to be sick. Instead, she struck out. "Congratulations. You drove him away, too."

It was either attack or scream. Crumple. Her father had been her only ally—at least until she'd gone beyond the pale.

Her mother didn't answer but studied Benjy and brushed one hand over his hair. Finally, she dragged her gaze up to her daughter's, now composed. Unflinching. Cold as she had always been when she focused on her problem child.

Once there had been love in those emerald eyes, but not in so many years Ria could barely remember it. She'd always come up short, forever disappointing this woman. Betsey was the perfect daughter, ladylike, unsullied. Hair neatly combed, dresses spotless. Just like their elegant, beautiful mother.

And once Ria had prayed every night to change, but the harder she tried, the more stunning her failures, until she'd quit altogether.

Make your peace, Ria.

It won't work, Dog Boy.

Even if she'd known what to say, her mother was already halfway to the stairs, holding herself with her trademark exquisite posture. "I'm going to get dressed," she said over her shoulder. "I'll alert Malcolm that you're here."

And then she was gone.

AFTER NEARLY A YEAR, Sandor Míklos Wolfe still did not take the miracle of America for granted, and Texas…ah, Texas. The sheer scope of it, the room to breathe and think and move…even a young boy's dreams of his lost father's homeland had not done it justice.

With the still-sharp pleasure of someone who'd spent his first thirty-four years in Budapest, sharing two rooms with his grandmother and a hall bath in a once-grand home with two other families, he glanced around the garage apartment to which only he and his new landlady possessed a key.

He shook his head at his good fortune. Humble this place might be to many in this country, but his grandmother, with her disdain for all things American, would have clucked her tongue and chided him for the bounty of it. Three rooms—count them, three for him alone—plus half the empty garage below, in which he hoped to set up a workshop. If only he could have provided Nani with such luxury before she died, but Hungary, though the most progressive of all Eastern Europe, now battled crippling inflation and unemployment instead of Soviet oppression.

He had American citizenship, courtesy of the father who had left Hungary right after Sandor's birth. Alexander Wolfe had been a graduate student who'd managed to obtain an extended visa to study the rich history of Hungary. He'd promised to send for his wife and child, but his demise in a motorcycle wreck had ended that hope. Eight years later, Sandor's mother had succumbed to pneumonia. Her single, much-cherished photograph of his father had been given into Sandor's keeping by his grandmother, who had sacrificed much to raise him. Once grown, Sandor had delayed the long-anticipated journey to his father's homeland in order to return the favor and care for her.

But Nani was gone now, freeing him to follow his dreams. The opportunities in the U.S. were breathtaking, he thought, as he descended the stairs he had already strengthened then strode across the driveway he had begun to clear last night in preparation for resurfacing. To succeed here, one only needed the will to work hard and the discipline to be frugal. He had plenty of both.

He closed the tailgate of the weathered pickup for which he had saved enough to pay cash. The space in its bed had been ample for the few belongings he'd moved from Cleo's storeroom.

And all of this new life and hopeful future, he owed to Cleopatra Channing's penchant for taking in strays.

"You worked quite late."

Sandor turned at the sound of his landlady, Billie Packard. Only slightly shorter than his own six foot three, rawboned and cantankerous, she could have passed for an aging Valkyrie, gray braids hanging over her chest, shapeless brown dress sporting an assortment of jeweled pins in rows like so many medals. He and Billie were still circling each other like wary dogs. "Did I disturb you?"

"No. An old woman doesn't sleep much." Her gaze encompassed the new lumber bracing the stairs and the open space where weeds had formerly overrun the asphalt of the driveway. "You only moved in last evening. I didn't expect you to start work this soon."

He shrugged. "These were first on my list." What he had done was only the beginning. Billie's old frame house in the Clarksville neighborhood near downtown had been neglected for many years. Sandor had spotted it—and the vacant garage apartment—on one of his late-night jaunts around the area near Cleo's shop, and he'd walked up to Billie's doorstep the next morning to propose a trade: repairs in exchange for rent. He could not sleep in Cleo's storeroom forever; she could use the space, but she would never ask him to move out.

At first, Billie had rejected the idea flatly, but Sandor had spent his whole life scrambling to make something out of nothing. On the second attempt at persuasion, he'd replaced two broken boards in her front porch; on the third, he had fixed a dripping faucet. Finally, he had realized that Billie couldn't afford the materials and had sweetened the deal to provide them himself if she would be patient with the time required to save up the money. He was deeply suspicious of the easy credit available in this country. He paid cash or bartered, period.

"So what are you doing up so early after working into the wee hours?"

"I am installing cabinets for Cleo this morning prior to proceeding to a new job site. I want to complete the work before she opens, to keep the noise down."

"The way you say her name—is she someone special to you? Tall, good-looking fellow like you probably has to fight off the women."

What Cleo was to him was none of her business, but he held his tongue. "She is my friend. I do repairs for her, nothing more. Excuse me, but now I must be off."

Billie's eyebrows rose, but she merely nodded. "I'll see you later, perhaps."

He tamped down his irritation and got into his truck. The truth was that he could easily have fallen in love with Cleo, though at fifty-one, she was sixteen years his senior. Unlike most American males of his age, Sandor did not think women achieved the peak of their beauty in their youth. But Cleo needed him more as a friend than as a lover, and he owed her too much to cross that barrier.

He would leave wooing her up to Colin Spencer, a nearby coffee-shop owner who was the most recent in line to moon over the elusive Cleo. She had always had suitors, from the day he'd met her, but she shied from any sort of deep involvement; however, Colin appeared to be wearing her down.

Divorce had broken something inside Cleo, though she covered it well. From what Sandor could divine, family had been her life, and her former husband, Malcolm, had been her world. Malcolm, whom Sandor had never met, was a fool to have let her go.

But the real culprit was the bad-seed daughter who had destroyed their family.

He drove the few blocks to the tree-shaded lot behind Cleo's exclusive gift shop on West Sixth Street and emerged to unlock the back door.

Once inside, he examined the revamped space with satisfaction. Drywall hung straight, joints carefully sealed. When the cabinets were set, he would paint, then lay the floor covering.

And Cleo would, as always, pay him too much. She said that he did not charge enough, but accepting even a penny from her, after she had let him sleep in her storeroom and hired him for odd jobs until he'd saved enough to move out, grated on him.

There was no one since Nani he admired more than Cleopatra Channing. Small and delicate, she seemed best suited to holding tea parties, but her appearance was deceptive. The dainty exterior obscured her inner strength; she had transformed herself from homemaker to formidable and admired businesswoman in the five years since her divorce.

Few people ever glimpsed the sadness inside her that was the legacy of losing her family. He considered himself privileged to enjoy her confidence, but even with him, she clung to the image she had cultivated—the smart, savvy, ever-poised retailer whose place had become the premier destination for that elusive, perfect gift.

Just then, he heard voices outside and realized that one of them was Cleo's. The other was probably Colin's. Because he was nearer Sandor's age, she was resisting Colin's pursuit, though she, too, was attracted.

Then Cleo's voice rose, sounded tense. Frightened.

Sandor crossed to the back door, just in time to witness Colin grab her arm and Cleo struggle.

"Don't," she cried.

"I was only trying—"

"Just—get out of here—"

Sandor was beside her in an instant. "Is something wrong, Cleopatra?"

"I—no, it's—"

He glared down at Colin. "Are you certain?"

Colin, normally easygoing, stared at her. "Cleo, I'd never hurt you."

Sandor believed that was true, based on his acquaintance with the man. Still, Cleo was upset, not herself at all. "Perhaps you could return later, Colin."

Colin's eyes were hot. "Yeah, sure. Here—" He shoved the pastry box he'd been holding at Sandor. Then his shoulders drooped. "I don't understand."

"I know." Cleo's normal poise was raveling at the edges, her eyes red rimmed. "It's not your fault, Colin. I just—things—" She gestured helplessly. "I'm sorry."

Colin took a step toward her to comfort.

Sandor caught his eye and shook his head.

Colin halted. Threw up his hands. "Have a good day." He left.

Cleo crumpled. "He's a nice man. He deserves better."

"As do you. Shh..." He clasped her elbow, led her into the shop and closed the door behind them. He settled her on the sofa in her office, placed the pastry box on the desk and crouched before her. "What has happened, Cleo?"

For a second, she attempted to draw herself up into the mask she usually donned with little effort. "Nothing's—" She abandoned pretense. "My daughter arrived on my doorstep this morning."

"Betsey is well?"

"Not Betsey. Victoria—Ria, as she asked to be called."

Ah. The demon child. Destroyer of families. Sandor had been told the story one night when he and Cleo were both working late after the shop had closed. Understood how much Victoria had devastated this woman who was his friend. "What does she want?"

"I'm not sure. Shelter, perhaps. Probably money, as well." She cast him a glance. "She has a little boy. They were both filthy and hungry. They've been living in her car for God knows how long."

Then she studied the ground, her voice barely audible. "He looks like David."

Now he understood why she was this upset. "So you will take him in and feed him because he is your flesh. You will care for him both for himself and for the son you can no longer hold."

Cleo nodded.

"And Victoria? What will you do with her?"

"She hates me still. There's so much anger in her."

"But if you send her away, you will lose the boy."

"Yes." Despair settled upon her.

"So much to fret over, even for you, the Madonna of Perpetual Worry." His attempt to lighten her spirits fell short.

"And now I have to call Malcolm." Dread filled her tones.

"How will he react?"

"He'll probably side with her, as always." She turned devastated eyes toward him. "I have no desire to fight with her anymore. I only—" Her face crumpled again. "I want my family back," she whispered. "The way it used to be."

Before he could comfort her, she straightened. "I was sure I'd put it behind me, but seeing her today, realizing that she hasn't changed... She has no right to that boy. She can't be trusted." Her focus sharpened with new purpose. "I'm going to insure that Benjy has the life he deserves. I will not stand by and let her harm another child."

Such stridence was uncharacteristic. Still, he chose caution. "You have little information about their relationship."

She tilted her chin. "I understand more than she does about being a mother."

"But you are not his." She should not get her hopes up. All Victoria had to do was leave, and the child would disappear, too.

Her eyes flashed fire, her voice whip sharp. "You have no children, Sandor. You can't possibly understand."

It was unlike her to go on the attack with him, a sign of how troubled she was. "This boy is not David. Saving him will not give you back your son."

Her expression told him that her mind was made up.

At least the defeated demeanor had vanished. Sandor decided to switch topics for now. "So what happened with Colin this morning?"

"Nothing." Her tone was carefully neutral.

"You are breaking his heart, Cleopatra."

A shocked gasp. "I have no idea what you mean." She rose abruptly and fussed with a teapot.

He chuckled. "Oh, my friend, you are so American sometimes. If that is your best impression of an elderly spinster, I am afraid you need more practice."

"Sandor, it's not what you—I mean, we aren't—"

"You think the attraction between you is invisible? Do not tell me—you have rejected him with some sort of argument about your remarkably advanced age."

She set down the teapot with a barely restrained thud. "I don't want to discuss this. It's—I'm…ridiculous." She quickened her steps toward the showroom.

"Cleo, stop. I apologize. I can see this pains you, and that is the last thing I want."

She stood with her back to him.

"Talk to me, my friend. Tell me what has happened to make you feel old again."

"It's just—" Resolutely, she faced him. "I am too old for him. It's a simple fact."

"He is an adult, Cleo. He knows his mind. And you are a beautiful woman, one who has been solitary for too long. Why can you not allow yourself a little pleasure? Who will it harm?"

"I can't discuss this with you, Sandor. It's not… proper."

Such a little Puritan. He resisted the smile that threatened. "And with whom can you?"

She did not yield the point. She had many acquaintances, but few close friends that he was aware of. "There's nothing to talk over. I've come to my senses."

"Cleo…" This was not his first encounter with her stubbornness. "Very well. I will drop it for now, but I will not cease to remind you that you are far from dead and merit much more than you allow yourself." He walked to the back door, then paused. "Please remember that above all I am your friend. I will be here, should you change your mind."

The tears she'd been fighting nearly got the best of her. "Thank you. You're very kind to me."

He shook his head sadly. "If only you would follow my example." He had much to accomplish today, and she had a shop to open. He would watch for a more propitious moment to continue the argument.

And he would do anything possible to protect her from the daughter who had been in town only a few hours but had somehow already managed to break her mother's heart again.

CHAPTER THREE

THOUGH SHE WAS EIGHT NOW, sometimes Victoria almost thought she could remember being a baby. She would catch a glimpse of her mother's hair when the wind had mussed it and it wasn't so perfect, and something about that sway of black against the curve of her mother's pale, perfect cheekbones—

Victoria could swear she recollected a rocking motion as she nestled safely against a slow, steady heartbeat while her mother's green eyes looked at her with love. Grown-ups would tell her that she couldn't possibly recall, so she never discussed it. But she knew. Once her mother had been all hers. Only hers, before Betsey arrived two years later.

But today was a special day. She and Mommy would have something called a Ladies' Lunch. Victoria's insides got squirmy, like a bunch of giggles wanting to jump out. Betsey didn't get to come, not even for a minute. Victoria was all dressed up. Both wore green-and-white-flowered dresses, but hers had ruffles and Mommy's was straight. Victoria was a little afraid to sit down, since she was a dirt magnet—at least, that's what

Mommy called her. *Victoria, dirt just seems to jump on you, no matter where you are. You're a dirt magnet, I swear.*

She'd sigh and shake her head when she said that. Then she'd shift her gaze to where Betsey, who never had one speck on her, even though she was a baby compared with Victoria. Betsey never did anything but play inside with her stupid old dolls. How could she get messy?

"Ready, sweetie?"

Victoria jumped up from the sofa, rushed across the wooden floor and skidded, then bumped into a table, making the lamp jiggle.

Her mother laughed and hugged her. "I guess you are. All right, let's go." She raised her voice. "Malcolm, we're leaving now."

Daddy appeared at the top of the stairs and whistled. "Maybe you two better let me chaperone. What knockouts you are—I don't think I'm letting either one of you out the door."

Then her mother's voice slid down, and she laughed that low kind of laugh that belonged to only Daddy. "You devil," she cooed, and her green eyes got brighter and her cheeks just a little red.

Daddy stared at her mother the way he never did anyone else, as if she was the biggest chocolate sundae in the world. "You be careful, hear me? I want you two back, safe and sound."

Mommy blew him a kiss and then winked at him.

He studied Victoria with great care. "You're gonna

break some hearts, Vic. You're as beautiful as your mother."

She would never be that pretty. No one could. Mommy should be a model or a fairy princess or something. Daddy called her Snow because he said she resembled Snow White, the fairest of them all.

But today, Victoria felt special, so she blew him a kiss, too. "I love you, Daddy."

"I love you, too, sport. You ladies have a great time. Bets and I will hold down the fort."

Victoria could tell that the great treat of having Daddy all to herself wasn't enough to make Betsey forgive not being included in Ladies' Lunch. Her lower lip trembled as she leaned into Daddy's hip while he stroked her hair.

They turned to go, and Betsey cried out, "Wait—" She ran down the stairs and threw her arms around Mommy's waist, her eyes filling with tears.

Mommy knelt and hugged Betsey, whispered in her ear and rocked her.

Victoria watched, holding her breath and wondering if Mommy would cave in and tell Betsey she could go, too. Betsey wouldn't skid across the floor and jiggle a lamp.

Her sister shook her head and sobbed. Mommy whispered again and hugged her once more, hard.

Then she rose and held out her hand to Victoria. Clasping it tightly, she blew Betsey a kiss. "Bye, sweetheart. You take care of Daddy for me, all right?"

"Yes, Mommy." Betsey's nod was barely visible.

Victoria waited for the magic to crumble, for Mommy to give up and say, *Oh, all right. Run, change your clothes quickly, Betsey.*

But she didn't. With breathtaking speed, they walked through the kitchen and out to the carport, then climbed into Mommy's car and drove away.

Off to their adventure, their Ladies' Lunch. Just Victoria and Mommy. No one else.

Mommy glanced over at her, smile white and dazzling against her scarlet lipstick. "Hold on to your hat, sweetie—we're going to paint the town red!"

Victoria laughed at the idea of a whole town of red houses. She made a vow that she wouldn't run, wouldn't spill, wouldn't yell and knock things over.

She would be a lady.

Just like her beautiful mother.

"RIA...WAKE UP, doll."

The first thing Ria spotted as she emerged from the dream was a rainbow arcing through the air. She closed her eyes. Tired. She was so tired.

"Come on, lamb, wake up and talk to me."

"Mother?" Then she blinked the room into focus and saw the wild tangle of long blond curls, the blinding fuchsia scarf fighting to keep her grandmother's wig under control. And failing.

Ria smiled. "Lola, what is that?"

"A healing crystal. You're my first experiment."

Ria bit back a chuckle and scanned her former bedroom for her mother.

Lola anticipated the question. "She's still at the shop. She's worried about you."

Sure she was. That Ria would steal the silver and drain the bar.

Ria struggled to rise. "I shouldn't have come."

One hand pushed her back gently. Blue eyes regarded her with sympathy. "Why did you?"

She discarded a slew of answers. Because she and Benjy had been living in her car for five weeks? Because screwed-up as she was, failure though she might be, she was a better mother than to let her child live in a car in winter?

Because, damn it, she'd promised Dog Boy that she'd go home, though she had been positive it wouldn't work?

In the end, she simply shrugged. "It doesn't matter. I saw the look on Mother's face. She'll take Benjy, but she doesn't want me here."

Lola didn't respond to that. "Where's his father?"

"He doesn't have one." Cleo hadn't had a father, either, so let Lola try to pontificate. The difference was, Lola had been sure who it was. Ria would never be completely certain. Benjy's sire could be hidden in any one of many hazy nights.

She waited for the recriminations.

She wasn't disappointed. Lola would understand raising a child alone, but even Lola wouldn't sympathize with keeping Benjy a secret for almost five years.

"Why didn't you tell anyone about him? Ria, honey, where have you been all this time?" Lola might be a flake, but right now, she was angry. Not as much as Mother, but then, no one looked down her nose quite as well as Cleo Channing.

Not all Ria's reasons made sense, even to her, so she settled for the obvious. "I didn't want the lectures. Or the meddling."

Blue eyes regarded her sadly. "I suspect you could use some of both. Ria—"

"Please, Lola. Not now."

Her grandmother subsided.

Ria rolled to her feet and rose from the bed, teetering. She raked fingers through matted hair and stared around the room as though she hadn't spent most of her life in this home. Actually, it didn't appear as though she ever had; Cleo had wiped every trace of her away. The double bed was the same one handed down from her parents when they got their king-size wonder, but the walls were freshly painted. All traces of the black with which she'd taunted Cleo had vanished. The room was a soft, buttery yellow now, the trim a gleaming white. African violets dotted the sills of windows covered only by sheer lace curtains Ria would once have yanked down in favor of blackout shades.

But it wasn't her room anymore; it was Cleo's. Careful Cleo, who always did everything right.

Everything but figure out what to do with a demon child.

"I can't stay here." She started across the room. Her only problem was the way the floor kept tilting.

"Running won't help, doll. You, of all people,

should know that." Lola's arm stole around her waist, and Ria looked at the two of them in the mirror on the opposite wall.

A hell of a pair. One wrinkled blond bombshell, one scarecrow with black spiky hair and fake Doc Martens.

"The red tips…I might have to try that," Lola teased. "A new image for me."

"Goes against type, Lola. Mamie van Doren would faint."

"Phhhpt—that bimbo. I could act."

Ria laughed, but inside she shivered, realizing for the first time that her grandmother wasn't ageless. Lola had bones now, not the flagrant curves of her B-movie past.

But Lola still stood tall, like Ria. They towered over the more delicate Cleo, over Ria's younger sister, Betsey, too.

Ria laid her hand over her grandmother's. "Where does Bets live?"

"She and her husband, Peter, have a house in Westlake and two darling little girls."

Betsey, married. Wow. "Junior Leaguer, right? Perfect house, perfect car?"

Lola smiled. "Perfect husband."

They shared a grin of mischief. For one second, Ria allowed herself a sliver of hope.

"I'm glad you're here, Lola."

"I'm driving your mother nuts."

Ria's grin widened. "So what's new?"

"She was getting into a rut. All she does is work."

"Why?"

"She's on her own now. She's got this monstrosity to support, and she wasn't willing to accept the money Malcolm wanted to give. Besides, she was never idle. She's done very well with her gift shop."

Ria conceded to fact. "No surprise there. She could organize World War Three in twenty-four hours, twelve if need be. Too bad I never liked being managed."

Lola's humor vanished. "Don't push her, Ria. She was a good mother to all of you—a better one than I was to her. Change things this time. It doesn't have to be a battle."

Ria faced the door and began to move forward. "It doesn't, no—"

But it always has been. Still, she'd used up all she had just to get here. What happened next?

Suddenly, she halted. She could ask Lola anything. "Where is Daddy, if he doesn't live here?"

Lola seemed uncomfortable. "He has a condo in Northwest Hills."

"What aren't you telling me?"

Lola sighed. "You'll hear it soon enough, I guess. He has a girlfriend."

Ria refused to let the hurt inside. "So? Daddy's a handsome man. Of course there would be women interested." When her grandmother's expression didn't ease, she persisted. "What?"

Lola shrugged. "She's about your age. Not that it

matters, except that this is the first one who's moved in with him."

Ria had to feel sorry for Cleo. "How did Mother take it?"

"She's a strong woman. Still..."

"What?"

"I always thought they'd get back together. Cleo would never verbalize it, but she might have, too. Not that she hasn't had her share of admirers, but—" Lola shook her head. "You only get one true love in this life, and the two of them belonged together. Still do, if you ask me."

Ria understood exactly who was to blame; it only compounded her sins.

She needed to see her son, the one thing she'd done right. Grasping the door handle, she looked at her grandmother. "I'll try with her, Lola. I'll let her set the tone."

Fact was, she was too tired to do anything else.

SANDOR RETURNED to his truck to get the next load of materials for the restaurant remodeling job, a small one but his biggest contract yet. A slim shape dashed from the other side of the truck bed, and the metal of his power saw glinted in the sun. "Hey—what are you—"

The boy scampered out of the parking lot and darted left at the building on the corner. Mindful of the character of this still-seedy fringe area downtown, Sandor hesitated long enough to lock his toolbox, then charged after him.

Because the boy was hampered by the weight of the saw, his gait was lopsided. Sandor's long legs narrowed the gap. The boy leaped for a fence and tried to scale it, but the extra burden gave Sandor the advantage. He grasped the boy's shirttail in one hand and his saw in the other, fury riding him hard. His own survival depended upon the tools he had painstakingly assembled as he could save up enough money.

"Lemme go—" the boy yelled, and a string of filthy words accompanied his struggles. He lashed out with fists and kicks, so desperate to escape that Sandor had to set down the saw to prevent the child from injuring himself. "You don't let me go, my brother gonna wipe the street with yo ass, mother—"

"Enough—" Sandor roared, cutting off the tirade. He gripped the boy's shoulders.

And recognized the expression. The skin might be darker, the garb different, but Sandor had an intimate acquaintance with the hunger and desperation. He forced his heartbeat to slow, his grip to ease.

The boy, perhaps twelve years old, tensed to run.

"Do not think of it. I will only catch you again."

A lower lip quivered, but eyes shouted defiance from beneath the sheen of unshed tears. "Go ahead. Call the cops, then. I ain't scared of you, moth—"

Sandor shook him again. "Watch your mouth. How do you expect anyone else to respect you if you do not respect yourself?"

The boy blinked. "You talk funny. Where you from?"

"I am as American as you."

The boy snorted. "I don't think so. I never heard no one talk like you 'cept maybe Arnold Schwarzenegger."

Sandor's mouth quirked. "I was born in Hungary, but my father was an American, a Texan, as a matter of fact."

"So yo mama talk funny like you?"

Sandor knew his English was, in fact, very good. He had studied it on the sly during the years it was forbidden; then, when the Iron Curtain had fallen, he had redoubled his efforts in preparation for the day he would finally manage to come to this country. "My mother is dead."

Sorrow dampened the boy's defiance. "Mine, too."

Ah, yes. He knew this boy. "I will let go of you if you promise to accompany me."

"Yeah, right. Like I'm so stupid I'm gonna walk myself right into the cop shop and surrender."

Behind the bluster, however, terror shouted.

"I will not have you arrested if you come with me."

"Oh, man, don't tell me you one of them pervs who like little boys." The boy's whole frame trembled even as he doubled his fists. "You lay a hand on me and I'll—"

Torn between outrage and laughter, Sandor spoke over the boy's bravado. "Do not be ridiculous. I am going to buy you breakfast."

"You—" The child gulped and hope blared from his eyes. Then he narrowed them. "Why?"

"Because I have been you." A child on the verge of starvation, stealing when he could not get honest work so that he and Nani could eat. His power saw would not bring much money at a pawnshop, but there were times when the smallest scrap was welcome. "My name is Sandor. What is yours?"

The child glanced at him from the corner of one eye. "Why do you care?"

He stifled impatience. "It is merely a courtesy. Did no one ever teach you manners?"

"Yeah, sure. I got an A in charm school. What they call that shit? Etiquette?"

He ignored the crack. "So you do comprehend words of more than one syllable that do not involve profanity."

"You are one weird dude, ain't you?" But the boy was smiling, just a bit.

"Then you will humor this weird dude and allow him to buy you a meal?"

"When I know what the catch is, yeah, maybe."

The boy's pinched look revealed just how wary he was, that he would risk losing a chance to eat. "Very well. There are two."

The child tensed. "Go ahead."

"One is that you will tell me your name." Sandor intended to learn much more about the child before he was done, but this would do for a start. "And the second is that once you have eaten as much as you want, you will stay here—" The boy's head shot up, naked longing warring with hesitance "—until it is time to break for lunch."

Wonder sparked past the caution. "Lunch?"

Sandor kept his chuckle to himself. "Which will be postponed long enough for us to make up for the delayed start I am getting."

"Us? What you mean, us?"

"A real man prefers to earn his way rather than to steal or accept charity."

"Wait—you gonna make me work?"

"I will not force you, no, but I have always found that food tastes better when one has earned it by honest labor. If you prefer handouts, you have chosen the wrong place."

"I didn't come to you." The boy shrugged when Sandor merely lifted one eyebrow. "Okay, but that was real dumb, you know, leaving your toolbox open like that."

Sandor nodded. "I accept your critique. I did not expect thieves to be up so early."

"I'm not—" The boy stopped in mid-sentence.

Sandor chose not to argue. "I should have been under way by now. One does not build a business by showing up late. A man is not a man if he does not honor his word when he gives it."

"You get those ideas in that place where you from? 'Cause I never heard anybody talk like you, and I don't mean just that accent."

Sandor shrugged. Trust was not easy for children deprived of the very basics of life. "I have time either to feed you or to engage in philosophical discussions, but not both." He released the boy's shoulder and bent to pick up his saw, then headed in the direction of the job site, holding his breath to see what the boy would do.

No footsteps sounded, but a voice did. "Jerome."

Sandor grinned, but quickly wiped it away as the boy neared. "I have learned in this country a taste for breakfast tacos, which have the advantage of being portable and thus can be eaten on the way back to work. How do you feel about them, Jerome?"

"You talk funny, but sometimes you make good sense, I guess." Jerome caught up with him. "So exactly what kind of work you got in mind? 'Cause I'm just a kid, after all. I can't be totin' them heavy pieces of wood or none of that shit."

"No cursing."

"What?"

"On my job site, there is no cursing." He glanced down at Jerome. "I assume you are strong enough to wield a broom."

"Well, duh…any fool can do that. Give me something harder."

"When you have earned it." Sandor could barely stem a laugh at Jerome's look of disdain.

"You really are some kind of strange moth—uh, dude."

At last, Sandor let his smile free.

CHAPTER FOUR

"CLOSE YOUR EYES," Ria told Benjy as she sluiced warm water over his foamy head, sliding her fingers through it to rinse out all the shampoo.

"Mom?"

"Don't open them yet." The past few weeks, washing hair had been a luxury. They'd been taking sponge baths in restrooms even before they drove across the country. She could still see the horror and accusation in her mother's eyes because this child was so filthy.

Benjy obeyed, but he was eager to talk. Squeezing his eyes shut, he continued. "Did you know Lola has a dog? And Aunt Cammie says that she wants to show me a park that's not far from here, and we might take Tyrone. Can I go, Mom? Please?"

Ria sidestepped the question. "I can't believe Tyrone's still alive. He must be a hundred years old." He'd once been sleek and black, so Lola had named him after Tyrone Power, with whom she swore she'd had one torrid night. But Ria had heard he was gay. The star, not the dog. For a moment she was tempted to laugh. Dogs couldn't be gay, right?

Thinking about that was better than trying to figure out why she was here. Not that it mattered. She didn't have anywhere else to go.

"Mom? Can I?"

"May I." *Oh, good grief. I sound like Mother.* "Okay, stand up." She smiled at Benjy and lifted him out of the tub to dry him.

"I'm big. I can do this by myself."

She started to protest that he seldom got more than half of himself dry, but she didn't. He was right. And she remembered how much she had hated being smothered.

"Be sure you dry behind your ears."

His expression was four going on forty. "I *know.* You can go now."

"But—" *I don't want to. I don't belong in this place. You're the only thing that's familiar. And this house is full of hurt. I don't want you hurt, Benjy.*

But even as she thought it, she recognized that no one here would harm this child. They were eagerly waiting to make up for the years they'd lost, a house full of women with no one left to nurture.

She would put up with as much as was necessary in order to give him safety. But she couldn't stay here long, just enough time to get back on her feet and then they'd be gone. She'd made good on her promise to Dog Boy. She'd been right and he'd been wrong.

Leaving was her ultimate trump card. The woman who had cast her out, who had preferred another child to her—that woman would do anything to see that Benjy stayed.

Because Benjy was her mother's chance to give all she craved to be doing for David. The good child.

Well, Mother, how does it feel now? The bad seed has something you want after all.

"I'll be just outside."

"Mom. *May* I go to the park with Aunt Cammie and Lola?"

She smiled and shook her head slowly. "You don't give up easily, do you?"

Benjy grinned back, resilient in a way she envied. "Is that a yes?"

Ria laughed. "That's a yes." She leaned down and kissed his nose. "Don't forget the ears," she whispered.

Then she left the room. But only far enough to stand a few feet along the hall. She slid down the wall and sat on the carpet, staring at a picture opposite, one of herself with Betsey and a very small David. Absorbed in trying to remember who that tall, coltish girl had been, she didn't register the door opening or the footsteps until she heard the voice.

"Vic—" Her father's voice. "I mean, Ria."

She whipped her head around, looked down the stairs and, for a moment, felt like that girl again, the one who thought this man could slay dragons. "Daddy…"

He didn't appear much older, except his dark hair was shot with silver. Tall, still with the lean frame of a runner, perhaps even more solid through the shoulders.

The first man she'd ever loved.

The last one she'd dared to trust, except for one scarecrow needle freak.

But this man hadn't been able to slay the dragon that lived in his house. Yet though his eyes held caution, they also sparked with something she'd never thought to see again. Love poured out from him in waves, and all of a sudden, Ria could remember what it had been like to be Daddy's girl.

"Come here, sweetheart."

Her vision blurred. Finally, she found the strength to rise and started down the stairs.

She broke into a run when he opened his arms to her.

He folded her into his embrace. Ria trembled and couldn't stifle a sob.

Malcolm tightened his arms around her, one hand caressing her hair. "Hey there, Vic," he said, calling her the old name of her childhood. "It's okay now. You're home. Everything's gonna be fine."

She burrowed closer, wanting so badly to believe it. For a moment, he stood there and simply rocked her as if she were still his little girl. *Oh, Daddy, Daddy...I'm scared...I've missed you so much....*

Abruptly, he stiffened. Gasped.

She glanced over her shoulder. Benjy stood at the top of the stairs, his black hair wet and spiking, his T-shirt damp. "Who is that man, Mom? Did he make you cry?"

She straightened, and wiped her eyes.

Before she could answer, her father squeezed her shoulder, then took the stairs two at a time until he neared the top and put his head at her son's level. "I'm your grandfather, Benjy, and I'm very glad you're here."

Benjy studied him solemnly.

The expression on her father's face could break her heart. She realized once again what a shock it must be that Benjy looked so much like David.

"Lola has a dog named Tyrone," Benjy said.

Malcolm grinned. "That old guy is still around?"

Benjy nodded. "Aunt Cammie and Lola are taking me and Tyrone to the park. If you won't make my mom sad anymore, you can go with us."

"I wouldn't like to upset your mom. She's my little girl, and I love her."

Oh, Daddy. New tears threatened. She'd been afraid to hope.

Benjy's head cocked slightly. "My mom's not a little girl."

"No, but she used to be your size. Even smaller."

Benjy was clearly skeptical.

"No kidding. She helped me build a tree house when she was only a few years older than you."

The eyes widened. "Where is it?"

"It used to be in the backyard. Want to go check if it's still there?"

Her son nodded, then belatedly peered past Malcolm for her approval.

Her father turned to her, too. In his eyes she caught sorrow and worry, yes, but mostly outrageous joy.

"Sure."

He held out his hands to Benjy while smiling at her. "Well, no time like the present."

"I don't got my shoes on," Benjy noted.

"How about a ride on my shoulders? Your mom liked that."

She had. For a second, she could recall the view from the dizzying heights of her father's shoulders.

Benjy seemed ecstatic but wary. "I don't know how."

Something sad moved over her father's face, but he banished it. "Piece of cake." He shrugged off his suit coat and climbed to the top step, then squatted. "Turn around, cowboy." He lifted her child, seeming not to have lost one ounce of strength in the intervening years.

Benjy squealed and gripped her father's hair as Malcolm stood up. Malcolm placed his hands on the child's legs to stabilize him. "Okay, sport, here we go. Watch the landing. We might have to duck."

"Okay." Benjy's voice was small at first, then increased with his delight. "Wow, Mom, see how tall I am!" He leaned over, and Malcolm quickly grabbed the banister to keep them steady. "What do I call you?"

Her father's smile widened by the second. "I never had a grandson before. What do you think?"

"I never had a grandpa. Nana Cleo said I could call her what her granddaughters do."

"The girls call me Gramps, but you don't have to. Pick your own. There's no hurry." Malcolm reached the bottom step and sought reassurance from her that he was right and she would stay. That they had time.

If Daddy lived here, she wouldn't hesitate to say yes. But he didn't, and her mother…

Ria wrapped her arms around her middle.

Her father, whose heart had always been far more open than Cleo's, tucked her stiff body against him and didn't press her. He shifted topics. "Your mom would remember where the tree house was. Let's get her to help us."

She let out the breath she'd been holding. The last thing in the world she wanted was to disappoint this man. He'd always been there for her, no matter how often she and her mother had been at loggerheads—at least until she had pushed him, too, past bearing.

But maybe they had a chance. Perhaps, if they didn't have to discuss the night she'd made even Daddy hate her—

"Focus on today, Vic—I mean, Ria. It's all we have," he murmured.

"Oh, Daddy." *I'm so sorry. I never meant—*

"Shh, sweetheart. Let's just take Benjy outside for now."

Gratefully, she softened into his hug, and he bestowed a kiss to her hair.

"Come on, Mom, show us where it was."

Ria let her father lead them through a house that finally felt a little like home, now that he was in it.

Until she recalled the girlfriend.

Why had he left? Her parents, regardless of her worst behavior, had never wavered in their love for each other, a love so immense that just realizing it existed had gotten her through many a terrified and lonely night. Where had it gone?

But she knew, somehow. Remembered the silences echoing with such pain that none of them had slept in those days before she could think of nothing to do but run away to save them all.

Perhaps her sins were even greater than she'd understood. Not only had she killed her sweet, kind brother, but she'd destroyed the love she'd been so sure would never die.

And that might be the worst crime of all.

Blinded by the horror of what she'd done to this man she loved so much, Ria tried to pull away before she did anything else to hurt him.

But her father refused to let go. Instead, when they neared the doorway, he tightened his hold on Benjy's leg and ducked, without once releasing the daughter who had cost him not only the son he cherished, but the woman he'd loved more than his own life.

And still, he had a heart big enough to welcome her back. To grin when Benjy squealed and jerked at Malcolm's hair.

To smile, as they entered the kitchen, at Lola and Aunt Cammie standing by the sink, mouths open and eyes wide. "Hello, ladies."

And to sweep her along with him as if she somehow still belonged.

As soon as they stepped onto the back porch, she spotted it. Though the years of weather and neglect had taken their toll, still, there the tree house stood, casting Ria back nearly twenty years to the weekend she and her father had constructed it.

"Daddy, make her stop it!" She'd been perched on one limb of the big old live oak in their backyard, waiting for her next chance to hammer a nail exactly how he'd shown her. Below, Betsey had picked up a piece of lumber.

Her father had glanced over his shoulder. "Vic, she's not hurting anything."

"But the tree house was my idea. We're building it, just you and me."

"Yes, it's mostly our project, but Betsey can help. It will be her place to play, too."

Tears stung her eyes. "Nothing is mine anymore."

Daddy glanced from her to her sister. "Want to help me over here, Bets?"

Miss Perfect nodded, and the pink bow in her neat pageboy shimmied. "Okay, Daddy."

"But—" Victoria protested.

The glare he cast her choked off her words. "Sweetheart, would you please get me a glass of ice water? I'm pretty thirsty," he said to Betsey.

"Okay, Daddy." She skipped daintily toward the house.

Daddy laid down his tape measure and walked over to the tree. "It's hard on you, having the new baby."

Victoria darted him a sideways look and shrugged. Thinking about David got her stomach all squirmy inside. She'd tried to hold him, but everyone just held their breath and made her more nervous. But there was this once when she'd been standing by his crib, and she could swear he wanted to tell her something special, and then he smiled.

But her mother said it was gas and picked him up and got all dreamy, and forgot she had a daughter.

"We've expected a lot from you because you're the oldest. Your mom appreciates your help, and so do I."

Some help. *Take Betsey outside, Victoria.* Or, *You girls go turn on the TV for a while.*

She shifted, and her scabbed knee banged the branch. She wasn't going to cry, though.

"I know you get tired of sharing things with Betsey, and now there's David. I had three brothers and two sisters and sometimes I got sick of never having anything to myself. I understand how you feel, but sweetie, that's what families do—they share. Good times and bad times, we go through them all together. We each have a part to play."

"David doesn't do anything. He just sleeps and cries and makes a mess. And we have to be quiet and Mommy spends all her time holding him." She blurted out the scary thing she couldn't shake. "If I was a boy, we wouldn't need him."

Sighing, Daddy lifted his arms to her. "Come down here for a second."

Stiff with misery that she shouldn't have said that out loud, nonetheless, she complied. He settled on the ground against the tree trunk and wrapped his arms around her. She burrowed close to his chest, her head tucked beneath his chin.

"Vic, I never wished you were a boy. You're my girl, remember? My special girl."

"Betsey's your girl, too."

"She is, and I love her very much. But you're unique, Vic. No one else can ever be our first child. There are so many things we three shared. Your mother cried when you were born, did you know that? Because she wanted you so much. And you know what else?"

She shook her head.

"I cried, too."

"You? You never cry, Daddy."

He was smiling at her the old way, like she hadn't made him mad. "Not very often. But that was a special time when you were born. You were so small and perfect and beautiful."

"Like Betsey is now."

He tapped her nose. "Like *you* are now."

A little bit, she wasn't so frightened anymore, and the relief freed the rest of the awful truth. "Mommy says I'm a mess. My clothes get dirty, and I skin up my knees. Betsey's always clean and perfect." She'd tried so hard to be like Mommy and Betsey, but she always seemed to fail.

"Betsey and you aren't the same person."

Victoria snorted. "You can say that again."

"But one is not better. I love you both."

Oh, Daddy...the hurt spilled out. "Mommy loves her better. And now there's David..." She wasn't blind—she'd witnessed how they both watched David as though he might disappear if they took their eyes off him for a second. As if he was the best gift anyone could ever imagine.

He held her chin lightly between finger and thumb. "Vic, your mother loves you. Don't you ever doubt that. She's just really busy and tired these days. I can change his diapers and get up with him, but because he's nursing, she still has to wake up to feed him. When he sleeps through the night, she'll get more rest. I promise this won't last long."

She wanted to believe him, but…

"Look, sport. Let's make a deal. You and I have designed this tree house and we'll do most of the building because we planned it. We're going to find a special spot inside it, and we'll carve a note that Victoria Channing is the architect of this structure. We'll work on it by ourselves, and we'll put it somewhere that only you and I know. It will be our secret. Even though you'll share this house with Betsey and David, once he's old enough, there will be a part of it that will belong only to you. What do you think?"

A bump inside her chest. "What would it say?"

"That's for you to decide. Does that sound good?"

So much that she was afraid to breathe. "Just you and me?"

"You're Daddy's special girl, aren't you?"

She imagined bringing friends over. *My daddy and I built this. We have a secret, only us two.* She ducked her chin and nodded.

"Just you and me, sport." He hugged her close, and hope swelled inside her. She wrapped her arms around his neck and squeezed tightly, wishing she never had to move from this spot. "I love you, Daddy."

"I love you, too. I always will."

She gnawed her lip and spoke. She would make him prouder. "I guess Betsey can help, then."

His eyes had that crinkle that said he was really happy. "That's my girl."

NOW RIA EDGED around the tree and peered beneath one corner of the structure.

And there it was, if timeworn. *Designed by Victoria and Malcolm Channing, June 1984.*

Love flooded her as her father boosted Benjy up onto the lowest limb of the old tree. Her son wobbled, and she had to force herself not to lunge for him, but Malcolm steadied him instantly.

Then he gave Benjy a finer gift and dropped his hands, letting her son feel the heady exhilaration of legs dangling over empty air, his head higher than anyone else's. Hero worship sparkled in Benjy's eyes. Her father laughed the way he used to laugh with her.

Ria's heart twisted. Too many people wanted to claim Benjy. It was all she could do not to snatch him down right now. She could show her child how to tackle ascending a tree, could teach him anything else he required. They didn't need anyone else. She and Benjy were a unit.

"Look, Mom, I'm way taller. I bet nobody's as high as I am." His head swiveled, and he glanced around the sloping yard. "This is cool, Gramps. Can I climb up to the part of the tree house that's left?"

"No," Ria answered him first. "It's too far up. You're not ready."

His lower lip stuck out. "I can do it. I *can*, Mom."

At that moment Ria confronted a facet of her son she'd encountered more and more often: his stubbornness. Sometimes her only advantage with him was her size. Heaven help her when she wasn't bigger anymore. "You've never climbed a tree before. Take it one step at a time."

"I'm not a baby. I'm big now."

"Benjy, don't argue with me. I said no, and that's that."

Benjy glared at her, his eyes watery. "I hate you. You don't want me to do anything fun."

Ria reeled from his words, embarrassed and angry at having to prove herself as a mother in front of Daddy.

Before she could answer, her father did, his voice stern. "Don't talk to your mother that way. She's only trying to watch over you. If you're truly big, then act accordingly."

Benjy's eyes went wide with shock. For a moment, his chin jutted out. Then an amazing thing happened. The child whose will was every bit as strong as hers bowed his head. "I'm sorry."

"Not to me. Apologize to your mother."

Tears trembled on his lashes. "I'm sorry, Mom." Then he faced his grandfather. "Don't be mad at me."

Ria wanted to go to him, but the two of them only

had eyes for each other. Her father laid one hand on Benjy's leg. "I'm not, I promise. But don't ever tell people you love that you hate them, no matter how angry they make you. You never know if you'll have a chance to make amends."

Ria stood off to the side, each word a dart that might have been aimed at her. In the dim mists of her past, she could hear that awful phrase being hurled in a voice that sounded too much like it belonged to her. "Daddy, I—"

Then another voice intervened, the tone sharp and peremptory. "What in the world is going on?"

Ria turned. "Hello, Betsey."

"Vicky?" Her sister, younger by two years, stopped and stared. "What are you doing here?" Every hair ruthlessly scraped back into a chignon, tiny pearls in her ears, crisp white cuffs and collar framing a black sweater that probably cost more than Ria's car was worth, Betsey was the perfect West Austin young matron. "You look dreadful."

Ria resisted the urge to check her faded jeans and threadbare blue flannel shirt, her scuffed secondhand boots. "Thanks. Nice to see you, too."

Betsey's high, perfect cheekbones pinkened. "I'm sorry. I didn't mean—" She glanced over at their father.

"Who's that lady?" Ria heard Benjy whisper.

"Benjamin, my man—" Malcolm scooped him off the limb and turned him sideways in his arms "—this is your aunt, Betsey. She's your mother's sister."

Benjy giggled as Malcolm tickled him. The smile her father wore took ten years off his face.

"Betsey, this fine young man is Ria's son, Benjy. Benjamin David."

Betsey sucked in a gasp at the name, but though her father's mouth tightened slightly, he brushed on past it. "We're trying to see how much work it'll require to restore the tree house to its former glory."

Betsey glanced at Ria. "*Ria? David?* How could you?" She shook her head violently. "I don't understand. You show up after six years without a word and—you're staying?" She gaped at her father. "And you're *smiling?* After what she put us through?"

Once they'd been so close. How many times had Betsey covered for her when she'd come home drunk and past curfew? Shame swept through Ria, but resentment stirred. What could this pampered stranger know of her life, of the battles Ria had faced? This woman understood nothing about loneliness so deep you wanted to die, about going hungry and sleeping cold and being so close to the edge you wanted to just let go and fall.

Betsey's face was bone-white and pinched. The expression she turned back to their father was a mixture of anger and pain and yearning.

Malcolm's tone was gentle but firm. "Watch what you say, honey." His gaze dropped to Benjy.

"Daddy, how can you just accept this? Especially when he—" She pointed at Benjy. "When he is the image of—"

"Not now, sweetheart." Malcolm pulled Benjy up and cradled him against his chest.

Her impeccable sister's composure was unraveling. Ria observed with fascination as Betsey became the image of Cleo earlier this morning, drawing herself up into impenetrable reserve. Her softhearted little sister was nowhere to be found.

Instead, a woman who was pure ice faced Ria. Only the eyes gave her away, brown like their father's but burning with a feverish glint. "I don't know what's going on, but I won't have it, do you understand me? You can't just drop back into our lives when we were all settled and expect us to act as though nothing ever happened. You destroyed this family, Vicky, and I won't let you do it again. We were doing fine without you."

"Stop it, Bets. Don't say things you don't mean," Malcolm intervened.

But her sister was in high dudgeon now, still staring at Ria. "Oh, I mean every word. David was your fault and Mother and Daddy's divorce was your doing, and I was left with nothing, no family at all. You ran out and I had no choice but to handle it." Her chin lifted. "Well, I did. We don't miss you."

"Elizabeth Anne, do not talk to your sister like that. If you can't be civil, then leave this house now."

Ria felt like a bystander at a train wreck. Except that the rushing air from its passage had knocked her off her feet. "No. I will. Benjy, come on."

Malcolm's voice went hard. "No, Ria." He didn't

loosen his hold on Benjy, who was regarding them all with wide eyes, his lip trembling slightly. "Shh, Benjy. It's going to be all right." One hand stroked the child's dark hair.

"How can it ever be all right with *her* around, Daddy?" Betsey shrilled. "She's never been anything but trouble. She broke your heart a hundred times. She killed—"

"Not one more word." Malcolm's voice was steel. "I will discuss this with you later." Then his tone gentled. "I think it's best that you leave now if the situation is so uncomfortable for you."

Betsey reacted as though she'd been slapped. "All I want is for you to be happy. I've tried to fix—" she shot Ria a look that was incredulous "—everything *she* destroyed." Her tone turned wounded. "How can you stand here and tell me that I should go and she can stay?"

Ria's legs were jelly. A loud buzz filled her head, and the tentative sense of belonging vanished like an early-morning mist. Everything her sister said was true. She had no defense to offer, no strength to try.

Her father came to her rescue, stepping in front of her where she stared down at the grass, tilting her chin up with one finger. "Families forgive, honey." He spoke to her sister, but he never took his eyes off Ria. "We have to go on from here."

Ria sought refuge in her father's warm brown gaze, caught in the light of a love she'd never expected to experience again. The hard shell of her loneliness cracked, rendering her more afraid than ever.

"Daddy, I'm—" *So sorry.* But Betsey was right. She'd forfeited the right to forgiveness long ago.

With Benjy on one hip, Malcolm gathered Ria against his chest, one strong arm around her shoulders. She burrowed in.

And heard Betsey's hoarse cry of pain, her footsteps as she ran away.

Ria huddled closer to the bulwark that was her father, her eyes stinging from the acid of her sister's anger. When she felt Benjy's small hand pat her head, it was her undoing.

"I can't stay, Daddy. But I don't know where—"

"Shh, sweetheart. You should have rest and food and time to think. It will all work out, I promise."

He was wrong. He'd always focused on the bright side, but her mother would not. Betsey had merely said what her mother was feeling.

But she was in no shape to leave yet. She had Benjy to consider, and he badly needed more time with enough food and shelter.

Ria leaned against her father and accepted his support, not kidding herself that she had more than a few days at most to figure things out.

But maybe…just for a little while…it would be all right to let someone else do the thinking for a change.

CHAPTER FIVE

THAT EVENING, Sandor kept his strokes even as he rolled paint over the last wall of the storeroom, but his mind wasn't on his work. Jerome had slipped away while Sandor had finished loading his truck, and he was worried about where the boy would spend the night. He knew nothing about the child except that he was clearly not getting enough to eat and had no supervision and that, despite his constant complaining, Jerome was a good helper. He never stopped talking, whether or not Sandor was silent, and he had a litany of gripes—no music, the weather was too hot even in October, his homies would laugh if they saw him wielding a broom…

But under the cover of his grumbles, he did the work.

And Sandor had intended to pay him as well as provide food; he also planned to make certain the boy had a safe place to stay.

But the boy had vanished, and Sandor had no idea where to find him. Now he had to pass the night imagining Jerome unprotected. For all his smart mouth, he was still just a boy, perhaps without any protection.

And there was not a thing Sandor could do, unless he was willing to bring in the authorities, something a man with his experience with corrupt bureaucracies would never do.

Then there was Cleo. Something more had happened today, but he did not know what.

He'd returned earlier, just in time to see a thunderous Colin heading back to his place. He'd heard Cleo talking on the phone and mentioning her ex-husband, but she'd slipped out the back door without her usual good-night. She was always thoughtful of his privacy, not presuming a right to enter without invitation even though the place was hers, but never before had she failed to alert him that she was leaving.

He wondered if he should intervene and warn Colin off. Cleo had had quite enough dumped on her lately, especially today. She was a remarkable human being whose beauty was more than her facade, but beyond her inner strength, there was a vulnerability that made him want to protect her.

Any man shallow enough not to appreciate the whole of her did not deserve her. He'd never met her ex-husband, but he scorned him, nonetheless. Betsey had told him of her father's much-younger companion, and Sandor found it pathetic, if typical of men that age.

Sandor would not do that to his own woman. When he found her, the mate of his soul he refused to believe did not exist, he would guard her and cherish her and love her all his days.

He had women who were interested, yes, but he did

not have time for a relationship yet; much more must be accomplished for him to be able to take care of his woman the way he wanted. It was why he had been cautious about forming any lasting attachments in Hungary. He wanted a family as much as any man—perhaps more than most. But he had known since he was a young boy that someday he would leave there, and uprooting a whole family was unfair.

So Sandor shied away from any deeper involvement and thus found himself less and less willing to attempt to satisfy his appetite with a candy bar when what he longed for was a full-course meal.

The hunger would wait. Must do so, though he was not certain whom he was waiting for.

For now, his concern was his friend Cleo. Perhaps he would call her, though he seldom intruded on her at home. But she had a houseful of guests—

And he was still worried about Jerome.

"GOOD NIGHT, Lola," Ria said.

"So early, doll?"

"It's been a long day." A long month…year. She wasn't sure what she'd expected when she set out to fulfill her promise to Dog Boy, but not this half-world she'd entered. Her parents divorced, her father warm and loving but lacking a place for her and Benjy, her mother with enough room but welcome only for Ria's son…her sister's hate, her grandmother's mixed reception, Aunt Cammie's predictable kindness.

Too much thrown at her and no clear path to follow.

"Sweet dreams," Aunt Cammie said.

Oh, if only, Aunt Cammie. She couldn't remember the last time she'd had a good night's sleep, much less the boon of pleasant dreams.

She glanced in on Benjy and smiled as Tyrone lifted his head from where he was curled into Benjy's side. She brushed her hand over her child's hair and kissed his cheek. "Sleep tight, my love." When she passed, she stroked Tyrone's fur. "Help me keep him safe, boy."

As she drifted off, she hoped that tomorrow would be better. That she'd wake up and somehow she would know what to do.

"RIA!" DAVID CRIED out from his perch behind the screen door. Every afternoon, he waited for her to come home from school. Some days it was kind of neat, but today she just wanted to be alone.

Victoria's best friend, Jill, waved at him as they crossed the front yard. "Hi, David," Jill called out. To Victoria, she said, "He's really cute."

Victoria shrugged. "He's all right." For someone who was always underfoot.

They reached the door just as her mother unlatched the screen. One day they'd found him by the street waiting for Daddy to come home. Mother had gone pale, gathering him up in her arms. First she'd cried, then yelled at Victoria, then scolded David that he was a daredevil just like his sister. Victoria had had to sit in her room for the rest of the afternoon just for forgetting to latch the screen door.

Little kids were so much trouble. David was almost two, but he was still a baby.

"Hi, Mrs. Channing," Jill said.

"Hello, girls. Where's Betsey?"

Victoria rolled her eyes. "She's with that dork, Scott." Betsey was only nine, a stupid fourth-grader, but she already had a boyfriend. She lorded it over Victoria, who was taller than all the boys and skinny, to boot. Victoria would never get breasts, never.

Her mother's eyebrows lifted. "Where are they?"

Victoria shrugged. "Somewhere behind us."

"You and your sister are supposed to walk home together. You know that."

David was pulling at her jeans. "Ria, Ria, come watch *Sesa Reet* with me." He stretched to his toes for her to pick him up.

"Not now, David." Her mother was still glaring at her. "Betsey's fine, Mom. She's always got a million friends with her. She'll be here in a minute." Never, on pain of death, would Victoria admit that Betsey was ashamed of her and didn't want to walk together. Victoria was the oldest, but Betsey was prettier and smarter and always, always did things right. The teachers loved her.

Victoria's teachers hated her. Especially Mrs. Goodman, the old bat who taught math and had already warned Victoria that she was calling her mother after school today to discuss her attitude.

"Ria," David whined, tugging at her arm.

"Victoria, I want you to go back and get your sis—"

"Stop it, David!" She shoved his arm away. He fell back on his rear, stunned, his mouth open.

"Victoria Grace Channing, don't you ever strike your brother. Go to your room this minute! I'm ashamed of you, picking on someone so much younger."

"I wasn't—"

"Don't back-talk me, young lady. In your room right now. Jill, I think you had better go on home."

Jill's eyes went wide. "Yes, Mrs. Channing."

Victoria started to protest her mother's refusal to listen, then cringed as David's big brown eyes filled with hurt and tears.

I had a bad day, she wanted to tell them. *I didn't do anything wrong, but my teacher hates me and Todd Caldwell told me I was ugly and I know I'll never have breasts and Betsey will always be perfect like Mother and no one ever asks what I want anymore. Just "Be nice to David" and "Where is your sister?" and "Victoria, why can't you behave?"*

But she didn't utter one word. Instead, she cradled her books into her chest and retreated to her room, wishing she were anyone but Victoria Channing, who had a gorgeous mother and beautiful sister and adorable little brother and a daddy who'd forgotten that she used to be his special girl.

HALF-ASLEEP, Ria cried out. Reached blindly. Rolled, and barely caught herself at the edge of the bed.

Heart pounding, she sat up. She gripped the spread, shook her head and blinked until she remembered where she was.

She sagged as despair rose like a smothering fog, settling over her until she knew she could not face one more day.

No. She shoved herself to her feet, then stumbled and grabbed the bedpost to right herself. *Help me, Dog Boy. Please.* She held her breath, listening.

But no one answered.

She straightened and forced herself to cross the floor, open the door. *Get out of this room, away from these thoughts.*

Down the stairs she went, headed for the kitchen—

In the doorway, she halted at the sight of her mother, one finger pressed to her lips.

Swollen lips. Recently kissed lips.

Daddy's face rose before Ria. Her promise to Lola fled in the wake of fury that all but blinded her. "Was he good?"

Her mother whirled. "What?"

"No woman looks like that unless she's been with a man. Anyone I know?"

Cleo tugged at her clothes as if checking to make sure she'd put herself back together. "That's none of your business."

Oh, God. Ria laughed, but there was no humor in it. She felt sick. First Daddy with a girlfriend, then her mother with some guy.

"It's true, isn't it? Who is he? My, my…maybe we

have more in common than I thought. This is a whole new wrinkle, Mother." With casualness she didn't feel, she strolled into the kitchen and leaned against the counter. "Want to tell me all about it?"

Cleo whirled on her, high color in her cheeks. "I don't have to explain anything about my life. You ran out six years ago and didn't have the courtesy to tell us you were alive."

"Am I supposed to believe you would have worried?"

"Of course we did," Cleo cried, pointing in the direction of Benjy's bedroom. "That little boy—you kept him from us. Why? And what are you doing back now?"

"I thought—" *Maybe things would be different. No—Dog Boy thought they would, but I never did.* Ria shoved away from the counter. "It doesn't matter. I was wrong. You still don't give a damn about me. You're only upset that I didn't tell you about Benjy." Desperate to get away, to think, she headed for the door. "Maybe he was better off, unaware of you. I sure was."

She was practically running for the door when she noted what she was wearing. With a quick reverse, she made for the stairs.

"Victoria, I do—"

Care? Don't make me laugh, Mother. Misery propelled her into her room, but not her room anymore, she thought, as she quickly donned the first clothes she found, then pounded back down the steps.

Her mother appeared in the foyer. "Where are you going?"

"Out."

"Where?"

Ria whirled, her jaw so tight the words barely slipped through. "I don't know, *Mother.* Do I have a curfew?"

"What about Benjy?"

Ria laughed so sharply it hurt her ears. "You'll take care of him, of course." She slipped halfway through the door. "And maybe, just maybe, you'll get real lucky and I won't come back. Then everything will be perfect in Cleo's little world."

"Victoria, I would never—"

Ria ran before her mother could lie to her again.

Her strides slowed when she got to the bottom of the hill on Twelfth Street facing Lamar. Traffic whizzed by in both directions, the hubbub of Austin traffic swirling around her. She didn't wait for the light but darted between cars, daring the drivers whose horns blared.

Go ahead. See if I care.

Miss me, miss me, now you gotta kiss me. The old schoolyard rhyme sang in her head.

Why did it have to be this way between her and Cleo? They'd been millstone and grain as long as she could remember, each grating against the other, grinding their relationship into dust.

They were mother and daughter. Shouldn't that mean something? Weren't mothers supposed to love their children, no matter what?

She loved Benjy, would defend him to her dying breath. Nothing would ever change that.

Where did we go wrong, Mother? When did you start to hate me? Was it before I killed your child? I can't recall anymore how it felt to be your darling.

A car came to a screeching halt inches away from her, the driver shouting at her as she stumbled across the street, blinded by her tears. "Hey, lady, what's the matter? You drunk or somethin'?"

She made a rude gesture and kept walking, hunched over in the night. A half block ahead, she saw a dingy bar with Joe's Place on the sign.

Trite. Seedy. Perfect. Ria pulled the door open and stepped inside, sucking in the welcome scents of beer and cigarette smoke.

I'll just nurse one along until everyone up there in Hell House is asleep. Then I'll go home.

Home. She faltered. Where was that?

Forget it. She dug into her pocket and counted out her pitiful funds.

"Scotch. Rocks."

When it arrived, she downed it.

Ria held the glass in her hand, rolling it and studying the reflection of the neon beer sign behind the bar. In the background, Alan Jackson crooned a song about remembering, about a couple who once had it all. As the bite of the Scotch quieted the beehive buzz in her brain, a molasses-slow melancholy settled on her shoulders, dipping down into a heart that was weary nigh onto dying.

What a mess she'd made of everything.

Except Benjy. Sweet, stubborn child of her heart. The luckiest accident of her life.

"What do I do?" she whispered.

"You dance with me, li'l darlin'. Ol' Cal here will make everything better." Lanky, with a dark mustache and smiling blue eyes, this stranger beat any other company she'd had tonight.

Ria summoned a cocksure grin. "I don't dance with just anyone, cowboy. Buy me another drink and we'll see."

Cal tipped back his hat and sat down beside her. "Barkeep, another one of what this lady's drinking."

And Ria lost herself in sweet talk and laughter, the day's edges smoothed off by whiskey. After another couple of drinks, she let herself fall into the sins of the flesh with a whimper of relief. Cigarettes she seldom smoked, too many Scotches to count, a dance now and again where she reveled in how Cal's eyes raked her body…pretty soon, the world righted itself, and Ria felt good again.

Good enough to get horny. Enough not to care where Cal's hands roamed. *Just keep the liquor flowing, barkeep, and I'll get through this night without thinking too much.*

When Ria got too dizzy, Cal led her outside, promising to take her home. In the dark parking lot behind the building, he pulled her into the shadows cast by trees overhanging the hood of his pickup.

"Come on, Ria girl, I promise you gonna like it."

"Maybe." *Just stop me from thinking.*

He had her jeans unsnapped and off one leg before she could blink, not even bothering with a kiss. She heard his zipper slide down, and she shoved at his chest. "You'd better have a rubber on that thing, cowboy."

Cal cursed and fished into his pocket. When Ria saw the deed done, she lifted one leg and wrapped it behind his hips. *Turn off, damn you. Turn off.* But her whirling brain refused. Ria shoved at him when he tried to kiss her. "No kissing."

"Just like a worthless whore. Hell," he growled. "Shoulda known you was worthless."

Ria slapped him.

"Be still, bitch." He grabbed her arms and tried to pin her to the hood. "I ain't finished."

"I don't care," she cried, and clawed at his eyes.

SANDOR FINISHED cleaning his paintbrush and raked his fingers through already tousled hair, muttering a few choice words in Hungarian. Perhaps a walk would clear his head; he certainly was not ready to sleep.

Without pausing for a jacket, he strode outside. Blocks later, little more at ease than when he'd begun, he noted that he'd reached Lamar and Twelfth, only a short distance from Cleo's house. He could hike up the hill and talk to her. See if she needed to discuss whatever had happened earlier.

But it was late, and he respected her privacy. So he turned right instead of left and headed toward downtown. A short block later, he crossed in front of a dingy bar on West Twelfth that had withstood the gentrification taking place around it. For a moment, he contemplated entering to seek out a beer. He reached for the door handle—

A scream cut through the darkness.

Sandor charged around the side of the building, where he heard furious words he couldn't make out.

Then the sound of a slap, flesh upon flesh.

"Be still, damn you," a man's voice growled. "You asked for this."

"Let me go—" a woman cried.

Sandor spotted them in front of a pickup, the woman half-naked and fighting. "Stop—" he shouted.

They didn't seem to hear him. She clawed at the man's eyes.

He dropped her, and she slid to the ground with a yelp, then scrambled to gather her things and retreat from him. "Get away from me."

"Goddamn you, leadin' a man on like that. Come here."

"Let her be," Sandor ordered.

The man turned in fury. "Get the hell out of here."

"Not until I speak with the lady." Sandor cast a quick glimpse toward her.

The woman rapidly straightened her clothes, sobbing with each breath.

"Are you hurt?"

She glanced up then, eyes wild, hair choppy and short and black, face shadowed with fear and pain.

"This ain't your business," the other man snarled. "Get back over here, Ria, and finish what you promised."

Ria? The man charged, and Sandor couldn't stop to ponder. He blocked the man's path, casting over his shoulder. "Go—wait for me in front."

"You goddamn drunken whore—don't you leave!"

Sandor didn't pause to see where she went. "You deal with me now, unless you are too frightened of someone your size."

Mean eyes narrowed. "I'm not afraid of anyone." He took a swing.

Sandor had no trouble dodging that blow or the next. Each maneuver only increased the man's rage.

"Bring it on. You too chicken to stand and fight?"

Sandor ignored the taunt, watching for the opportunity.

Then it appeared. He moved in under the man's guard, hooked a foot around his ankle and dropped him on his back on the pavement.

His opponent didn't move, mouth gaping like a fish's as he sought the breath that had been knocked out of him.

Sandor chose mercy. "No man is worthy to call himself such if he mistreats women." He cast a disparaging glare, then turned to go.

He made it only a few feet before a bellow of rage preceded heavy footsteps. He whirled and met the charge.

Fists flew, and the skin on them broke. To continue

the battle was not his choice, but Sandor never backed down when trouble was brought to his door. He avoided physical violence as a means of resolution, but that did not mean he could not acquit himself well.

"Break it up, you two," a voice shouted. "I've phoned the cops."

Sandor's opponent lifted his head, registered the situation and spit a violent curse. "This ain't over," he warned Sandor. "But you're not worth going to jail for, and she's sure as hell not."

With that, he took off running for his pickup. Tires squealed as he drove out the back way.

Sandor swiped at a cut on his mouth and glanced at the owner of the voice. "Is there a woman waiting in front?"

"The one who was all over that guy?" The older man shook his head. "Of course not. She's long gone. Best you make yourself scarce, too."

Sandor shook his head and wondered if he'd just encountered Cleo's bad-seed daughter.

RIA RAN AND RAN, until her lungs burned and her stomach heaved. Halfway up the hill to the only place she knew to go, she stopped and was sick in someone's bushes.

Whore. Goddamn drunken whore. The refrain repeated again and again with every step she took.

Finally, she arrived outside the house that had once been home, looking up at the window of the room where her son lay sleeping, and wondered if she should make things easier on everyone and just go away.

She opened the front door and crept inside, but lost her balance and thumped against the wall.

Aunt Cammie appeared in her robe, her face creased with worry.

"Sorry, sorry." She snickered, her voice high, half-hysterical. Ria backed away, ashamed to have Aunt Cammie see her like this, smelling of sex and booze and cigarettes.

"I—I'll take care of myself, Aunt Cammie."

"You certainly will not." Her quiet aunt, who slipped around in shadows, stood her ground. "You think you're the only one ever met hopeless, child? I'm going to put you to bed, and you don't be fretting any more tonight. Tomorrow is soon enough, or the next day. Answers aren't that easy, not for most of us."

Ria nodded toward the house. "They are for her."

Aunt Cammie smiled sadly. "No, they aren't. Your mother just hides it better than most." She pulled Ria closer. "Now, come on."

"I—I smell bad. This guy—"

"Shh, sweetheart. I'll draw you a nice bath downstairs, where no one will hear you."

"I'm so tired, Aunt Cammie."

"Lean on me, child. There's love waiting for you to take it."

"Oh, Aunt Cammie, if only you were right." Nonetheless, Ria let her tiny aunt shepherd her to bed.

Not home, no, but shelter. At least for one more night.

RIA STIRRED, pushing against the smothering blanket of despair, the bone-deep chill of knowing that nothing would ever be okay again.

With fingers frozen by fear, she scrabbled at the door handle of the car, shoving hard with muscles that had turned to water.

Finally, the door opened. She turned to get David out.

He wasn't there. He never was.

"David," she screamed. "Where are you?"

You killed him. You should have died.

The faces hovered, accusing. Her mother's uncombed hair, her vacant stare, her beauty gone haggard. Her father's frame bowed under the weight of being strong for all of them.

"Daddy," she wept. "Mother, I didn't mean—"

But no one could hear her.

She was alone with the sickening knowledge.

That no one would ever love her again.

RIA SAT UP in the bed with a gasp, trying to figure out where she was. "Benjy—" Faint tendrils of light crept beneath the window shades.

She scrambled from the bed, her limbs leaden from the dream. Her vision grayed, and she grasped at the doorjamb.

Then she heard her son giggle, heard her mother's low, husky laughter.

Her fingers tightened on the wood, and she readied

her jellied muscles to go down the stairs to spirit him away. To recapture the only thing good in her life.

"Go back to bed, child." Aunt Cammie appeared before her, silver hair in tiny pin curls, quilted robe zipped to her throat. She laid a hand on Ria's shoulder and squeezed. "We'll care for Benjy. You need to rest."

The small hand stroking her back now imparted a comfort Ria was desperate to claim. "He's my son. I have to—"

Aunt Cammie led her back to the bed. "You don't have to do anything right now but sleep and heal." With careful, efficient movements, she straightened the bedclothes and urged Ria onto the mattress with a gentle but unshakable hand. Then she tucked the covers around Ria as though she was still a child.

Tears sprang to Ria's eyes. No one had cared for her in so long. "Aunt Cammie, I—"

Wise blue-gray eyes peered out from a lined, gentle face. The faint aroma of talcum powder clung, as always, to Aunt Cammie's skin. She was not a pretty woman, certainly nothing like her once-glamorous sister, but she was beautiful from the inside out. "Shh, Ria. Time will solve everything. You just rest now. Later, I'll make you cinnamon toast loaded with sugar, the way you always liked it when you came to visit."

Ria tried for a smile. "Don't let her take him away from me."

The silver head shook slowly. "Your mother loves you, child. She isn't your enemy."

Aunt Cammie was too gentle. She didn't understand that some things were beyond forgiveness.

Ria clutched at the older woman's wrist. "Promise me you'll watch out for Benjy. If I sleep, you'll keep him safe?"

Aunt Cammie frowned faintly, but her voice was soothing. "He is surrounded by people who adore him."

"Promise—" Ria struggled to rise.

Two small hands settled her back on her pillow. "All right, Ria. I promise." The voice was firm and unyielding. "Now, you rest. You're safe here, and so is your child. You're home now."

Home. For them, yes. Even for Benjy. But not for her. Ria drifted off to sleep, dreaming of the day she'd find the place where she belonged.

CHAPTER SIX

THE DAWN SKY WAS RIMMED in coral as Sandor descended the stairs from his apartment, frowning. He had planned to be at the restaurant early. His agreement with the owner stipulated that he would work around their prime serving hours, which required him to finish by ten in the morning. If he could arrange it, he would be welcome to return for two hours in the afternoon, after the lunch rush and before dinner, as long as he stayed out of the way of the kitchen crew. He had lost time yesterday morning while feeding Jerome, and he wanted to make it up, though he was well ahead of schedule.

But he could not get the woman from the parking lot out of his mind. Even his worries over Jerome occupied second place.

He flexed his right hand and winced. What if she had, indeed been Cleo's troubled daughter? In the leaf-dappled shadows cast by streetlights, he had caught only a glimpse of her face, but even as disheveled and frightened as she had been, there had been something about her….

She had her mother's eyes. Taller by several inches, lacking anything approaching Cleo's elegance, she was still striking in her own way, ragged hair, scruffy clothes and all.

Still, Cleo's gaze, though sorrowful since her daughter's arrival, still held optimism. Power.

The woman last night was all but bereft of hope. He had known others like her, many of them, in his homeland. No enemy or oppressor could destroy a nation or a person more thoroughly than despair. It kept people docile; futility made them weak.

Yet, he recalled, she'd had enough spirit to fight her attacker, even if the bar owner swore that she'd all but laid herself on a platter for the man Sandor had battled.

Thus, she still must possess a flicker of optimism, however deeply buried. He could testify from experience that the tiniest spark could be nurtured into a roaring blaze. His presence in this country was proof of that.

She could be saved.

Sandor didn't like the direction of his thoughts. Even if this woman proved to be her child, Cleo commanded his absolute loyalty.

Her daughter was on her own.

He dismissed her from consideration and focused on scanning the streets near the restaurant, searching for signs of Jerome.

LATE IN THE AFTERNOON, Ria heard the piano and Benjy's laughter. She went downstairs to investigate and couldn't stifle a grin at the sight before her.

Benjy, Aunt Cammie and Lola had obviously returned from walking Tyrone. Now her son stood on her mother's precious cherry dining table in his sock feet, gripping a wooden spoon as Lola demonstrated the fine art of pretending it was a microphone.

Aunt Cammie was noodling around on the piano, her normally shy smile widening.

"Let's hit it," Lola called out. "Time for some Aretha Franklin—give us a chord, Cammie."

Aunt Cammie complied.

"Follow my lead, sweetie. Since you don't know the words, just sing out *woo-woo* whenever the mood strikes you," Lola instructed Benjy.

Benjy giggled.

Ria would have walked the entire cross-country trip on foot just for this moment. For the carefree look on her child's face.

Then he spotted her. "Mom, come sing!"

She shook her head. "I'd rather listen."

"Oh, no, you don't," Lola said. "I was going to hunt you down if you didn't show up soon." She brandished another wooden spoon. "Get over here."

Benjy chimed in, and Aunt Cammie threw herself into playing music that called to a part of Ria craving to let loose for a while, to stop worrying and simply live in the moment. To remember what fun was like.

And she actually did love to sing. When she wasn't raising hell in high school, track and choir had been her favorite moments of the day.

Everyone in this room cared about her, she realized. Not one of them would make fun of her or ask her for anything but to join in the merriment and leave it at that.

The huge smile on her child's face when she accepted her wooden spoon and moved to stand beside her grandmother, facing the antique mirror on the opposite wall, was all the validation she needed.

The music swelled past her grandmother's off-key voice and her child's giggles. A bubble of happiness rose inside her as she closed her eyes and sang…and with profound gratefulness, Ria let the music bear her away.

Aretha led to The Supremes, and Ria couldn't remember the last time she had felt this light and free. They laughed and clapped and stamped their feet on the floor. She caught the sight of them in the mirror—

And froze as she spotted her mother.

Who had gone just as still.

Ria tensed for disapproval. Beside her, Lola swiveled, caught by Ria's sudden silence.

But Benjy felt no such constraint. "Nana, sing with us! We're The Supremes."

Aunt Cammie kept playing, and Lola advanced on Cleo, grasping her hand. "Here, take my mike. I'm loud enough without one."

Cleo clasped the spoon in her hand, an odd look of indecision on her face. She darted a glance at her daughter, and suddenly, it dawned on Ria that her mother might be as afraid of derision as she herself was.

After last night's bitter exchange, neither had reason to trust the other's kindness.

The thought of the evening before sapped the joy from the moment, as Ria remembered, through the scrim of her drunken behavior, all that had happened.

Her mother was right to hate her. She despised herself.

Then Lola started singing again, and Benjy chimed in with his *woo-woos,* interrupting only to say, "Please, Nana."

Cleo stared at her daughter, waiting.

The moment spun out, and Ria realized that, this once, she had the power. She could slap at her mother again…or extend an olive branch, though she had little hope of it being accepted.

Inhaling deeply to steady herself, Ria scooted over to make room. With a dazed expression on her face, her mother slipped in beside her.

And the music entwined them all in fragile new tendrils of hope.

LATER, WHILE AUNT CAMMIE cooked on the stove, and her mother prepared a salad with Lola observing as she sipped a glass of wine, Ria found herself with the luxury of nothing to do but teach Benjy about setting the table. The golden glow of the last hour lingered, and inspiration struck her.

"Sweetie. Let's go outside."

Her mother peered at them curiously but refrained from commenting.

"We'll be right back."

"What are we doing, Mom?"

"I thought we could make a centerpiece for the table for Nana."

"What's a centerpiece?"

Nothing could demonstrate more vividly the difference in their rearing. Cleo had always decorated the table, though sometimes more elaborately than others, while Ria had done well to provide food for her son, much less the niceties.

She explained as they gathered—small brown acorns from the live oaks, red and green nandina shoots, a few pecans and the first golden leaves of fall, though Central Texas still felt more like summer.

Back inside, she sought other ingredients: a bright ruby apple, a fat golden pear. Assorted cups and saucers and napkins. Goblets and candles. With them, she and Benjy built a series of platforms, draping the napkins over some, nestling acorns inside goblets, nandina spikes in a glass, scattering leaves here and there.

When she moved to the side, her mother gasped.

Ria tensed. *It looks dumb. I should never have…*

But her mother surprised her. "It's extraordinary, Vic—Ria," she stammered. "How lovely."

Stunned, Ria shrugged. "Just something I made up."

"It's beautiful. You have real style. None of those items is unusual by itself, but the composite is amazing."

Ria was thrilled but wary of hoping for too much. Petrified to disturb the fragile peace, she turned away.

"Let's go wash our hands, Benjy. Dinner's nearly ready, right, Aunt Cammie?"

"Yes, dear. Only a couple of minutes more."

Her mother averted her face, but not before Ria saw the hurt and withdrawal. Before she could do anything else wrong, Ria whisked her son from the room.

During dinner, Ria berated herself and tried to figure out how to recapture that precious moment of her mother's praise, but she couldn't. Lola kept the conversation going until dessert, though both Ria and Cleo said little.

Ria's tension had ratcheted so high she was ready for escape.

But just then, her mother spoke. "Ria, may I ask you a favor?"

Ria stiffened. "What?"

All eyes but Benjy's were on them. He drove a little car around the edge of his plate.

Cleo hesitated, then forged on. "I could use a new display at the shop. I'm wondering if you would be interested in a job."

Ria blinked, too staggered to speak. Why would—

Cleo rushed ahead. "I'm shorthanded right now, and it's usually my responsibility, but if you could spare the time, it would free me to catch up on the paperwork that's been mounting because I've had to be out front more."

All Ria could manage was, "Why?"

"One of my assistants quit, and Betsey doesn't work but two days a week—"

"No," Ria interrupted, "why me?"

Cleo gestured to the centerpiece. "I like your flair."

"Why would you trust me?" There had to be a catch.

Lola cast Ria a chiding frown.

Ria stared right back at her grandmother. But even as she hedged, the prospect of the job glimmered before her, tempting and lovely.

"We could make it a trial run. I'll pay you, of course, but if you enjoy the work and the display is effective, we could make it more permanent."

Because she wanted it so badly, Ria snatched at objections. "Betsey will hate it."

"It's not Betsey's shop. And your sister will adjust."

She was terrified to care this much, so she played it cool. "I may not be around long."

But though her mother's eyes had lost the gleam of enthusiasm, she persisted. "Even once would be a big help to me."

But what if I fail you again? What if you hate it? Ria was far more scared to try than to get the hurt over with quickly. She ventured one last objection. "I don't have anywhere to leave Benjy."

Her mother wilted a little more.

But Lola jumped in. "Cammie and I would love to baby-sit," Lola said, turning to Benjy. "Tyrone needs watching, and I think you're just the man for the job, Benjamin, don't you?"

Benjy smiled. "Sure, Grammy."

Cleo and Ria exchanged startled looks. *Grammy?* From the woman who refused to be called by anything but her stage name?

Lola sniffed regally, daring them to comment. "Then it's settled. Tomorrow your mother will go to the shop with Nana, and we'll have ourselves some fun."

Cleo's expression was carefully neutral and polite. "I'd like to get started before we open. Will eight or eight-thirty suit you?"

Did she really dare do this? With her heart flip-flopping in her chest, Ria nodded. "I'll be ready." Then she rose from the table, hoping her legs would hold her. "If you'll excuse us, Benjy, it's time for your bath."

She escaped before either she or her mother could come to their senses.

HE SHOULD take the final step, Sandor thought the next morning, and move his wood-carving tools to the garage below his apartment. Billie was willing, and the space was there.

But this was the work of his heart, and he had produced the best pieces of his life here in Cleo's domain. Was it the light, the location or the sense of shelter he felt? His mouth quirked in wry amusement. He, Cleo's self-appointed protector, felt safer in this place where he had first found a new home. A fresh chance.

Which was why, no doubt, he had given up the attempt to sleep at three in the morning and driven to the shop. Billie might say she slept like the dead, but the only work he could do there would generate a great deal of noise.

So he had risen and dressed and sought refuge from his worries in this place. He stared at the piece he'd been crafting, on and off, for weeks now, knowing from the first moment he had breached the rough exterior of the block of wood, that it would be his finest effort. Sinuous and golden, a woman's form had emerged, and spoke to the deepest part of him.

He did not know her; she resembled no flesh-and-blood female he had met, but somehow, she evoked a response he did not altogether welcome.

She stirred the man who had become nearly a monk, so obsessed had he been with creating the existence he had waited thirty-five years to live, and made him realize that in some ways, he was still waiting.

He had work, a handful of friends, a few women, though he could have had more. Women seemed drawn to him for various reasons—the accent, the cultural difference, perhaps even his detachment made him seem a challenge.

But sex, though a fine physical outlet, was lonely without the accompanying bond.

"Good morning."

At the sound of Cleo's voice, Sandor started and dropped his chisel. He had completely missed the peal of the chime she kept at the back door. "Good morning." He turned and found himself echoing the grin he had not seen on her face in days. "You seem happy."

"I am. My daughter is—oh!" She broke off in mid-sentence as she glanced behind him. "Sandor—" She stared at the figure as if mesmerized. After a long span, she glanced up, eyes wide. "It's incredible. Absolutely stunning. Such power." She put out a hand, then drew it back, curling her fingers. "It's not even finished, and I want to touch it so badly my skin tickles. Look—" She held out an arm. "Goose bumps. My word, Sandor." Her smile could have eclipsed the sun. "You have no business pretending to be a handyman. If you don't give the galleries a chance at this, I will absolutely have a fit."

He laughed, both delighted and embarrassed. "I cannot begin to tell you how the prospect of your tantrum frightens me."

She joined him. "Smart aleck." Then she sobered. "I'm serious, though. How often have I told you how remarkable your work is? You should be doing this full-time, and I should be shot for taking advantage of you for so long."

Advantage? "Cleopatra," he said, very seriously, clasping her hand. "You cannot possibly believe that. You saved me. You gave a perfect stranger a chance. Thanks to you, I have had the opportunity to make a life in this strange and beautiful country as I dreamed of doing since I was a small child." He covered both their hands with his other one, as if pledging fealty. "There is no possible way for me to repay you, but there is nothing I would not do for you in the attempt."

Cleo's eyes glistened, and she squeezed his hand. "You owe me nothing, Sandor. You're my friend—it's what friends do." She gestured toward the piece. "I'm completely serious about this. If you don't put together a portfolio and show it around, I swear I'm going to do it for you. I can't wait for Ria to see this."

He blinked at the pride and joy in her tone. "Ria?"

She whirled to face him, both hope and fear in her eyes. "She'll be here—" she glanced at her watch and frowned faintly "—very soon. She promised to get under way well before the shop opened."

He checked the time. *Then she had better hurry.* But he kept silent, wondering what was transpiring.

"I'm going to have her design a display. She has an amazing eye." Cleo seemed oblivious that she was chewing at her lip. "Oh, Sandor, I wish you could have been there last night." She touched his arm. "I think there's hope for us."

The woman before him was not the same Cleo determined to snatch a grandchild from a neglectful mother, or the woman broken by the loss of a son. This one was nearly manic in her excitement, floating on both nerves and forced optimism.

She would not welcome speculation about her daughter's whereabouts two nights ago, possibly the same woman who was late, even granted this chance to mend fences. The daughter who would bruise her mother's heart again.

So though Sandor had intended to leave, he would stay and assess the situation himself when Ria arrived. And hope to find no resemblance at all to a half-naked woman caught in the seedy shadows of a parking lot.

RIA HAD CHOSEN to walk to the shop, only eight blocks away. She was late, and every step closer tempted her to go back. She had changed clothes three times before returning to her first instinct, black jeans and a man's white shirt tied at the waist. She'd tried her lone dress, but it only heightened the contrast between her and the ever-elegant Cleo. The morning was cool, and she had donned Dog Boy's black leather jacket as much for reassurance as for warmth.

Why had she agreed? It would be a disaster, this ill-fated attempt at a truce.

She needed the money, but there were far easier ways to earn it than trying to please her mother. Ria attempted to forget her nerves and forced herself to study the neighborhood that had once been so familiar.

Austin had grown explosively in her absence, it appeared. A block down, the ramshackle prairie-style home where crazy old Mrs. Hunt and her twenty or more cats had lived now sported a revamped second floor, a wall of windows on the front taking in the downtown skyline. What had happened to the animals that had once wound around Mrs. Hunt's ankles while she sang in her shaky trill?

A Volvo and a Land Rover were parked in the driveway now. Gentrified prettiness where once there had been shabby soulfulness, tattered but durable, not glossy and new. Ria shuddered.

Realizing she'd slowed her pace, she again fought the urge to turn back. Then she remembered Lola's pleased expression when Ria had accepted her mother's offer.

Give her a chance.

It won't work, Lola. It never does.

But Ria thought about how her mother had hung back from participating in the singing last night, how for a moment she had appeared almost…uncertain.

Her mother's voice wasn't strong, never had been. She didn't carry a tune that well—about the only thing she didn't do to perfection. So she hadn't sung very loudly, and she might never have joined them at all, except for Benjy's urging.

The experience had been awkward, like a junior-high dance. Oh, Lola was perfectly comfortable, but then, Lola had never known a shy moment in her life.

She and her mother had both felt self-conscious, however. It was Benjy's aching eagerness that had tipped the balance. Had brought Cleo into the music and kept Ria from running out of the room.

For a few minutes carved out of a lifetime, they had had fun together, Ria and her mother. And she had let that fragile peace sway her into this fool's errand.

She turned the corner and saw her mother's car in the alley behind the row of trendy shops. Sucking air into lungs that had slammed shut, she marched toward her fate as surely as any victim ever faced a firing squad.

The back door was open, and she could hear voices. A man's rumble, and woman's merriment, which, she suddenly realized, belonged to her mother.

She couldn't recall the last time she'd heard her mother laugh like that.

Clenching fingers over sweaty palms, Ria edged inside the door of what at first seemed to be only storage. To the right was an open space with the unmistakable aroma of fresh paint.

Ria glanced to the left, to an area lined with shelves, and did a double take.

In the center of the bright glow cast by a skylight stood a large block of wood, not finished but already sculpted into graceful lines…hypnotically sensual, erotic in a way Ria had never dreamed wood could be. A woman's curves were emerging from the wood, so alive Ria could feel the breath suspended inside the grain.

She walked closer, her hand rising toward it.

"I prefer that you not touch."

The voice startled her, and Ria whirled.

"Body oils discolor the wood." The man moved like a lion stalking, all tawny hair and muscular grace.

"I'm sorry. It's just so—"

One eyebrow lifted. He looked at her oddly but didn't speak, as if waiting for her to continue.

"Sensual. Pure."

He evidenced no pleasure in her compliments. Unfriendly hazel eyes pinned her. "Some would call that a contradiction in terms."

"They'd be wrong."

The predator's gaze eased only slightly. "I agree."

A strained silence ensued. Finally, Ria spoke. "You're obviously the artist. I'm—"

"Cleopatra's cub," he supplied.

Not even her father was allowed to call her mother Cleopatra. Who was this man?

"Ria?"

Her mother's voice startled her. Ria turned, expecting censure for being late.

Instead, a quiet pride glowed as Cleo nodded toward the piece. "I see you and Sandor have met. Isn't his work amazing? Sandor Wolfe, this is my—"

"Daughter. She could be no one else. The eyes, the hair, she is unmistakably yours." The resemblance didn't please him. His accent was one Ria couldn't place, but his voice sounded oddly familiar. His tone was polite, but his body spelled out warning in the step he took to be closer to Cleo, as if a guardian, a bulwark.

In that instant, Ria had a sinking feeling that this was the man who had given her mother the look she'd worn coming home late the other night. Faintly bruised lips. Soft eyes. Mussed hair.

He must be her mother's lover, this much-younger warrior with knife-blade cheekbones and warning eyes, his powerful body hovering behind the dainty Cleo.

This man who could make a piece of wood live and breathe.

She lifted her chin. Glared at him.

He dared to stand where Ria's father should be. In that instant, Cleo and Malcolm's divorce became real, and it seemed more wrong and hurtful than anything since David's death.

His gaze hardened. Became fierce, almost savage.

Dear God. Were those her mother's curves in that wood?

She couldn't be here. Ria readied herself to leave before she heard her mother's voice.

"Sandor, would you please excuse us?" Cleo began with her usual ice-cold control, but an undertow tugged at Ria, echoing what had persuaded her into agreeing to this mistake last night.

Her mother's uncertainty. A tremor in her voice so faint Ria might have imagined it.

And defiance mixed with a plea.

He didn't move, and his stare was palpable, as intense as that of a hunter marking prey. He scanned her from head to foot, his contempt clear. Dared her to leave. Waited for her to rebuke her mother, then he would strike, quick and merciless. Only his caring for her mother held him back now.

Amazing. He protected Cleo because he thought she was vulnerable.

Your mother just hides it better than most. Was Aunt Cammie right? Did the perfect Cleo have a soft underbelly?

Change things this time. It doesn't have to be a battle.

But the big guy was spoiling for one, she could see.

To rob him of the pleasure of throwing her out, she would stay. She faced her mother. "Where's the display you want me to do?"

Cleo's shoulders relaxed. "Right through here." She turned to lead Ria into the store.

The guardian drew back barely enough to let her pass, insolence mixing with a challenge.

Ria was the interloper, the odd man out. She wanted to be anywhere but here.

Sandor joined Cleo and entered the shop. The ice queen and her man-at-arms, his hand protectively at her back.

Ria straightened and stepped across the threshold, feeling like nothing so much as a green soldier on his first foray into enemy territory.

UNABLE TO FIND an excuse to remain that was not transparent, Sandor left a few minutes later, disturbed on more accounts than he'd expected.

The first, of course, was simply how off balance Cleo was in her daughter's presence. Though she worked very hard to maintain her usual aplomb, he saw her hands shake and her eyes dart nervously as she sought to interpret the most minute reaction from Ria.

They were two boxers, dancing in the ring, each measuring the other and waiting for the first punch to be thrown, stiff and uncertain until that happened. Their relationship was nothing like Cleo's with Betsey; those two did not always agree but were easy together. They could work in serene silence or chat for hours on any manner of topics.

Ria and Cleo were nearly paralyzed by each other, as if a single word could topple their shaky détente.

And oddly enough, Ria seemed far more rattled than her mother. The rebel who had sundered a family was nowhere in evidence.

She seemed, in fact, vulnerable to a frightening degree.

But appearances could deceive.

Sandor decided right then not to move the rest of his things just yet.

Cleopatra's daughter would bear watching.

CHAPTER SEVEN

"WATCH ME, MOM. Look at how fast I am." Benjy raced across the porch and down the steps. "Count how many seconds to the mailbox. You can see me, right?" He paused, hands on hips. "Maybe you should come down here."

"I wouldn't miss it." Though Ria wasn't sure she could move from the rocking chair. She hadn't stopped for lunch, even at her mother's urging, eager to finish the display as quickly as possible and get out of the atmosphere that fairly pulsated with tension.

Too excited to wait for her, Benjy charged down the sidewalk, his legs churning, and like a double image, she glimpsed him as a toddler taking his first steps.

The fat, dimpled legs had lengthened and slimmed. For an instant, she could almost visualize him at fourteen instead of four.

Anguish arrowed straight into her heart.

It wasn't Benjy she was picturing. It was David.

She propelled herself from her chair, swooped down and grabbed Benjy, nuzzling his neck and growling in a way she knew tickled him.

"Mom, you have to—" He dissolved into giggles. "Not now, Mom." But he snuggled closer, and the power of her love for him robbed her of breath.

To think just how close she'd come to not having this miracle in her life was terrifying. Alone and pregnant, she'd believed she only had one choice.

But she hadn't counted on Dog Boy.

"You sure about this, Ria?" Dog Boy's voice had penetrated her fixation on the stained waiting-room floor.

"Don't you want this baby?"

"No, of course not. I'm barely making ends meet as it is. I have to find a place to live. I just—" Wonder. *What do you look like, little one?*

Ria bent over, rocking slightly in the hard orange plastic chair.

Dog Boy knelt and covered her hand with his own. At least his fingernails were cleaner these days. His voice turned soft. "Talk to me, Ria. You positive you can do this?"

The swirls of puke-green in the ancient floor matched the walls. Dusty plastic ivy on the scarred table floated like an island in a sea of torn magazines. But she could barely read the titles through the film over her eyes.

Your mother is just…sad, she could hear her father's deep voice, dark with its own pain. *She lost the baby.*

The barrier holding her memories at bay buckled.

She wanted to call Daddy, ask him what to do. But she was too old for that now…and too unwelcome.

"I don't know," she whispered. *Talk to me, baby. I'm afraid. I can't live with any more guilt. Any more blood on my hands.*

Dog Boy jumped up, jerking her to her feet. "Come on."

"What are you doing?" She registered the jitter that was so much a part of him, but the warmth of his hand on her arm made her feel more alive.

"You're not so tough. That's your dirty secret. You act like you got brass balls, but you don't. I'm taking you out of here before you do something you'll regret."

Hope and logic rattled sabers in her head. "I have to, don't you see? I can't support a baby. I can barely fend for myself."

"I'll take care of you."

She blinked. "You?" A scarecrow still, his eyes burning with the fever of methamphetamines racing through his blood, he was the least likely savior she could imagine.

He held her shoulders with a grip that belied his thin frame. "Yeah, me." His chin jutted in defiance. "I got a place. Got a job. You can stay with me, save up your money for when the baby comes."

"You're a needle freak, Dog Boy. I can't—"

He shook his head abruptly. "Not anymore. Starting now." His look was as serious as she'd ever seen from him.

"Give me a chance, Ria." His hands squeezed her shoulders. "Let me do something right in my life."

She tried to figure out how she could possibly be this

crazy, while within her a seed of wistfulness grew. "How could we possibly—"

"Listen to me." His voice was low and intense. "Something inside you is gonna die if you go through with it. This is your chance, girl—giving a life to make up for the one you lost."

"You have no right—"

He shook her once, hard. "You owe me. Those scars on your wrists say so."

She'd told him too much, her story welling up like the scarlet staining the bandages he'd made from his shirt until he could get her to the hospital. In the long hours of that night when she'd wanted to die, he'd forced her to survive.

The tears broke free then, dripping on her hands. "I'm so scared, Dog Boy. I have no idea how to be a mother."

He pulled her against his bony shoulder, their heights a match for each other. "We'll manage. We got brains as good as any. Maybe we don't know much about families, but we'll learn."

Ria sobbed against his neck. "This isn't about sex, is it? 'Cause I can't have sex with you, Dog Boy. You're the only friend I have."

Laughter rattled in his throat. "I told you once, girl. You're not my type."

He rocked her, and she gratefully surrendered. "This is crazy."

"No," he murmured, drawing her with him toward the door of the clinic. "This is right."

NOW SHE PRESSED a kiss to Benjy's hair, and thanked whatever kind fate had sent an unlikely carrot-topped angel into her life. He had lived up to his word, even though his past had, in the end, caught up with him.

"You're the only good thing I've ever done," she murmured to her son.

Her heart seized with fear, and she understood in a way she never had before that what she felt at the thought of never knowing Benjy could only be a shadow of the grief her parents had suffered. Ria tightened her arms around her son, burying her face in his hair. "I'm sorry." In silence, she pleaded. *I accept that I'm guilty, but please...punish me some other way. Don't steal this precious life from me, even though I don't deserve him. Anything—I'll suffer anything else. Let all of them hate me forever, but please, please keep him safe.*

All the while aware that she, of all people, had no standing to make bargains with God.

Benjy, with that spooky sense he sometimes had, grew still and cuddled closer.

Though her instinct was to cling harder, Ria leaned back to give him some room.

But she couldn't let him go just yet, not while terror choked her. So she settled for stroking his beloved face as she beat back her fear. "You are the best boy in the world."

He grinned without a trace of hesitation, accepting it as his due. "You always say that."

"Because I always mean it. I love you so much, Benjy." Her throat closed again.

Ria forced herself to gather up the ragged edges of her heart. He was a child, and it was her job to comfort him, not the other way around. She started to speak, but had to clear her throat first.

"So..." She reminded herself that despite all the uncertainties and questions and mistakes, at this very moment, there was nothing to fear. Benjy was safe. "Okay." *Let him go now, Ria.* So she mustered a smile, and, in the doing of it, felt herself settle. "You're ready?"

As quickly as that, he became a normal, energetic four-year-old again and jumped down from her lap, his grin wide and confident. "Yep. I'm gonna be really fast, you'll see."

"I'm sure you will, sweetie." Bless him. Being with Benjy was a sure cure for any ailment. "Ready, set, go!"

She counted the seconds faithfully, the way, as a child, she'd avoided cracks in the sidewalk to insure that her mother's back wouldn't get broken. *I'll be so good. I'll do everything right, I promise.* The litany repeated in her head as she called out the markers to the child she loved more than life.

Benjy was about to round the mailbox when he stopped in his tracks. "Gramps! Mom, Gramps is coming!" He jumped up and down and waved.

She saw her father's wide white grin as he pulled to the curb. He emerged from the car and caught Benjy in his arms for a hug. Benjy's words tripped over themselves as he related all the events of his day to his grandfather, and Ria was cast back in time to how David had always thrown himself into Daddy's embrace.

How did you survive it? she wondered.

Then realized two things simultaneously. One, her father had lost more than his son.

And two, that, unlike her father, she would not be strong enough to go on. Losing Benjy would take away her one reason to live.

Don't think about it or you'll go mad. She tried to listen to that voice, but all she could hear was the drumbeat of dread. *If anyone deserves to lose a child, Ria, it's you.*

Benjy hasn't done anything wrong, she cried out. *He has the best heart in the world.*

But so had David.

"Ria?" Her father's voice broke into the web of soul-stealing fright. "What's wrong, sweetheart?"

"Oh, Daddy, I—" She nearly threw herself at him to let him soothe away her terrors as he always had.

But she didn't deserve his comfort. Her son still lived.

So she dissembled. "I'm fine. Just a little tired after working at the shop."

Malcolm's eyes widened. "Cleo's shop?"

Perched on his back, Benjy spoke first. "Nana gave Mom a job making stuff pretty."

Malcolm's forehead creased, and Ria explained.

"So you and your mother survived working together."

"More or less."

"I'm glad." He nodded his approval. "She's trying, honey. She really wants things to be different this time."

Ria thought of the glowering Hungarian and his territorial air and wondered if her father would be championing her mother if he knew.

But the same second, she discarded that thought: Daddy had a girlfriend living with him, much as she detested the idea. She granted his point. "It was nice of her to offer me the chance. It's just…hard."

"Gramps, did you come to play with me?" Benjy queried.

"I sure did, but I wanted to see your mom, too."

"So if she watches us play, that counts, right? Want to climb to the tree house again?"

Malcolm looked at her for an opinion.

She smiled back. "Go ahead. I'm fine. I'm going to check on helping Aunt Cammie with supper."

Her father hugged her and pressed a kiss to her hair. "I'm proud of you, Ria."

She leaned into him and soaked up the rich pleasure of those words.

"So can we go now, Gramps?" Benjy's feet drummed the air in his excitement.

Malcolm chuckled and squeezed Ria once more, then lowered Benjy to the ground. "The tree house needs some work yet, and we'll do that on Sunday, but for now, I have another idea."

"What?"

"You like to play football?"

Benjy's eyes opened wide. "I never played it before."

Malcolm cast her a surprised glance, and Ria cringed. Dog Boy had taken sick not long after Benjy had learned to walk, and she'd been too caught up in, first, survival, then working to support all of them, to even think of something like sports. And Dog Boy hadn't had the strength.

But her father simply said, "Then it's time to give it a try. I've got a football just your size in the car. Let's get it." He held out a hand, and Benjy slipped his smaller one into his grandfather's clasp, chattering as they walked.

Ria watched them go for a minute. How absorbed they were in each other. Once she would have been jealous, but at this moment, she could only feel happy for a little boy who should be granted truckloads of love, if there were any justice.

Smiling, she went inside.

SHE'D SET THE TABLE and made a salad, but again and again, she was drawn back to the window to observe the two males she loved best in the world. Benjy was in his element, and her father's face had lost ten years as he laughed and played, patiently explaining football to a little boy who soaked up both information and affection like drought-stricken land absorbs water.

Her mother's car turned into the driveway just then.

Cleo emerged and opened her arms to Benjy, who fell all over himself recounting what he and Gramps had done.

But what struck Ria most was the pain and tenderness on her father's face as he looked at Cleo.

And the longing on hers as she cast sideways glances at him.

"Nana, I made a touchdown! Gramps couldn't catch me, could you, Gramps?"

Malcolm's gaze jerked away. "Too fast for me, sport." He grinned, eyebrows waggling. "But I'm feeling lucky now." He rubbed his hands together gleefully. "Let's see whatcha got, big guy. Bet you can't do it again."

Daddy helped her mother rise, and for a moment, both of them seemed paralyzed. "Snow—" he began.

Snow. How many times had she heard Daddy call Mother that, his tones alternately light with teasing and ripe with what she now understood as seduction? It was his fondest name for her, the one unique to them, dating back to before her birth. The day they'd met, he'd said she looked like Snow White, and the name had stuck.

"Come on, Nana," Benjy called out. "Mom can be on my side, and you can be with Gramps."

Then both of them noticed her. She had come outside and was standing on the porch. Ria's attention went to Malcolm's hand on her mother's elbow, and a tiny seed of hope rose. Could the love between them merely be sleeping and not extinguished?

"Gramps, you ready? Nana?"

Cleo glanced over. “Benjy, I’m sorry. I have groceries in the car, and Aunt Cammie’s waiting for them.”

“We’ll help,” Malcolm said. “We’ve got work to do, my man.”

Ria descended the steps to join them. Her father reached inside the car and parceled out bags, saving the heaviest load for himself. Her mother preceded them and held the front door as they formed a train and made their way inside.

Malcolm stopped before her mother, nodding for her to precede him. “Beauty first, Snow.”

Once her mother would have lifted to tiptoe and kissed him. Ria felt like a voyeur, but, barely daring to breathe, she remained nonetheless, silently willing her mother to close the gap between them.

Instead, Cleo shook her head. “No. Go ahead.” She took a step backward and stared at the ground.

Malcolm started through, then paused, as if about to say something.

Ria decided to gamble. “Daddy?”

They both jolted. Turned.

“Would you stay and have supper with us? Aunt Cammie says there’s plenty.” *Forgive me, Aunt Cammie. If I’m wrong, I won’t eat a bite, I swear.*

Daddy looked at her mother, as if she had the final word.

Ria tensed. Nudged a little. “Mother? You don’t mind, do you?”

Before she had a chance to respond, Malcolm did. “I’m sorry, Ria. I wish I could, but—”

Suddenly, all three of them knew the words he didn't utter. He had a home to go to. A woman who waited.

Ria's spirits took a nosedive. She wanted to cry.

Cleo's back straightened, her voice brisk and neutral. "We'd better not monopolize any more of your time. Ria, why don't you grab one of these bags and I'll carry the other, so Malcolm can go."

Malcolm's hand stopped hers as she reached for the sack nearest her. "I'm sorry, Ria." His words were directed at her, but his gaze never left her mother. "I really wish I could." He seemed truly remorseful.

Frantically, Ria sought a solution, but before she could find one, her mother drew back. "Perhaps another time," she murmured.

And with careful steps, she headed for the kitchen.

Her father watched her mother leave, and Ria's heart broke for him. For both of them.

THE NEXT AFTERNOON, Ria trailed through the empty house, lost in thought. She worried at her lower lip as the idea for a new display formed.

Lola, Benjy, Aunt Cammie and Tyrone were off on their daily walk to the park, a jaunt that lasted longer every time. The older women had limitless patience with every side foray Benjy wanted to make, and he relished the attention.

The display idea shimmered in her mind, a fantasy of snow and ice for the corner window on the street. Should she ask her mother if she'd be interested?

Ria's hand hovered over the phone.

No. She'd go to the shop, instead. Then she'd be able to demonstrate with her hands, freed of the limitation of drawing word pictures.

But as she arrived at the front door, her steps faltered. She didn't have a key; she couldn't lock the house. Her mother's house, where she was only a visitor.

Mother might not like the idea, anyway. She hadn't asked Ria to do another display. For all Ria knew, the one she'd created had been dismantled.

She stepped back, feeling foolish, her idea melting like ice in the sun. Disappointment turned the sunny day gray. She hovered on the edge of indecision, but slowly, the picture formed again in her mind, niggling at her hesitation.

It would be stunning. Cleo didn't have to pay her for it if she didn't like it. And the memory of her mother's delight over the initial arrangement warmed something deep inside her.

She'd just walk by the shop, see if what she'd done was still up. If it was, she'd go inside and talk to her mother about this new one. But first, she'd check on whether her mother still hid a key outside the back door, so she could lock the house with it.

A few minutes later, she was on her way, thankful that her mother was a creature of habit. As she covered the blocks between the house and the shop, excitement unfurled inside her. The materials wouldn't have to cost much, but this would be a showstopper. And if her mother was willing to spend a little more on supplies…

Ria's head was whirling by the time she bypassed the alley behind the shop and rounded the corner so she could view the space beside the front door.

Her display was still there.

Her heart gave a little leap. She checked the corner window to assure herself that she'd remembered the area accurately. Then she squared her shoulders and headed up the steps from the street.

The tiny golden bells sang as she opened the front door, her steps quick as the image brightened in her head. She scanned the cash register area, looking for her mother.

From behind her left shoulder, a voice spoke, "Good afternoon. May I help you?"

Ria froze and turned to confront her sister.

"Oh. It's you." Betsey's ready smile slid away.

Ria stepped backward. "Is, uh, is Mother here?"

"No. She's gone to the bank."

"Oh." Ria cast her gaze around frantically as she wondered whether to leave or stay. "Will she be long?"

"I don't know. Probably not, but sometimes she runs other errands."

Ria eyed the back door, wondering if she could just go back there and wait.

"Was there something you needed?"

Her impulse was to escape. That was stupid. She was the oldest. Betsey was a cream puff. "No, I...uh, I just wanted to ask her about something." *Don't run, Ria. For Benjy's sake, stay.* "I'll wander around while I wait."

"It could be a while." Betsey stood as rigid as a soldier at attention. Every atom of her body denied Ria welcome.

"I don't mind. Benjy's at the park with Aunt Cammie and Lola and Tyrone."

Her sister opened her mouth, then closed it without saying anything, simply nodding.

Ria watched her depart, every hair in place, her clothing understated and gorgeous and probably costing the earth. Her mind went back over the years, trying to recall if she'd ever witnessed Betsey mussed. Were her daughters just like her, or was maybe one of them a little awkward, prone to climbing trees or getting dirty?

"Daddy said you have two girls, but I don't know their names or ages."

Betsey faced her, clearly skeptical, but ever the perfect hostess she responded. "Elizabeth is four and Marguerite is three."

"Do they look like you? Do you have pictures?"

The tiniest of frown lines disturbed Betsey's perfect face. "Do you really care?"

The edge in her voice tempted Ria to give up. Instead, she dug deeper. "You're my sister, Betsey. Of course I do. I never meant to hurt you."

For a moment, Betsey's eyes betrayed the slightest scramble, the faintest hint of softening. "You hurt all of us, Victoria," she said with quiet ferocity. "And now you're doing it again. When will you disappear this time? Or do you expect Mother and Daddy to support you? She can't afford to keep giving you charity work, you know."

Charity. Was that all it had been, or did Betsey only desire to return the hurt?

Not that she wasn't justified. Shame washed over Ria. She'd earned her sister's contempt many times over as Betsey helped her hide her misdeeds.

"Bets, I—"

The bells sang out, and a customer stepped inside.

Instantly, a mask slid over Betsey's features. "Good afternoon. How are you today, Mrs. Johnston?"

"Oh, Betsey, darling, I'm so glad you're here. I must find a quick hostess gift for the perfectly dreadful wife of one of William's executives."

"I'll be right with you." Betsey turned to Ria, her voice lowering. "Do you still care to wait?"

Ria shook her head. "Just tell Mother I'll talk to her when she gets home."

Betsey merely nodded and glided over to help find a gift for a dreadful hostess.

Ria slipped out the door with careful steps until she made it around the corner.

And then she ran.

THAT NIGHT AT DINNER, Cleo glanced across the table. "We've sold a lot of merchandise off your display. The way you evoked an old-fashioned Christmas from a child's view from beneath the tree provokes an emotional response. More than one person stayed there a long time with a wistful expression on her face."

Ria ducked her head. "I had an idea for the corner window, but…the shop is fine. You probably don't need it."

"If you'd like to tackle the project, I'd be very happy to have you do so. What did you have in mind?"

Cautiously, Ria broached her idea, breathing an inner sigh when Cleo's eyes lit. For a few precious minutes, they spoke as allies instead of foes. She was dizzy with the richness of it.

"Could you start tomorrow? We should have most of what you need."

Ria hesitated. "Will…" She hated herself for being a coward. "Who's working tomorrow?"

Sympathy sparked in her mother's eyes. Betsey must be scheduled. "Perhaps that isn't the best day, but oh, how I'd love to have that up right away."

Ria looked down at her plate. "I could—" She swallowed deeply. "If you would be willing to let me, I could start it tonight, after Benjy's in bed." She toyed with her water glass. She'd stolen from her mother's purse, all those years ago. Cleo would never trust her with her shop.

"Oh, Ria, I don't think—"

She shoved back from the table, gripping her plate in white-knuckled hands. "I understand. Let's just forget it." She reached for Benjy's plate. "About ready for your bath, sweetie?"

"Ria." Her mother's voice was strained.

"Do I have to, Mom?" Benjy's face screwed up in a frown.

"Hurry up, Benjy," Ria snapped. Then she bit the inside of her cheek and reached deep for composure. She smiled at her son. "Let's fill it really high, so you can play whale, okay?"

Benjy's eyes widened. "Okay!"

"Go get your pajamas, and I'll meet you in the bathroom in just a minute."

Her son's chair slid backward in a rush. "I should show Gramps how long I can hold my breath. Can we call him, Mom?"

"Ria—" Her mother's hand reached out as she passed.

Ria dodged her touch and kept walking. "I don't think Gramps can come tonight, but we'll talk to him about it the next time he's here. Deal?"

"Yeah!"

"All right, then head up those stairs."

He paused on the second step. "Wanna watch me, Nana?"

Ria saw Cleo ruthlessly smother her distress before she faced her grandson. "I'd love to. Just let me visit with your mother for a minute, and I'll be there."

"Okay." He raced up the stairs.

"Ria—" Her mother rose to follow her.

Ria caught a glimpse of Lola's warning and Aunt Cammie's pleading expression. She stopped in the doorway to the kitchen. "What?"

Her mother's hesitation lasted only a second. "If you really don't mind getting started tonight, I'll call to check if Sandor's still there working. If he is, he can let you in." She inhaled audibly. "Otherwise, I'll give you my key and the security code, and you can just leave the key on the kitchen counter if you return after I'm in bed."

With hands suddenly gone nerveless, Ria crossed the few remaining steps and set the plates on the counter before she dropped them. Swallowing hard, she faced her mother, seeing the strain on her face. The look in her mother's eyes that begged Ria not to make her sorry.

"Thank you," Ria said softly. She had to leave the room before she lost the battle to tears. "I—I'll just get Benjy's bath started."

With slow, careful steps, she walked through the other door to the kitchen and headed up the stairs.

SANDOR WAS THERE, Cleo had discovered, but she had given Ria her key and code anyway, saying that though he often worked late into the night, she didn't want him to feel obligated to stay.

Ria would have preferred to walk, but her mother had asked her to drive, even offering her own car in place of Ria's rattletrap, which Daddy had gotten running, at least temporarily. Cleo couldn't know how innocent the neighborhood was, compared with the places Ria had lived in their years apart. Hiking the few blocks was child's play, even at night.

But Ria complied, unwilling to disturb the delicate filaments of a new peace.

Of course, Sandor would make sure she didn't steal

anything, but the key and the code were olive branches offered across a chasm Ria had never expected to bridge. Even if the glowering Hungarian stood sentinel every second she was there, Ria didn't care.

As she approached the back door, he appeared in the opening, the light from the alley washing over his handsome, forbidding features.

Ria straightened her shoulders and marched forward.

He blocked her path.

"If you'll excuse me, I'll get to work."

He didn't budge. "You will not break her heart again."

Ria wondered how long she would have to fight the sins of her past. "Please let me by."

He clasped her arm. "She is more fragile than you recognize."

Ria frowned at the echo of Aunt Cammie's words. "Just because you've got the hots for her doesn't give you the right to lecture me." She started to brush by him, but his grip tightened. "Let me go."

"Never speak of her that way. You understand nothing."

Ria jerked from his grasp, then placed both hands on his chest and shoved hard. The day's nerves boiled over. "I understand how a woman looks when she's been with a man. I saw her the other night and how you are with her. It doesn't take a genius."

"Do not pass judgment when you have no facts. Your mother has many admirers, but I am simply her friend." Hard, warning eyes stared down into hers. "I'll watch out for my friends."

"And you're so sure I'm going to hurt her."

"You have no regard for your own survival. Why should you care for hers?"

"You don't know the first thing about me." The way he was looking at her…something about his voice, his accent…

The pieces tumbled into place. "You. At Joe's Place." Oh, God. "You'll tell her."

He shook his head. "I see no reason to upset her. I do not believe it to be inevitable that you must wound her. You have a second chance and, with it, the power to make the future different from the past."

"But you believe I'll fail."

"Not necessarily." His fierce eyes gentled. "You do, however."

Ria flinched from the truth of it. "I don't give a damn about your opinions. Just stay away from me, and I'll do the same." *And quit trying to get into my head.*

"Did he hurt you?"

To understand he meant the man at the bar took her a second. She ducked his scrutiny. "I'm perfectly fine." How much had he witnessed?

Then she heard how she sounded, snapping at a man who had come to her rescue, even if she couldn't help wondering what he would have done if he'd realized who she was. Chagrin assailed her. How easily she had already fractured the night's delicate new promise.

She eyed the floor. This man would never like her, but for her mother's sake, she made the effort. "I'm sorry. I appreciate what you did. I—I had too much to drink and…" She remembered more than she wanted to about her behavior.

"There is never a good excuse for forcing a woman."

Startled, she lifted her head, but his expression was grim. Still Ria persisted. "I brought it on myself." Then a thought occurred to her. "Did he hurt you?"

He did a double take, then surprised her with a smile that gleamed white against the golden skin. His face lost some of the harsh angles, and she was struck anew by how gorgeous he was when he wasn't glowering.

"He posed no serious threat to me." His gaze narrowed. "But he knocked you to the ground. Did you seek medical attention?"

She shook her head. "I didn't need it." Or any other kind of attention. She wanted to forget that night. To wipe it from his memory would be even better.

He studied her, and she braced for the lecture.

But instead, he gave her his back. "I must work. If you require something, let me know."

And just like that, he dismissed her. She was nothing to him, yet moments before he'd been kind and concerned.

Or maybe she'd seen what she wished for, not what was real. Disapproval was what he did best, second only to his skill at threatening.

He might be part of her mother's life, but he didn't have to impact hers any more than she allowed, except that he possessed knowledge that would set back her détente with her mother.

All the way to square one, this man could send them, merely by speaking a few words. Perhaps she'd better tell her mother herself first.

The second the thought entered, she rejected it, easily able to picture her mother's disappointment. She'd seen that expression too many times in her life, before it had hardened into hatred.

She would never manage to be like her mother, so cool and elegant and lovely, but right now, Ria would settle for not being despised. She had found one thing she could do that made her mother look at her with new eyes, and the part of Ria that still dared to hope wanted to build on that, not destroy.

She stared at Sandor's broad back and wondered what his angle was, how he could be leveraged into remaining silent. One thing she'd learned in L.A. was that everyone had an angle; to get what you wanted required figuring it out, that was all. No one did something for nothing.

She didn't have enough information about Sandor to guess, though, and that frightened her. The ground beneath her feet turned to shifting sands again, and she considered walking right back out the door.

But that would be the Ria everyone knew.

Everyone but Benjy, who thought she was wonderful.

And Dog Boy, who had believed in her. She'd been her best self in the odd little family they'd made, had proved that she could stick, for once in her life.

But now her dearest friend was gone. She missed him desperately.

Benjy, though, wasn't. She couldn't bear for him to view her as everyone in this place did. So despite how badly she wanted to flee, she made her way slowly toward the supplies Cleo had described.

And did her best to ignore the man who had witnessed the Ria she couldn't ever seem to leave behind.

CHAPTER EIGHT

STRANGER AND STRANGER. For a second there, he had experienced the urge to comfort her. Make certain she had escaped that night without harm. Encourage her to speak of it; let her spill out the fear and nerves still lurking behind her bravado.

In an odd way she reminded him of Jerome, posturing to conceal the frightened creature within, letting swagger blind those unable or unwilling to peer deeper.

And lonely, even more so than her mother. Cleo guarded her heart, yes, and did not share it easily.

But the woman he'd been prepared to loathe on sight, the woman he would have welcomed the opportunity to punish for what she had cost Cleo…

This Ria Channing was broken inside. Operating on sheer willpower. He realized, in a sudden blinding and surprising insight, just how razor-thin was the edge on which she was balanced. How easily she could be sent tumbling.

For all the months he had known Cleo, he had harbored the wish to avenge her by whatever means would restore her to wholeness. Find the missing piece of the puzzle that dimmed her smile and weighted her heart. More often than not, he had imagined the solution would involve some sort of terrible justice being dealt to Cleo's faithless husband and hateful child, causing each to experience the agony they had visited upon her.

But only a blind man could look at Ria and not see that she had an intimate acquaintance with torment. It was there in her lightless green eyes, in the haunted hollows of a face as lovely as her mother's, the ragged, red-tipped black hair that topped a too-gaunt frame.

One would have to be a monster to heap more suffering upon this woman, and Sandor had never found joy in harming others.

But neither could he forget the pain she had caused and the lives she had wrecked. Her sister, who was a fine person and who alone had stayed to care for what was left of their family. Even her father, though Sandor found him harder to pity, as Malcolm had too easily managed to replace Cleo. The man had still lost his son.

Most of all, of course, there was Cleo, whom he wished daily to truly repay for all she meant to him—friend, older sister…at times the mother he'd lost too young.

So, deprived of a clear choice in how to treat this complicated woman, Sandor shoved his fingers through his hair and stalked back to work.

HE WAS STILL THERE when Ria finished. As she cleaned up the fragments of ribbon and wire and tape, she wished she could just walk out the front door and not have to see him again that night. Every second that she'd labored, she'd been all too aware of him.

He confused her. His presence was too strong. He was fierce, yet in an odd way somehow…kind.

And she had to pass him to depart. She should tell him she was leaving, but maybe she'd just slam the back door and let him find out that way.

Then she got mad that she allowed him to unnerve her. Jaw tight, she closed the shop door and locked up. As she crossed the concrete floor, the glow from his work space caught her eye.

She turned toward it, and something deep inside her shivered.

He was engrossed in what he was doing. His long fingers caressed the wood, trailing down the grain with exquisite tenderness, yet his other hand gripped a sharp chisel, and the muscles in his arm stood out in relief.

A study in contrasts. Cast in golden light, he was anything but a handyman; he seemed a creature of another time, a different world. For a moment, the creative spirit inside her had to stop. To simply…look.

He walked around the piece slowly and scanned the wood.

Then he saw her and went still.

"Are you showing your work anywhere?"

His eyebrows rose, then snapped together. "No."

"Why on earth not?"

"My reasons are my own."

"But you can't seriously want to spend your time doing plumbing and painting walls when you are capable of beauty like this."

"All work is honorable." His voice was stiff with wounded pride.

Off on the wrong foot again. "I'm sorry. I only meant..." She threw her hands wide. "I give up. I'm out of here." She turned to go.

"It is not practical, this carving. My efforts are directed toward building a business now."

She blinked. "Beauty doesn't have to be practical. That's not why people buy it."

"So you think it is beautiful?"

"Of course I do."

For a heart's beat, she spotted a hunger in him and understood that even he had vulnerabilities.

Just as quickly, he erased any trace of them. "I do not trust luxury."

Ria cocked her head. "What do you mean?"

"Your life has been pampered. You cannot understand what it is to see those you care for lack medicine or the simplest necessities."

She couldn't help the laughter that clawed from her throat. She clapped a hand over her mouth but couldn't stem it.

He glared at her. "Starvation and want are not cause for humor."

Ria perched on the fine edge of hysteria, until tears streamed down her face. Nothing was funny, yet all of it, both of them, were ridiculous. Of the myriad sins she was guilty of, he had indicted her with possibly the only one that was patently untrue.

He dismissed her with a disgusted wave and stalked out.

"Wait." She grabbed for his arm.

He jerked from her grip, his eyes flashing fury, and shoved past.

She lost her balance, fell against the doorframe and rapped her head on the wood.

He lunged and steadied her, looking stricken. "I am sorry. I did not mean…let me see your head." He drew her near as his fingers combed gently through her hair. "Where does it hurt?"

Mortified and woozy, unsettled by the physicality of him, Ria tried to withdraw, but with only one hand, he restrained her easily. "Let me go," she said, horrified to hear her voice crack. He smelled like sawdust and sweat and healthy male. He was so sure of himself. A part of her craved to bury her head against that broad chest and seek shelter. She leaned toward him the merest inch, letting her brow rest, just for a second, against the cotton.

He stiffened. She jerked back.

"This needs ice." He towed her toward the kitchen area.

She pulled away. "I'm fine." But as she backed toward the outer door, a hot rush of moisture stung her eyes. She paused with her hand on the knob. "You're right to despise me for many reasons, but you're dead wrong about one."

"And what might that be?"

"I understand exactly what it's like to go hungry. How much worse it is to be impotent to provide for someone you love. There is no other force on earth that would have brought me back. I'm only here for the sake of my son."

"Your mother loves him."

"Yes," she said softly. "He reminds her of my brother."

"Yes. David."

Her head rose. "You know about—" She closed her eyes. "Of course you do. What else has she told you?"

Before he could answer, she held up a hand. "Never mind. I know how she thinks. What she must have said."

"Do you? I wonder."

"What do you mean?"

"This shop is the center of the life she painstakingly rebuilt after you and your father abandoned her. All the love that had nowhere to go was invested here. It is no small thing that she would give you free rein here."

"I wonder if she'll ever forgive me." Ria shocked herself by uttering the thought. She waited for him to use the words against her.

"She does not know, either."

Tough but honest. Instinctively, she attacked to dodge the pain of his confirmation. "So what else have you learned through pillow talk?"

His breath escaped in a huff. "I will tell you only once more. I have never been her lover. Do not slander her to me again."

His protest had the ring of truth, yet her mother had come home the other night clearly marked by a lover's kisses. "Then who is?"

"That is not your business or mine. I tire of discussing it."

"And I'm sick of your preaching." She spun and grabbed the door handle.

"So you will run, is that it? Do you ever stay and fight for what you want?"

Her heart drummed in her throat.

"Do you have any idea what you want, Ria?"

She shut her eyes against the longings crawling up, ready to spill.

But not to this man, this arrogant bastard who—

She whirled. "What about you?" She jabbed a finger in the direction of his carving. "It's obvious that working with wood is where your heart is, yet you brush it off as impractical."

"I have plans. There are steps." His eyes were amber now, lit with both determination and yearning.

Who was she to say his path was wrong? "What steps?"

He frowned as if unsure whether to trust her. "I came to this country with nothing less than one year ago. Your mother gave me a place to sleep and let me work. More than once, she fed me what she pretended was excess food." In his voice was a mix of shame and gratitude and affection. "Now I own tools and a pickup truck. A few days ago, I moved into a garage apartment, where I will trade repairs for rent. With these hands—" he held them out, and once again she saw the strong, lean fingers, the wide palms "—I have done honest labor, first for Cleo, then for other merchants. Now I have a larger job, remodeling a restaurant named Finn's. Soon I must hire helpers."

Ria saw in him the pride of achievement, which she had seldom felt herself, except when she looked at Benjy. She had discovered within her the capacity for hard work, but hers had been only a succession of low-end jobs, whatever was required to put food on the table.

This man had a dream, and she had no right to call it unworthy.

Then his statement hit her. *Soon I must hire helpers.* And Betsey's: *She can't afford to keep giving you charity work.*

"Hire me." The words escaped her before she could think.

"What?"

"You'll hire help, you said. I need a job."

"You have one, making displays for your mother."

"I can't mooch off her forever."

He stared at her for so long she was ready to take back the request. *Never mind* hovered on her lips.

But then she got mad. "I know how to work hard. I might have had it easy as a kid, but once I left here, I've been a maid and a waitress and flipped burgers and—" She frowned. "You don't believe me?"

"None of those involves construction skills. I cannot afford the time to train you."

Never had she wanted so badly to give up. His disdain couldn't be more obvious. So why didn't she?

Because she was tired of losing things, damn it. Her pride, her self-respect...friends and family and—

"I'll work free the first day."

She could nearly see the pragmatist take over. You didn't get much more practical than free labor.

His eyes narrowed. "You still have no skills."

But her mind was spinning in high gear now, though she hadn't the faintest idea why she persisted. Except that she was so far out on this limb that the risk was actually sort of energizing.

What the hell. You're at the bottom. Nowhere to fall.

"I can clean. Job sites have to be swept, don't they? Trash picked up?"

One faint glint, that was all, but she'd scored a point, she could tell.

So she pushed it. "I can drive, so that means I could run errands, pick up lumber or—" She lifted a palm. "Whatever." He was thinking about it; she saw that. "I can paint. Any idiot can wield a paintbrush."

His eyebrows drew together. "There is an art to a proper paint job. One does not simply slap it on a wall."

"You just want to keep the fumes to yourself, right? Like the high?" *Oh, shut up, Ria. You almost had him, then you make a stupid joke that he won't even think is funny.*

But he grinned, a wide slash of white that could squeeze the walls of your lungs together. "You are serious."

Her breath whooshed out in a gust. "Deadly."

"I do not understand. We do not like each other. Trust each other." His brow beetled. "You think I am lying about not being your mother's lover."

"I've worked with plenty of people I couldn't stand." She wanted to clap her hands over her mouth again. Stupid, stupid.

But she had a sense that if she gave up now, she was lost. "Okay, say I believe you that you and my mother aren't—"

"Do so, then."

"What?"

"I speak the truth. Always. I value it in others. If you believe me, then look me in the eye and say it."

Oddly enough, she found that she did. "I don't have to pretend I like you, do I?"

The white slash again. "I do not wish to associate with liars."

She'd been one so many times in her life there was no hope of counting.

But maybe that was another step down the road to a new Ria, one Benjy could respect.

So she nodded at Sandor. "I believe that you and my mother are not lovers—"

He interrupted. "And never have been."

She rolled her eyes. "So is this like an oath taking? Hold-up-your-right-hand, repeat-after-me kind of thing?"

He chuckled. "I only seek to set the record straight."

"Fine. Not lovers, now or ever." She paused. "And maybe I could like you someday."

His mouth quirked. "Perhaps I could like you, as well, but I do not rush into hasty decisions."

No kidding. But she kept quiet. "When do I start tomorrow and where?"

He hesitated for an endless second. "What about your son?"

Her heart quailed at the thought of leaving Benjy all day, no matter how well cared for he'd be. "My grandmother and great-aunt would do back flips. They can't get enough of him." Though neither was young, somehow the hours with him revitalized them both—not that Lola needed much more energy—and he blossomed under their cosseting. Ruthlessly, she forced her mind away from the pleasure she, too, had experienced in the days since they'd arrived. With a roof over their heads and food to eat, she and her child had begun to relax for the first time in many, many months.

Dog Boy had rallied what little strength he had until the very end, making sure that for at least part of each day, things were as normal as possible, for Benjy's sake.

But Benjy was a sensitive little boy forced to be more serious than any small child should have to be. He had learned too early to be quiet and careful in a house where death hovered over them every day.

"You are not ready for full-time employment," Sandor observed. "You are pale and thin. You should rest."

"I can't." Somehow she had to start building. For too long, her life had been a slide toward destruction. She lifted her eyes to his. "And I'm stronger than I look."

He frowned, but perhaps he saw the plea she could not afford to hide. She needed this, whatever it took.

The inner debate seemed to go on forever.

Finally, he exhaled loudly. "Your mother gave me a chance when she had no reason to trust me. I can do no less for her daughter."

Ria's pride was stung. She wanted to succeed on her own account, not because of some imagined debt to her mother.

Take it, you fool. His reasoning doesn't matter. He's saying yes.

So she stifled a retort, tilted her chin up and put out one hand. "You won't be sorry."

Slowly he accepted the handshake, her fingers swallowed up by his.

In the instant of contact, her skin against his, an unfamiliar creature inside her shivered. Caught up in the sensation, she nearly missed his next words.

"I promise you only the one day. Anything more will have to build upon that."

Oh, how she wanted to puncture his arrogance and cynicism.

But she had earned every micron of his doubt. Only her performance would erase it. From some hidden reserve, she mustered the composure not to take the bait.

Imagining her voice as her sister's or her mother's, she kept her tone cool and neutral. "Give me the address and the time." *And I'll show you, you smug bastard.*

"Five o'clock."

A.M.? She blinked but didn't ask. "Fine. Where is it?"

"I will pick you up at your mother's. It is only the one day, after all."

She saw him anticipate her loss of temper and kept her eyes squarely on his, visualizing her mother's poise as if she could slip inside Cleo's skin. "I'll be ready."

As temper and nerves threatened to topple the lid she'd jammed on both, she departed. She had approximately four hours to sleep. She would show him, damned if she wouldn't.

But no way would she race out the door. Instead, she took her own sweet time in leaving.

CHAPTER NINE

SANDOR HAD TO GIVE her credit when he pulled up to the curb in front of Cleo's house at five minutes before five the next morning.

Her eyes might be bleary and her step a bit slow, but she was waiting on the sidewalk for him, dressed in an ancient pair of jeans that hugged her slim hips, and a baggy, paint-stained T-shirt. On her feet, she even wore sensible running shoes. Her look of determination had him pausing to reconsider his assumptions about her.

"Good morning," he said as she climbed into the passenger seat.

She glanced sideways and mumbled something in a husky tone that shouldn't have had his insides stirring.

But it did. Her speaking voice was low and pleasant, when she wasn't using her sharp tongue to ward off anyone who might come too close. This faint rasp, though…a man could clearly imagine the pleasure of hearing it in the embrace of night.

"Here." She thrust a thermal cup at him, and the

edge was back. "I made coffee. Don't talk to me until I've had a cup."

Ah. The prickly woman hadn't vanished after all, though she had managed to surprise him. He had intended to stop and buy them both breakfast to make up for advancing the start time an hour as a test.

Assuming she showed, which he had not truly expected her to do. "Have you eaten?"

She frowned. "I hate breakfast."

"You cannot work on an empty stomach. Breakfast is the most important meal of the day."

Ria squinted at him and sighed. "You're going to make me talk, aren't you?" She lifted one shoulder. "Fine, but you may not like the result."

"Your ill temper does not frighten me."

She sighed more dramatically. "Too much to hope, I guess." He thought he saw her mouth quirk, though in the dim light from the dash, he could not be sure.

"We will stop for food."

"Not on your life, pal. We have work to do."

Cheeky. Irritating and bewildering as the woman was, any flash of humor was a surprise. "I am buying."

She stiffened. "I don't need charity."

"I will not get my money's worth if you faint from hunger."

"You're not paying me today, remember? Anything I accomplish is a bonus."

"I am the boss. Taking orders is part of your job."

"Ja wohl, mein Fuhrer." She snapped a smart salute.

"Wrong nationality." Sandor covered his chuckle with a cough. "But the obedience is welcome."

He could practically hear her teeth grinding from where he sat.

To her credit, she did not argue but simply sipped in silence.

He did the same and was impressed to discover that the difficult woman at his side made an extraordinary cup of coffee.

Perhaps, once she acknowledged that she was not suited to his type of work, he could mention her to Colin and obtain her a position more suited to her physical strength.

In the meantime, he would see that she ate, and at the end of the day, he would pay her, as well, before sending her on her way.

BUT RIA SURPRISED HIM. She was indeed stronger than she appeared. Though he had only been able to force one breakfast taco down her—and she had complained bitterly through every bite—she kept up a steady pace all morning. It was nine-thirty, the time he would normally be forced to stop and begin cleanup so the restaurant employees could prepare for the lunch rush, but today he would easily be able to continue his own efforts for another half hour. Ria had not only cleaned up nearly before the sawdust hit the floor, but she'd also noticed when he needed a piece of lumber or more nails and had had them ready to slip into his hands as though they had worked together for years.

And had remained silent the entire time.

Unlike Jerome, who had completed each task requested but initiated nothing and chattered every minute.

Sandor cast yet another glance toward the doorway, wishing he knew where the boy was.

"What are you looking at?" Ria asked. "You expecting Immigration, or did you ask the cops to keep an eye on me?"

He brought his attention back to the board he was nailing. "I do not fear Immigration. I am an American citizen."

Her eyes widened. "But you've been here less than a year, you said."

"My father was American, thus I was entitled to citizenship."

"So he spent his life in Hungary?"

"No."

She frowned. "What happened to him?"

"He left right after I was born to return to this country."

"But—" Abruptly, she closed her mouth. "It's not my business."

He bent the next nail. Jaw tight, he pried it out. "He promised to send for us, but a motorcycle accident claimed him. My mother died when I was eight. My grandmother raised me."

"I'm sorry."

He glanced at her and saw that she was. He shrugged. "No matter. It was all long ago."

But she continued to study him, and her eyes were both warm and sad.

"I do not need your pity." He hammered the next nail with one powerful stroke.

Then bent another one. With a low curse, he stalked to the doorway and shoved it open.

Just in time to see a small form skitter around the corner.

"Jerome," he shouted. "Wait."

Small footsteps pounded a retreat.

Sandor charged after him.

RIA QUICKLY MOVED to the door and peered outside.

A skinny black child ran across the parking lot, nearly making it to the edge of the fence before Sandor caught him. The boy tried to break away, but Sandor held his wrists, talking to him while the child squirmed.

A few months after she had landed in L.A., her musician boyfriend had dumped her in a tough part of town following a bitter fight. Even if Dog Boy had had a phone, she wouldn't have had enough money to phone him, much less pay cab fare, and she hadn't eaten for more than a day.

She'd shoplifted a candy bar, and the angry store owner had called the cops. While they were waiting, he'd loomed over her, one huge hand fisted to cuff her, the other one so tight on her wrist she'd been sure the bones would break.

She could still feel the greasy terror crowding her throat.

"Stop that," she yelled, and raced across the parking lot toward Sandor. "Don't hit him. Leave him alone."

Sandor was bent over, speaking to the boy, and when she launched herself at his back, she toppled him to the pavement and cracked her own head on the hard surface.

She squeezed her eyes shut as pain radiated through her skull, but not before she saw that the child had escaped.

Sandor leaped to his feet. "Jerome, she is hurt. Go inside and call an ambulance." Then he went to his knees beside her. "Ria, can you talk to me? How badly are you injured?" He glanced over his shoulder at the boy frozen to the spot. "*Now,* Jerome."

"Don't. I'm okay." Ria sat up with one hand pressed to the back of her head. Jerome's wide eyes stared at her.

"Dude, I don't know where you got this wildcat woman, but I like her." He grinned. "She pretty skinny, though. Not much meat on her."

"Be quiet," Sandor snapped. "Look at me, Ria."

She blinked. "I thought..."

The boy shrugged. "That's nice, girl, you coming to my rescue and all."

"But he was..."

Sandor grasped her chin. "Let me see your pupils." He shifted his focus from one to the other. "Close your eyes for a moment."

"Stop ordering me around."

"Hey, that's what I tell him. Man got his mind set on watching over me, but I don't need it, I say."

"Close them or I will do it for you."

Her mouth tightened.

"Might as well, girl. Man won't give up."

She huffed out a breath and complied. "Is this okay, master?"

The child giggled. How old was he? Not more than eleven or twelve, she thought. And completely unafraid of Sandor. She felt like an idiot.

"Now, open them."

She took her sweet time, and the boy winked at her. She couldn't help smiling back.

Then Sandor began probing her skull and grazed a sore spot.

"Ow!"

"The ice machine, Jerome. You recall where it is. Please place some cubes in a towel or something. I will carry her inside."

"Carry—" But before she could complain, he had lifted her, standing easily as if she were no burden. His arms were strong beneath her, his chest broad and deep. She could see a patch at his jaw where he had missed shaving. His beard was shades darker than the honey-gold of his hair.

And suddenly, she was a little breathless.

He didn't speak to her but simply carted her into the cool interior that was as fragrant with sawdust as he himself, his own scent compounded with honest sweat and something elementally…male.

It had been a very, very long time since Ria had been this close to a healthy adult of the opposite sex—not since a couple of aborted attempts at dating when Benjy was very small and Dog Boy had pushed her out into the world again.

Her life, for so long, had been as caretaker, first for a tiny infant and then also for a dying man, a struggle to watch over both while working to support them all. Dating and sex had receded so far into the background that she'd ceased to think of herself as a woman.

The last several months, Dog Boy had required constant monitoring they couldn't afford. Rather than send him to some warehouse for indigents, she'd sold everything but the essentials and Benjy's pitiful few belongings, then scrimped and stretched the meager bankroll to enable her to be with him full-time until the end.

After that there'd been the grieving, the awful, howling pain of losing her only friend.

And the dread of fulfilling her promise to return to Austin.

Ria had learned early exactly how to deal with the male of the species. Sex was the bottom line; with it might come affection or at least protection, but neither ever lasted. It was a tool a wise woman wielded when needed, without expecting too much.

She would use it now if that would help, but this man was not like any other she'd encountered. She had no confidence in his reaction, and she was through embarrassing herself in front of him. "Put me down."

He glanced at her but didn't relent.

"I'm not an invalid, damn it. I'm fine." She began to struggle.

His arms tightened, rolling her into his chest. "Shh," he soothed. "Take it easy."

Her body seemed to have a mind of its own as it curled into his strength. Hot tears squeezed from beneath her lids, and a terrible longing choked her. Didn't he know how kindness could hurt? Couldn't he understand that to weaken would kill her?

She slammed an open palm into his unyielding chest and shoved. "Let me go," she gasped, breathing hard as if she'd run a race. "Don't…I can't…"

His grip loosened only a little, but she scrambled onto her feet and backed away, one hand out to ward him off.

And because she was shaky and scared, she brandished the only defense she had. "If you wanted your hands on me, all you had to do was say the word. Buy me a drink after work, and we'll see what happens next."

Equal measures of disgust and anger—laced with pity, damn him—mingled in his expression. The air around them crackled until Ria felt sick to her stomach. She dragged her eyes from his and sought the pile of trash she'd been sweeping. "You said we had to be finished by ten, didn't you, *boss man?*" With trembling fingers and blurred vision, she grabbed the broom and went to work.

"Here's the ice, Sandor." Jerome's tennis shoes squeaked on the concrete floor.

Ria's strokes stalled out as the atmosphere built until she expected it to explode in chain lightning and rolling thunder, but she didn't turn around.

When Sandor finally spoke, his voice was quiet and low. "Please put it in the cooler, Jerome." Tight, but kind to the boy.

"But she—"

"If you will carry that bucket to my truck, I would appreciate it." She heard the clack of several boards lifted at once.

Why didn't he yell? Throw something? Grab her again? Anything but this deadly, patient restraint. She kept sweeping as she heard his heavy footsteps recede.

"Whoo-ee, girl." Jerome whistled. "You crazy or just mean? Dude only trying to help you. What's wrong with you?"

She thought she could wait the boy out; if she didn't respond, he'd lose interest and leave.

No such luck. He walked right up and planted himself in front of her so that she had to stop.

"What?" she snapped.

"Hey, you cryin'."

"I am not." She brushed her eyes with the back of one hand.

"Are you okay?" He sounded so young without his swagger.

Suddenly, she could hear the echo of another young voice, Dog Boy's, asking that question six years ago. Smell again the odors of the bus station, dense with hopelessness and diesel and urine. Hear the rumbling of the metal monsters waiting outside as she tried to read the bus schedule through the haze of tears.

But all she'd been able to see was the hard truth in her mother's face, the moment when she knew even her father would trade her life for David's. In a heartbeat.

Oh, David.

No way to forget the pictures in her mind. Quit hearing the scream of twisting, ripping metal, the roar of the other engine.

The silence.

Where her brother's voice should have been.

"Are you okay?" A hand had touched her shoulder.

She'd screamed and jerked away.

Bloodshot blue eyes greeted her from within a face framed by red, scraggly curls. "Hey, didn't mean to scare you. It's just that you were, like, crying, man." His clothes were at least two sizes too large, swallowing his scarecrow build. He was just a kid, somewhere near David's age, and he hadn't had a good meal in weeks, she'd bet.

His fingernails were dirty but his touch gentle. She wanted to slap his hand away, but something kind in those blue eyes held her in place.

"Where ya goin', girl?"

She shook her head. "Don't know yet."

"Traveling light." He nodded at the single canvas bag she'd packed in haste. "Fight with a boyfriend?"

She smiled bitterly, turning away, trying to ignore him. "I wish."

He shrugged. "Your story's your own." He nodded

around the dingy waiting room stinking with a long hot day's sweat, ripe with the acrid scent of losers. "I'm Dog Boy. You got a name, little girl lost?"

"What the hell kind of name is that?"

"As good as any," he said with a shrug. He jittered on the balls of his feet, his gaze skating over the faces in the room. Then suddenly, he pinned her with the intensity of a spotlight's glare. "Hey, you got no plans, come with me."

"Where?" She frowned. Not that it mattered. She had no destination. Just away. As far as possible.

"L.A., baby. LaLa Land."

Her eyes narrowed. "You don't seem like the L.A. type."

"Ain't only pretty boys in Hollywood. Somebody got to wash the dishes."

"I don't like washing dishes."

"Babe, with your looks, that won't be a problem. Anyway, what you got to hold you here?"

A hot poker stabbed her chest. "Nothing."

"Then what you waitin' for, girl? Come with Dog Boy to Lotusland. Milk and honey, sunshine on the beach, a million dreams just waitin' to come alive." His expression turned crafty. "I got a friend, a musician. Used to play the Sixth Street clubs. We'll have us a place to crash."

"Why me? You don't know me."

"I'm a sucker for tears, what can I say?" He smiled.

"That's bullshit." She glared at him. "Is this about sex, is that it?"

"Jesus Christ, what's your problem?" He danced in place, his wiry body snapping with energy. "I just thought you could use a friend. Hey, I been there. My old man threw me out when I was twelve."

L.A. was as good as anywhere else. She had barely a hundred dollars to her name. But she had to get one more thing clear. "Just until I find my own place. I pay my way and I don't owe you a thing. And you keep your hands to yourself."

He held up both palms in surrender. "Whoa, chill, girl. Don't get your panties in a wad."

"No, you hear me. I make my own rules now. I don't belong to anyone. You don't like it, tough. I can go anywhere. I don't need you."

"What you walk into here, Dog Boy? You don't have to put up with this shit." He stared at the ceiling as if answers would fall from the sky.

Then, with the guile of an elf, he lifted one eyebrow and cocked his head, staring down at her. "Amazon Girl, looks like this is your lucky day. Seems like my spirit guides say that I ain't had enough crap yet in my life and you're exactly what it takes to get my quota full. One thing, though—you got a name?" His crooked smile couldn't be ignored as he asked the question again.

For the first time since the car crash, she felt a faint stir of hope pierce her leaden despair.

Oh, David. If you can hear me now—I'm sorry. Dear God, I miss you.

"Ria." David's name for her. It was all she would

take from this place where so much had gone wrong. "My name is Ria."

"I like it." He swept into a courtly bow. "Prince Charming at your service. Your chariot awaits, my lady."

"HEY—WHERE YOU GO, girl?" Jerome snapped his fingers in front of her face.

Ria shook her head, suddenly exhausted. "I've got to get out of here."

"You can try, but he'll just hunt you down. He been all over this part of town after me. I watch him, but I hide."

"Why? He likes you. He wants to help."

Eyes years older than his body stared into hers. "'Cause he's an innocent, you dig? He big and strong, had a hard life, yeah, but he don't see the world like you and me do. He still think he can fix things. People."

These eyes were brown and not Dog Boy's pale blue, but she recognized a kindred spirit, another soul forced to grow up too early.

"Are you using?" she asked him.

Jerome frowned and stepped back. "Mind your own business."

She gripped his upper arm, barely skin over bone. "Look at me. More than pot?" She shook him gently, still grasping tight. "Tell me you're too smart for needles."

He jerked away. "What's it to you?"

"It's an ugly way to die, the garbage that comes through a needle. If Sandor wants to fix you, you let him. Everyone needs friends."

He glanced at her sideways. "Even you?"

"I already used up one more than I deserved." She thrust the broom at him. "Tell him—" She cast about for an explanation Sandor would swallow.

Then realized he wouldn't require one. She was acting exactly as he'd expected.

But Jerome was right. In a sense, though Sandor had known hardship, he maintained an optimism she had lost long ago. What if her behavior discouraged him from his belief that he could save this child?

"Hey." She held out a hand before Jerome got too far. "Give me that."

The boy returned, his forehead crinkling as he watched her finish sweeping the pile into a dustpan. "Girl, you a head case."

"What do you know?" Ria shrugged but smiled at him. "You're just a kid."

Jerome grinned back. "So…you gonna be here tomorrow?"

Ria rested one fist on her hip. "I will if you will."

The boy laughed and scampered out the door.

CHAPTER TEN

"WHY DID YOU allow him to leave?" The anger on which Sandor had slammed a lid bubbled up once more, rattling and blowing steam.

Ria swept the last of the dust into the pan. "It's a free country. You ought to appreciate that more than most."

"He is a child. I have searched for him for days." Only rigid discipline kept him from shouting as the sounds of the restaurant workers filtered in. "He is in trouble and you simply let him walk away."

"He'll come back." She picked up the trash bag and moved toward the door.

He grabbed her shoulder and whirled her around. "You cannot be sure of that."

She was oddly calm. "I was on the streets, too, Sandor. Older than him, but I understand what it's like to have things dangled in front of you and be afraid to grab them."

"He is too young to be on his own."

Her head cocked. "What age were you when you were scrounging for food for your grandmother?"

"That is different."

"How?" She seemed honestly interested.

"There were no gangbangers in my country. No children carrying guns and murdering other children for a pair of expensive shoes."

"Then why did you leave?"

"I wanted the freedom to make my own decisions, to determine my own fate."

"Maybe that's all Jerome wants."

"Were you on the streets because that was your wish?"

"I had nowhere else to go." Her eyes darkened, and in that instant he regretted bringing up her past.

"I can help the boy, Ria. But only if I can locate him."

Her chin jutted. "He'll be back, I'm telling you."

He wanted to believe her. "You cannot be certain."

Her mouth curved. "Want to lay money on it? If I'm right, I get a raise."

"I have not hired you yet."

"I surprised you, though, didn't I? You didn't believe I could work this hard. You have no idea what I'm capable of handling, Sandor." Her smile widened, though nerves jittered in her gaze. "And the only way to find out is to tune in for tomorrow's episode."

He glanced toward the door, then back at her. "This job will last only another week or so."

"Then you'd better get busy hustling up the next one, hadn't you, boss?" She winked at him and strolled off.

Sandor stared after her. Who was this woman, by turns terrified and belligerent, fragile then mischievous?

Soft, oddly so for someone who was barely more than bones. And seductive, though she would believe it was her blatant offer of her body that lured him, when in fact the glimpses of her courage scaled the barriers of his distrust.

He shook his head. In that, she resembled no one more than her mother, and the observation would infuriate her, he did not doubt.

For that reason, perhaps he should say so, to keep her at a distance. He was Cleo's friend, and he could not allow himself to become confused in his loyalties.

Perhaps he could convince Ria that the day's labor was finished, though he could use a second set of hands for the gutter repair he had in mind to do at Billie's. As quickly as he considered the ruse, however, he rejected it. Ria was a good worker; he must give her that.

And he was a practical man. One did not reject a useful tool when it was right at hand.

Even if that tool disturbed him in ways best not considered.

RIA CARRIED the last of the trash to the Dumpster and walked back to the pickup, gnawing her lip. She needed this job for reasons she didn't want to think about too hard, and arguing with Sandor was not likely to impress him. As for teasing him, well, he was far too serious himself not to hold that against her. Tackling him and accusing him of harming a child—even worse.

Great way to get on his good side, champ. She

clenched and released her fingers as she waited for him to emerge.

Then she got mad that his opinion of her mattered.

Who was this guy, anyway? The Slavic god peering down from his perch, secure in his right to judge others. Rigid in his standards, determined to dislike her.

She let out her breath in a whoosh. *Not fair.*

He'd cuddled her, damn it. What was that about? She was a grown woman, not a child, and she'd—

Liked it, be honest. Savored the sense of safety, of refuge. Wished for more.

Her nostrils flared as she drew herself upright and wrapped her arms around her middle. Refuge was not her destiny; hadn't she learned that again and again? She wasn't a child anymore—she had borne one. Her job was to get her act together and provide refuge for him.

"Do you intend to stand there all morning, or are you ready to work?"

She jolted. He waited on the other side of the pickup, his expression unreadable. "I thought it was time to quit so they could serve lunch."

"We can come again this afternoon for an hour or two if I can obtain the proper materials, but I have another repair to accomplish now. Or have you had enough?"

Ria narrowed her eyes, wondering how this other job had suddenly materialized, sniffing the air for the scent of pity.

Then she decided it didn't matter. "Of course not.

I'll last as long as you can." Truth to tell, she was more tired than she'd expected. Somehow, relaxing her guard once she'd made it to Austin and Benjy was safe had made her more exhausted, not less.

But she had a great deal of experience with working past her limits. She opened the door on her side and got in. When he hesitated, she cocked her head.

"So what's the holdup? We have a job, boss man. Get it in gear."

He never cracked a smile, but he closed and locked the toolbox, then settled into the seat beside her and turned the key in the ignition.

A few minutes later, after a silent ride, they pulled into the driveway of an old house in the Clarksville neighborhood that had certainly seen better days. The siding had last been painted long before her birth, she was sure, weathered to a silvery gray, with scattered patches of green clinging to the shutters.

But the driveway gleamed pristine and new, the asphalt a raven's-wing black.

"You've already been busy, I see." At his lifted brow, she nodded to indicate the driveway. "I bet it's hard to figure where to start."

He nodded. "There is much to do to restore this place."

She thought of the transformation in her mother's area, just as close to the center of the city. "Please tell me this isn't for some stockbroker and his wife."

He stared at her. "Why?"

She shrugged. "I liked this part of town the way it was. Too much of the old Austin is vanishing."

"Change is the lifeblood of this country. It is one of America's charms."

"To you, maybe. There's nothing wrong with a little shabbiness. It lends character." She gazed out the window and spotted a woman as tall as most men, decked out in a flowing, tie-dyed dress and sporting thick silver braids nearly to her waist. "Oh, wow." She couldn't help grinning. "Now, that's the Austin I know."

"Wait—"

But Ria was already leaping from the truck. "Good morning," she said. "I love your house."

"Ria—" Sandor called out.

She kept moving forward, ignoring him. The woman was probably Lola's age but had chosen to accept the natural order. No blond hair, no nips and tucks. Her face was lined and noble, free of any makeup. Jeweled pins and beads scampered across the bodice of her dress. An old hippie, Ria thought with delight. "Have you always lived here?"

The woman glanced over Ria's shoulder just as Sandor's hand dropped onto it. Ria tried to shake him off, but his grip only tightened.

"Who's this?" The woman frowned.

"Good morning," Sandor responded. "Billie Packard, my landlady, this is Ria Channing. My assistant."

"I don't like having strangers in my house. You didn't tell me you'd have strangers."

Ria's enthusiasm drained away. "I can go."

Sandor restrained her. "She is a good worker. And now you have been introduced."

The woman focused dark, piercing eyes on her. She was nearly Sandor's height, and though Ria was not short herself, she felt the woman's presence looming over her as if she were her mother's diminutive stature.

Sharp beak of a nose, skin tanned like leather, rangy build, this woman was earthy and magnificent, as far from the polished, glitzy Lola as was possible.

"Let me see your palm."

Ria blinked, but something about the woman demanded obedience. She stuck out her right hand.

Billie tilted it from one side to the other to catch the light. Slowly, she traced the lines, and the touch was faint enough to tickle, but instead, a warm hum followed the path drawn by her forefinger. "Hmm," the old woman said, muttering.

Mesmerized by the blue-purple veins trailing over the back of the woman's finger, tunneling beneath the skin and twining over tendons standing in relief, Ria waited like an acolyte for the old woman to impart a crumb of wisdom.

But as much as she yearned to know her future, the prospect unnerved her. As desperate questions fought to reach her lips, she yanked her hand away.

Before she could escape, the woman spoke. "He's taken you on, too."

Ria stuck her hands in her pockets. "I don't know what you mean."

The old woman pointed downward, and Ria saw two

cats twining around Sandor's ankles, rubbing and begging for attention. One was a big scarred yellow tom, the other a half-starved calico female. "Boy been here less than a week, and as if it's not enough for him to decide he's going to adopt my house as a charity project, already every stray animal in the neighborhood has figured out who's the easy touch."

"I'm not a stray." Ria frowned. "I don't need handouts. I'll earn my keep."

A raucous belly laugh issued from the woman's throat. "Good for you. Girl after my own heart." She faced Sandor. "Hear that, boy? This one's got spirit. Might just give you a run for your money."

Still caught in her own outrage, Ria nearly missed the color that flared on Sandor's face.

"There is much to be done." Mouth tight, he strode to his truck and removed an extension ladder.

He's embarrassed, Ria realized. It was almost enough to snap her out of her fury. To make her forget the itch in her palm.

Sandor strode toward the corner of the house, carrying the heavy ladder with ease. Ria started after him, then paused.

"What did you find?" she asked Billie, cursing herself for being unable to let the subject go.

A pause. "You're going to meet a tall, handsome stranger." Billie's gaze strayed toward Sandor, and she cackled.

Ria grabbed the old woman's wrist. "Don't be flippant with me. You don't understand what I've done, where I've been." Aghast at herself, Ria started to release her grip.

But Billie placed her other hand over Ria's, and something ghosted across her eyes. "Palmistry is a parlor game, nothing more." But her tone said differently.

Ria searched the old woman's eyes to uncover what was truth and what was lie. The dark orbs were faintly milky at the center, and Ria wondered exactly how much Billie could see.

"He's waiting for you, child."

A shiver danced over Ria's nape, across her shoulders and arms, twitching her fingers. She couldn't break the contact, yet truth, as elusive as a night creature's glissade through moonlight and shadow, taunted her. Lured her.

"Ria." Sandor's voice, both low and impatient, jolted her.

She looked up, then quickly back to Billie.

But Billie was ambling toward the front porch, taking her prophecies with her.

"Wait."

Billie didn't respond.

"Ria." Sandor clasped her upper arm. "She is old. She tires easily."

"But…" She tried to wriggle from his grasp. "I have to…"

"Ria," he repeated her name, his voice gentle. "There is no magic. She has no answers that you do not possess inside yourself."

She does. She has to. Ria stared at the ground. *I don't know anything. I never have.*

"Would you like me to drive you home?"

There again, the compassion. *He's taken you on, too.*

Finding her path had never seemed more impossible. Mere feet in front of her, the road disappeared into mist.

This one's got spirit. Might just give you a run for your money.

Dear God, she was tired.

Benjy. All that counts is Benjy.

Ria fixed her inner vision on the small face that was her world. She lifted her head and studied Sandor. "What do we need to do first?"

Hazel eyes searched her own. Finally, he nodded. "Several downspouts have broken loose. If you will hold each straight at the bottom, I will reattach them." He hesitated, then seemed to reconsider.

He walked toward the ladder.

Ria followed. One step at a time. It would have to be enough for now.

SHE WAS FALTERING, but the stubborn woman would not give up. Sandor tightened a screw in the last gutter strap and peered over the roof at Ria. "You are not drinking enough water." Though it was September, the day was quite warm. He wondered if fall would ever make an appearance.

"I'm fine." She released the death grip she had on

the metal, and one of his too-large gloves slipped off her hand and landed in the dirt. She bent, then straightened, and swayed slightly.

Sandor glanced at his watch and swore. Nearly two o'clock, and they had not taken a lunch break yet. He was accustomed to going all day without eating if he was too busy, but she should not. She was much too thin to be holding on from anything but sheer will.

"Move," he ordered. "I am ready to climb down."

She stepped aside without an argument, so he was certain that she was truly exhausted. At the bottom of the ladder, he clasped her arm. "Come with me."

"Where?"

He stopped long enough to grab the cooler and pour her some water. "Drink." Her normally porcelain skin held an unhealthy tinge. The absence of sweat worried him nearly as much as her torpor. "Why did you not tell me you felt ill?" He jerked the bandanna holding back his hair and soaked it, then began to sponge her skin. "Sit down."

She raised glazed eyes to his, and he swore again and lifted her into his arms.

"You can't keep hauling me around like a sack of feed."

He wanted to feel relief that she was able to joke, but he was too busy cursing himself for not paying more attention. He concentrated on climbing the stairs to his apartment.

"Where are you taking me?"

He remained silent, balancing her in one arm while

he probed his pocket for the key. He managed to unlock the door, then regretted bringing her up here because he had, as usual, refused to leave the one small window air conditioner running, to save money. It was hotter in here than outside.

He made a quick decision and crossed to the bathroom, then turned on the shower. Disregarding his own clothes and sparing but an instant for regret at the toll to his shoes, he paused only long enough to unbuckle his tool belt, then stepped into the small metal shower stall, with her.

Ria's eyes flew open. She shrieked. "What are you doing? This water's freezing!" She struggled against him, but Sandor simply tightened his hold and dunked her head under the spray.

She came up hissing like a wet cat. "You bastard." She slammed a fist into his chest, her green eyes spitting.

Relief swept through him. She was completely alert now, if furious. "Be still. You will injure yourself."

"No way. I'm saving my strength to hurt you," she spluttered.

Then she stopped. Stared.

Threw back her head and began to laugh.

The merriment made her appear so young that Sandor abruptly wished he could have known her as a girl. Before life—and her own mistakes—had fractured her fragile sense of herself.

The hilarity relaxed her, and suddenly, he was very much aware of her as a woman, of the admittedly faint contours beneath his hands. She was more bone than curve, more wraith than siren, but he still had no doubt that it was a female he held.

The frigid shower did not help on that score. Against his will, his body reacted to her. He lifted her away so she would not be able to tell.

Too late. Her eyes widened, the pupils going dark.

Somewhere beyond cold water and wet clothing, another level of consciousness emerged. Hovered between them. Dared not breathe.

This time she managed to scramble from his embrace, her hip brushing his body as she escaped the shower and stood dripping in the middle of the tiny room.

He could not break the gaze that bound them.

Neither could she, though she looked like nothing so much as a doe ready to sprint away.

No. Not a doe. Not in that T-shirt so wet that he could see the shadowed curves of her breasts. Sandor swallowed hard and managed to shut off the water. Thrust a towel at her.

And beat her out the door.

SHE WANTED to go home. Escape.

She wanted to pounce. Feast.

Ria untied her shoes, grateful that they'd been mostly stuck beyond the reach of the spray, and removed them, staring down at her soaked jeans and the T-shirt plastered against her body.

Ineffectually, she dried with the towel, but finally resorted to yanking off the shirt and wringing it out in the ancient, cracked sink. A small, hazy mirror hung above it.

Ria caught a glimpse of herself and blinked. She appeared…

Alive. Hectic spots of color on her cheeks, eyes dancing.

Dancing? Forget that. She was mad as hell, that was all. How dare he just shove her under ice-cold water and—

And step into it himself. His shoes must be soaked. His shirt and jeans sure were.

His jeans. His body. He'd responded as if—

Whew. She exhaled and refused to think anymore about what had just happened. He was male, that was all. She had enough experience with the other sex to know that a guy could hate a woman and still get aroused.

She just hadn't known she could, too. Hate, that is, and still feel a jolt of lust like she'd never—

Be honest, Ria. You don't hate him. In fact, you…

No. No way. She still wasn't sure she believed he hadn't been involved with her mother, so she certainly wasn't going to be attracted—

Okay. She believed him. But he despised her.

So he charged up these stairs as if you weighed nothing because he can't stand you?

Oh, man. She was so confused. She had to leave. Surely she'd proved to him that she could do the work and didn't have to stay all day.

Benjy. Remember Benjy.

So Ria stood very still and breathed deeply, in and out, for ten measured repetitions. Then she slipped back on her damp T-shirt—no way was she asking to borrow anything—and pulled it out from her chest.

She mopped up the floor as best she could and straightened the painfully neat counter, where only a toothbrush, razor and bar of soap lay.

Then she inhaled another lungful of air, grasped the knob and opened the door.

Sandor was removing a dry shirt from the lone bureau and turned.

Oh, my. What a chest. More of that golden skin, acres of it, and a dusting of hair. She stood transfixed.

He yanked the fabric over his head. "I will make you a sandwich."

"No, that's all right." But he had already left the room. Ria realized she'd never made it past his chest to see his expression, but from the sound of his voice, he didn't welcome the ogling.

She spared a second to peruse the small space, which contained only a double bed—surely too short for his frame—the bureau and one straight-backed chair. Nothing on the walls or windows. The cell of an ascetic.

Was this really his place, this wood-carver who could make the viewer weep with the beauty of his work? Did his artist's soul not wither and die here?

"Come and drink more water," he ordered.

Artist. She rolled her eyes. Tyrant, more like it. Brute. Insensitive and—

"Ria—" His tone was quiet but echoed with warning.

She rounded the doorway. Caught his look. Grabbed the hem of her damp shirt and prepared to draw it away from her body again.

No. She'd forgotten every last lesson she'd learned about handling men. She still had to have a job; she'd obtain it by whatever means necessary. She deliberately threw her shoulders back to take advantage of what meager curves she possessed.

He noticed. But though his nostrils flared in response, he didn't react as she'd intended.

"Eat." Sandor slammed the plate down in front of her. "Do not move until you have consumed it and the glass of water. Then I will take you home."

"You can't do that."

One eyebrow arched. He had beautiful eyes, even when he was glaring at her.

"The day isn't over. I told you I can handle the work."

Sandor reached into his hip pocket, retrieved a worn wallet and counted out several bills. "I will pay you for a full day." He thrust them at her.

Something inside her collapsed. She stared at the money instead of him. "What about tomorrow?"

"Ria…" His voice was too gentle.

Every last bit of hope started to unravel. "Don't do this to me," she whispered. She dashed at the moisture gathering in her eyes. Raised her head.

Glared. "I can't quit, damn you."

He glanced away. “You are a hard worker.”

“But?”

His eyes were kind and sad. “Ria, you require more time to rest and recover.” He gestured toward her. “You are half-starved.”

She didn’t need to examine her pitiful excuse for a figure. “I’ve always been skinny. So what?”

“I will speak to a friend about a job in his coffee shop, once you are stronger.”

“I want this one.”

“I am trying to tell you—”

That I’ve failed. Again. “I get it.” With dull resignation, she cast a look of longing at the sandwich she hadn’t yet tasted. She rose. Left the money where it was.

“I can walk from here. It’s not that far.”

“You will let me drive you. First, you will eat.”

“I’m not hungry.”

Impatient, he raked his fingers through his hair. “You must have food.”

She shrugged. “I need lots of things, Sandor. But they’re not your problem.” She crossed to the door. Decided against a Pyrrhic victory. She was tired. “If you insist on driving me, then let’s go before you lose any more work time.”

He picked up the money. Extended it toward her.

A growl came from her throat. “Don’t you dare.” She whirled. Raced down the steps.

Nearly missed one for the film over her eyes.

“Ria,” he said from the top. “I have no desire to hurt you.”

She paused at the bottom, gripping the banister as her head spun. "Then get in the car and drive."

With a muttered oath, he locked the apartment door and pounded down the stairs after her.

CHAPTER ELEVEN

VERY EARLY THE NEXT MORNING, Cleo shifted the bag to her left hand as she reached to unlock the shop. Before she could slip the key inside, Sandor jerked the door open. Took the bag.

"Don't you ever go home?"

He smiled faintly. The sight of her, after a long, sleepless night, warmed him. "The advantages of living nearby."

Cleo studied him and frowned. "You look terrible. What's happened?"

"Nothing." He glanced away. He should be at the restaurant any minute, but perhaps Cleo's unexpected arrival was a sign that it was time to tell her the decision he had wrestled with during the dark hours.

"Sandor." She restrained him with a hand on his wrist. "You're disturbed."

He shrugged. "Restless night." Difficult one, too, and not only because of this woman's daughter. His last reason for remaining had vanished. Ria was troubled, yes, but he no longer believed she would harm her mother intentionally. Instead, he probably owed both

Cleo and Ria an apology for mishandling Ria the day before. Regardless, he did not know how to break the news that he was moving out.

Or whether he or Cleo would mind more, though he suspected it would be him. For the moment, he merely stood aside and swept his arm out to demonstrate how he'd passed the night.

Her brow beetled. Then suddenly, her puzzlement cleared. "You've finished."

Sandor nodded.

"Let me see." Eagerly, she headed for the doorway, then stopped in mid-stride. "Oh. Oh." One hand pressed to her heart.

Pride stirred. It was the best work he'd ever done. In the morning's golden light, the wood seemed to glow from within, the grain exploding with vitality, every curve alive.

"I could swear she's breathing. It's exquisite. Oh, beyond that— I don't have the right words. Lovely. Stunning. Sandor—"

"It is yours."

She froze. Whirled, eyes wide. "You don't—I can't—" She was stammering. "Sandor, it would be wrong for me to accept such a magnificent piece. You could sell it for so much. This will be the centerpiece of your first show."

He was not ready for that step. "You do not want it?"

"Of course I do, but—"

"If such an opportunity comes, perhaps I would ask to borrow it, but it is yours, now and always."

She opened her mouth to protest, but he shook his head. "There is more to tell you." He hesitated, not ready for this step, either. "It is time, Cleo."

She sighed. "You're leaving."

He nodded. "It is…difficult." He studied this woman who had changed his life. "Being here has been a gift. I can never repay you for all you have done for me. Please do not refuse my poor gesture. It is not enough, but it is a beginning."

"You can't believe you haven't given me back as much. All that you've done around here—" She gestured. "And you've been my friend when…" Bittersweet sorrow crossed her features. "You've always been there when I needed one."

"That will not change. I am your friend, now and ever."

For a second, she hesitated, and he was afraid she would ask him not to go. That he would have to explain about her daughter and how she confused him. How he might have made things worse for her by blundering with Ria.

Because he felt such conflict within himself, he was determined to spare Cleo any more uproar in her life.

She smiled softly. "I'm glad."

"So you will accept this?"

She contemplated the figure again, and he wondered what she was thinking.

"All right." She turned back. "But I insist on loaning it to you when you have your first show. Which, I might add, should be sooner rather than later." She struggled for a smile. "Provided, of course, that I approve of the security arrangements."

He met her shaky grin with his own. He had taken one glimpse of her locks and replaced them all the first day, then bullied her into updating the archaic security system.

"You will call me when anything must be done around here." Not a question, though it was probably wiser for him to stay away.

"Just try refusing." Her voice wobbled a little.

He cleared his throat. Sought a new topic to give them both time to recover. "How was your afternoon off? What did you and Benjy do?"

Her eyes telegraphed her gratitude. "Malcolm showed up with Elizabeth and Marguerite, wanting to take Benjy to the park. The kids begged me to go, too."

"And did you?"

"Yes." Then Cleo was off and running, chattering about the things the children did, how they'd first circled like adversaries, then had become a pack of rolling puppies. "And now we have plans for a slumber party. The kids want Malcolm to attend."

Sandor caught a glow on her face that he had never witnessed before. "And do you wish it, as well?"

She glanced away. "Of course not. They're too young to understand that it's impossible."

She didn't seem aware that her heart was in her eyes. "Poor Colin. I begin to see the problem."

Cleo stared at him. "What do you mean?"

"His age is not the only strike against him. I can hear it in your voice. You are still in love with Malcolm."

"That's ridiculous. We're divorced, Sandor."

"Since when does the heart pay attention to a piece of paper?" Though he wished hers would; Malcolm had hurt her.

"He has someone else now. He lives with her."

"He is spending a lot of time at your house lately."

"That's for Benjy."

"If you choose to believe that." He bent to her. "I do not want him to hurt you. He walked away from you once."

"Because I asked him to go, not that it's any of your business."

He frowned. Why would she have done such a thing?

Before he could respond, she continued. "It wouldn't work. Too much has happened. We've grown apart."

"You are afraid."

"I am not."

But he could hear in her voice both fear…and yearning. Cleo was so courageous. Why would she simply give up? "He is not worth fighting for?"

"He's got a younger woman. She's beautiful—tall and blond."

"You are beautiful, and you could have a younger lover, too, but you do not accept him. How do you know Malcolm does not have his own longings for you? Living together signifies nothing."

"I don't intend to discuss it."

She deluded herself; hope was written all over her features. He was all too aware, though, of how stubborn Cleo could be, so he pressed no more. "If that is your wish."

"It is." The phone rang.

"I must leave for the restaurant."

"But..." She glanced at the instrument.

"Go ahead. I will return later for the rest of my tools."

She hesitated. Looked so vulnerable. "You won't leave without saying goodbye, will you?"

His chest tightened. "Of course not." He found a smile for her. "I will see you later, my friend. Answer your call."

She did so, but without ever removing her eyes from him as he departed.

Once outside, he felt as alone as he had in the beginning. He had to remind himself that he would cross paths with Cleo again, that he knew other people now.

That this was the best course for all of them.

"PLEASE, MOM, please?" Later that afternoon, Benjy's big brown eyes rebuked Ria's foreboding. "Let's invite Elizabeth and Marguerite to feed the ducks with us. They'd really like it, I promise."

But their mother won't, she wanted to tell him. No way on earth would Betsey let Ria take her precious daughters anywhere. He hadn't stopped talking about his outing with her nieces and her parents the day before.

"Listen, Benjy, I'm sure Elizabeth and Marguerite are fun to play with, but you'll meet new friends."

"Please, Mom. Just call, okay? Please?"

He asked for so little. He'd dealt with so much. But Ria already knew how Betsey would react, and it would break this child's heart.

But those soft brown eyes only asked her to try. How could she not?

"All right," she sighed. "I'll check."

"Call their mom now, okay?"

Ria got the number from Aunt Cammie, but Betsey wasn't home. She was at the shop, and the girls were with their housekeeper, who required permission to let them leave with anyone but Betsey or Peter.

With a leaden heart, Ria decided against phoning, hoping to gauge her sister's mood better in person. She left Benjy with Aunt Cammie, afraid to let him hear whatever Betsey had to say.

When she arrived, her heart sank as she spotted Sandor's pickup. She nearly wheeled the car in the opposite direction, still unnerved by what had happened in his apartment.

But Benjy was counting on her, so she parked and trudged inside.

The steps past Sandor's workroom door loomed as if a thousand yards long. She attempted to pass without glancing over, but her eyes betrayed her.

The piece was gone.

Ria's steps faltered.

Then Sandor moved into view.

Ria hurried on. She had challenge enough, dealing with her sister. No way was she ready to talk to this man.

Once inside, Betsey noticed her immediately, but she was busy with a customer and merely nodded.

Ria pretended to browse, wishing whoever it was would scram so she could get this over with. Idly, she began to tidy up the shelves closest to her.

Finally, the woman made her purchase and left.

"Mother's not here right now," Betsey supplied, stopping several feet away. "She had a meeting with her accountant."

Ria swallowed hard. "I came to see you."

Betsey's brown eyes widened. "Me? Why?"

"I, uh—" Ria glanced down at the floor. "This isn't for me, Bets. I know how you feel about me, but he's—Benjy hasn't done anything to you. He's innocent in all this."

"What do you want?" Suspicion colored every syllable.

Her spirits sank. "Never mind. It doesn't matter. I already know your answer. I'll figure out some way to explain it to him." She forced herself to walk slowly toward the back door.

"Wait—"

Her sister's hand grasped her arm. Ria noted the perfect French-manicured nails.

"Ask me, Vic. Don't you ever get tired of running away?"

Ria sagged. "Don't you ever get tired of passing judgment?"

What little sympathy had been in her sister's eyes turned to sparks. Betsey's temper had always required much to ignite it, but it burned hot—and long—when it did. "It's so easy for you. Whip through like a hurricane, then leave everyone else to deal with the damage. You're the most selfish person I've ever met. You have no idea what you've done, do you?"

She fought not to cower. "It was six years ago, Betsey. I never meant for it to happen. Do I stay on trial forever?"

"David's dead. Mother and Daddy are divorced. You caused all that."

"You don't think I hurt, too?" Anger punched a hole in resignation. "I made a mistake, the biggest one of my whole screwed-up life. I'd sell my soul to bring him back, to return to the moment before we got in that car. I have no idea why I lived and he died. I wish I hadn't. And I'm sure you do, too. But he's still gone." She spun and stumbled, blindly seeking the way out. "And I can't figure out how to make any of it better."

"Go away," Betsey suggested. "Don't ever come back. We were doing fine until you showed up."

Ria tried to see her sister through the haze of agony. Her voice dropped to a whisper. "I can't do that to Benjy."

Benjy. Oh, God. She hadn't even gotten as far as asking. Suddenly, she laughed, though it hurt all the way up her throat.

Betsey grabbed her arm. "Leave him here. We'll take care of him."

Ria jerked away. "Abandon my child? With you? You hate his guts."

"I don't. He's not to blame."

"But I am, right, Bets? It's not enough that I pay every second inside my heart. I have to beg for forgiveness that you and Mother are never going to give. Only Daddy—"

"You let Daddy alone," Betsey snapped. "He's got enough problems on his hands with Vanessa and the baby. Having you around only makes things worse."

Ria gasped. Blinked, not sure she'd heard the word. "Baby?"

Betsey shook her head angrily, spots of color high in her cheeks. "Forget I said anything." She turned away.

Ria stepped into her path. "Daddy's going to have a child?"

Betsey visibly drooped. "He isn't telling anyone yet." Her chin lifted. "But the last thing he should have to deal with is your histrionics. He has a new family on the way."

"But...but he loves Benjy, and—" *And he loves me. And he looked at Mother as if—*

Ria felt sick. Her father wouldn't need them anymore. She knew how that worked.

"Mother and Aunt Cammie and Lola will watch over Benjy." Betsey's voice softened. "He's innocent, and he deserves a better situation than you've provided him. Daddy and I will help. He'll have plenty of people to love him."

"I'm his mother," Ria whispered. "*I* love him." *I need him.*

"Enough to give him the life he deserves? Will you ever straighten out your own? And even if you did, how long do you expect Mother to support you?"

Just then, the bells at the door jingled, and a customer stepped inside.

Betsey pasted on a smile of welcome. "I'll be right with you." She turned back, her eyes dark pools of pain. "Vicky, I'm sorry. I shouldn't have told you about—" Was there a small plea in her expression? "Wait for me. I have to deal with this." She headed for the customer.

Ria didn't wait. Couldn't. She stumbled into the back room, tripping on the leg of the sofa.

Strong hands steadied her. "Sit."

She blinked. "Go away." But she complied and dropped her head into her hands. Next to her sister, Sandor was the last person she wanted to see right now.

"I think not." Sandor closed the door, then stood before her, hazel eyes filled with something that might have been sympathy. "I will get you water."

"You heard."

He nodded. "Here." He thrust a glass into her hands.

She drank because she couldn't think what else to do. "Is she right? Should I leave him here?"

"Betsey is not a bad person. She has borne a burden for all these years, trying to be the perfect daughter, to keep things tranquil. Your presence makes that difficult."

"So I just desert my child?"

"I did not say that. Only you can answer the question of where he is better off."

"It would make life so simple for everyone, wouldn't it? Daddy has his little nest, Betsey hers, Mother needs no one. But I—" She doubled over. Her heart would surely explode from the pain. "He's all I have. The only thing I've ever done right."

"He is not all you have." His voice was filled with pity.

Rage rescued her from weakness. "What the hell do you know? Don't patronize me."

His own temper kindled. "You have the power to change everything, yet you fall into self-pity, instead."

She lifted astounded eyes to his. "I have no power. I'm the one who owes a debt that will never go away. I'll wait until my dying day for forgiveness that won't come."

"I, I, I. Me, me, me."

She jumped up. Slapped him.

He caught her shoulders in a merciless grip.

The moment teetered on a razor's edge.

Abruptly, he released her as if disgusted. "Go on, little girl. Run. Hide from growing up."

She couldn't speak, could only look at him, the stain of shock coating her skin like acid, burning away the protective shield of her suffering.

"Go to hell," she growled. Then she pulled the threadbare fragments of her pride around her.

And walked out the door.

But once outside, she didn't dare go home to Benjy yet. He was too sensitive to her moods.

And she'd disappointed him.

Again.

She couldn't get into her car yet, either. Walking might help. Maybe a run. And along the way, she'd search for a pay phone to call Aunt Cammie so Benjy wouldn't be waiting. She had no idea how she'd explain it to him, but maybe if she walked long enough, she'd figure it out.

Or maybe she should do as Betsey suggested.

And just keep going. For good.

SANDOR RESTRAINED himself from following her only by extreme force of will. She worried him as much as she enraged him. He'd been wrong: she was a bomb with the timer ticking, and another woman he cared about deeply could be destroyed when the casing shattered.

When instead of going toward her car and Cleo's house, she turned left on the path that would lead to Joe's Bar, he muttered a curse.

Then walked to the phone, found a number and dialed.

In a few terse sentences, he secured the agreement of Hank, the owner, to keep an eye out for Ria and any trouble that might follow her.

He heard Betsey weeping and realized that someone else was as shattered.

So he headed inside, wondering if Cleo would be so sorry to see him go after all.

RIA RAN until her lungs burned, up and down tree-shrouded side streets, but the slide show of her mistakes wouldn't leave her.

Coming in drunk and sick to her soul after losing her virginity in the back of a car.

"Hey, what's wrong with you?" Eric Madsen's handsome face frowned as he pulled up his jeans and zipped them.

"Nothing." Victoria huddled against the car door, wishing she were anywhere but here. It was stupid to want to cry, but she did.

The star wide receiver stared at her for a minute in the dim greenish light of the dashboard. "Listen, I didn't realize you were—I mean, everyone thinks—"

That she was a slut. She had a rep, a creature that had grown beyond the creator's ability to manage it.

She wanted to curl up in her own bed. She should have realized it was bullshit, all that stuff about souls meeting and rockets exploding. Her mother had lectured Victoria to save herself for something that didn't exist, at least not anymore. Her parents had it, but she never would.

Betsey's brown eyes dark with disappointment as Victoria stumbled on the porch. Snickered.

"Hush. You'll wake everyone, and then you'll be grounded again."

"I don't care." She swallowed the sobs clogging the back of her throat.

"I said be quiet. Do you want Mother to hear you?"

"You mean the Virgin Cleopatra? Have I got a surprise for her. You ever seen a penis, Bets? Oops." A ragged laugh escaped her. "Sorry, didn't mean to shock your lily-white ears."

"Oh, Vicky," Betsey sighed sadly. "You didn't."

"Hey, what am I saving it for? Mother lied to us, sweet pea. No knights in shining armor left." She flung one arm out in a dramatic gesture and hit a lamp.

Betsey grabbed it before it could fall. When she faced her sister again, her eyes were bright with moisture.

"Oh, Bets, I'm sorry." Her sister still took her side every time, risking herself to keep Victoria out of scrapes. "Of course you should save yourself. There will be some good guy for you."

"Vicky, you'll have one, too," Betsey whispered urgently. "You just..." Her voice trailed off.

But Victoria knew. "Yeah, well, ain't gonna happen. Anyway, time for good little girls to be in bed." Desperate to escape and be alone, she charged past her sister, lost her balance and slammed into the banister.

"Vicky." Betsey's eyes were swimming in pity now.

"Don't you dare feel sorry for me," she muttered furiously, then relented. "Bets, I can't be like you. Only one perfect child per house." Then she cast a glance up the stairs toward her brother's room. "Or maybe one of each gender." She shrugged. "But not me, nossir." Grasping the rail, she tried to haul herself upright.

Betsey was already slipping next to her and holding her tight. "Just be quiet, okay? I'll get you in bed."

"No!" She nearly shouted but stemmed the impulse instantly. "Shower. I have to take a shower."

"You'll wake them up. They can't find you this way again."

Betsey didn't understand that everything was different now. Messed up even worse than usual. "I don't care." She turned, held her sister's gaze. "I have to get clean, Bets. I have to."

Her innocent sister studied her for an endless second, and Victoria wondered what she saw. "Okay. I'll manage it somehow."

Victoria leaned her head against her sister's, weak with relief. "I don't deserve you, Bets. I'm sorry."

"Shh," Betsey soothed. "Now, please be quiet."

Unsteadily, Victoria drew one finger across her lips as they'd done since childhood.

But this time, Betsey didn't smile.

RIA RAN ACROSS the street and nearly got hit, so lost in memory she was. As the driver shot her the finger and tires squealed, she stopped on the other side, leaning on her knees while she caught her breath.

That night had been only one of many, but it had been one of the worst until

No. Don't go there.

Instead, she recalled the horrible scene that had ensued when her parents had awakened and she'd been trapped, still dressed and smelling of sex and beer, in the small bathroom.

Her mother's disgust.

Her father's heartache.

And David…oh, it had killed her to have him see her that way.

David stood there, black hair standing in unruly tufts, his brown eyes wide and scared. "Mommy?

Daddy? Ria, are you hurt?" He brushed past them, clasping her around the waist.

Her eyes had filled with tears then. With one shaking hand, she stroked David's hair, then leaned down and kissed his head. "I'm fine, David," she said in a shaky voice sliding down into dull resignation. "We're all okay. Let Mom and Dad put you to bed while I take my shower, then we'll go to sleep." Her look dared them to argue.

Her mother's eyes were bright with her own tears. "Victoria, I can stay and help you."

"No, Mother. You can't." She turned around and twisted the shower knob, filling the room with the sound of water.

Behind her, she'd heard her mother. "Come on, David. Let's go back to bed."

Before they passed, David peered up at Malcolm, all the trust in the world in his big brown eyes. "You'll make sure Ria's okay, Daddy?"

Her father's anguished gaze caught her, and she could only stare back, wondering what pretty lie he would tell.

"Of course I will, son." But she could see that he didn't believe it, any more than she did.

THERE WERE TOO MANY more of those memories. She shouldn't have returned from L.A.

But she didn't know where else to go.

All she was certain of was that nothing had changed. She would never be more than an embarrassment at best, a total screwup at worst.

Just then, she noted where she was, half a block from Joe's Place. She walked in the door and tasted the thick, dark air of forbidden pleasures. Soaked it in, slid beneath the viscera and rolled in the pulsing warmth of anticipated sin.

It wouldn't last. It never did. But for a while, she could be what she really was: bad. Bad to the bone, stained umber with iniquity, scarred with the pain she'd wrought.

There was no use fighting anymore. *I tried, Dog Boy. I told you it wouldn't work.*

Why did you have to die, my only friend?

So she stood at the jukebox and fed in quarters, swaying to the music, lost in its spell. For a while, the others left her alone, as the ancients once avoided coming close to those on whom evil had left its mark.

But first one, and then another, the men drifted toward her, lured perhaps by the air of corruption, the sweet, seductive smell of sin and lost hope.

And Ria gripped the jukebox with fingers gone nerveless…and laughed, daring each of them to want her…to touch.

Finally, one of them did, sliding up behind her, placing his hands on her hips. She glanced over her shoulder with a look of pure contempt. But when his fingers slackened, she slapped a hand over his, pressing it back into her flesh, the sensation reminding her that she was alive, if blackened in her soul.

Then she scanned the group and smiled, licking her lips. "Sorry, boys. Maybe later."

She slid her body around and grasped his shoulders, rubbing across the front of him, feeling his response. She laughed again, but when he leaned down to kiss her, she grabbed his hair and yanked his head back.

"Ow!" His eyes sparked with anger. He shoved her away. "You bitch, what the hell do you think you're doing?"

She grabbed his shirtfront and reeled him back in. "I may not be much, but I'm not easy. Come on, big boy. Show me what you're made of."

"You're crazy, you know that?"

Ria laughed again. "No secret there. Tell me something new." Then she flicked her fingers against his chest with a sharp pop. "Hey, now. Show me what you got." Suddenly, she was ready for violence herself. Anger filled her throat, choked her, stopped her breath.

"You want rough, babe?" He stepped forward and yanked her to him. "I'll give you rough."

Before she could react, his mouth assaulted hers. Ria shoved at him, lifting her knee to do some damage.

Abruptly, the man flew backward.

Sandor stood before her, his eyes unreadable, violence shimmering in the air around him.

"Hey." The other man rose from the floor. "She's mine. We were just getting started."

Sandor advanced on the man, speaking low. Whatever he said, the guy backed away. Sandor cast one glance around the room as though daring anyone else to act.

"Who do you think you are?" Ria asked. "Leave me alone."

"Shut up," he muttered furiously. "Let me get us out of here in one piece. You have the blood up on every man in this place." With no gentleness, he yanked her behind him and out the door.

On the sidewalk, she tried to stop and face him. He dragged her forward, all but throwing her bodily into his pickup.

When he rounded the hood, she scrabbled for the door handle, but she couldn't open it before he got in.

"Do not dare."

"I didn't need your help. I was having a good time."

"You were courting gang rape."

"What's it to you?" Her heart beat so fast she was dizzy with it.

He turned onto a deserted side street and slammed on the brakes. "Fine. Go. Take care of yourself."

She shot a look at him. His jaw was hard, but his eyes were surprisingly gentle…and far too knowing. He scared the hell out of her.

Once again, she struggled with the door handle.

He leaned across her and opened it with one quick stroke. "Go on. Return to that place, or another like it and do your worst. Then there will be a clear field for your family to gain custody of your child."

"I hate you." She slid out and slammed the door.

Started walking on legs turned to rubber, with a heart ground to glass.

And slid to the pavement, her face in her hands.

She heard his footsteps, saw through her fingers as he crouched before her.

"You throw it all away, a bounty others would treasure. A family. Friends."

She lifted her head at that, struggling against despair. "I have no friends. I don't know anyone but my family."

"You know me."

"Your loyalties are to my mother."

"Your mother is concerned about you."

"Hah." She tossed her head. "Not after she talks to Betsey. Damn sure not after you tell her about this."

"What makes you think I will?"

"Why would you help me out?"

"You need a friend." His jaw flexed. "I am volunteering."

Ria began to laugh in earnest then, though all too soon laughter assumed the high notes of hysteria and became hard to stop.

Sandor grimaced. "I am glad you find me so humorous."

She shook her head helplessly, reaching upward for assistance to rise.

He grasped her hands and pulled her easily, then he jerked one wrist toward the light.

Ria tried to snatch it away, but he held firm, one finger tracing the silvery scar. He dropped that wrist and grabbed the other one, studying it, too.

His eyes flared. "When did you do this?"

She jerked her arms away, crossing them over her middle. "It doesn't matter."

"It matters if that child was with you."

Ria's head rose swiftly. "He wasn't."

"Was he born?"

"Why do you care?"

"Answer me."

"No, not that it's any of your business."

His shoulders relaxed. "Good. I did not think you would do that to him." He studied her. "It was the pain of David's death?"

She'd never talked about this to a soul but Dog Boy. "What's it to you?"

"It would kill your mother to hear this."

"Hah," she snorted. "My mother wished I were dead from the instant she lost David." She turned to walk away, but her legs wouldn't carry her. "I don't want to discuss it."

"But you should. The accident is a festering sore in your whole family. Have you never talked about it?"

Her shoulders shook with derision. "The Ice Queen? Deal with something painful? You don't understand her after all."

"Do not speak of her that way."

"That's who she is, who she's always been with me. Never with Daddy or Betsey or—" She couldn't say the name.

"David?" Sandor moved to stand in front of her.

"Don't."

"You gave your son his name. You use his pet name for you. Why will you not discuss him?"

She gripped her arms tighter around her waist. "Leave it alone, Sandor." This time she did start walking away. But she owed him one thing and paused. "Thank you for the rescue, Sir Galahad."

He stood there like a still, silent mountain, as immovable as granite. For a moment, all she wanted was to cling to that strength, to hold on to the last rock before the sea swept her away.

She couldn't do that. Wouldn't. But for some reason, she could ask him the question she could ask no one else.

"Do you know where he's buried?" she whispered.

His head tilted slightly, his gaze sweeping over her face, a relentless golden searchlight.

"You do not?" To her exquisitely sensitive ear, his voice contained no condemnation.

She shook her head. She'd never told even Dog Boy how much she wanted to go, or that she'd never been.

"I was...sedated." She looked away. "I've never been sure if it was for my sake, or because they couldn't bear to have me at the funeral."

He studied her, then stepped a little closer, his voice low. Gentle. "I will take you there."

She blinked. "Now?" Was she ready?

Would she ever be sure if she didn't try?

Ria spoke from behind clenched teeth, fingers digging into her sides. "Maybe. Yes." She inhaled sharply, then let out the breath in a whoosh. "I don't know."

Sandor nodded as if satisfied. In a courtly gesture, he touched her elbow lightly and guided her to the truck, then assisted her into the seat as though she were made of spun sugar.

The trip passed in silence. When he stopped the pickup, she emerged from the prison of memory, just barely whole enough to be glad that the cemetery was an old one. No sterile modern field of plastic flowers and tractor-mowed grass.

Sandor turned off the engine but didn't speak. He settled back against the cushion, and Ria had the sense that he would wait forever, if needed.

She stared out the window at trees older than this city, at the ragged counterpane of grave sites and their chess-piece monuments. Somewhere out there was the boy she'd killed through inattention, through reckless disdain for their mortal lives.

For a moment, she was frozen by the sound of glass and metal, by the screams she had never been able to distinguish as hers or his. In the moonlight, she almost thought she spotted dancing wraiths, spirits shaking fingers at she who dared disturb their sleep.

Knuckles white around the handle, she spoke over her shoulder, forcing out more words than she could bear.

"Show me."

She heard his door open, saw her own move. Felt his hand pry hers from the metal that kept her anchored in this world. Sensed the warmth of his touch on her elbow against the frozen landscape of her heart.

Sandor walked. She followed, every wary step bringing her nearer to the reckoning she must face.

He glanced over his shoulder and noted her lagging behind. Fell back until she reached him, then wrapped one arm around her shoulders and tucked her into his side. Paused for a moment while she curled into the comfort.

He waited patiently for her to decide. She clutched a fistful of his shirt and shivered.

"Ria, you do not have to do this," he murmured. He brought her into the circle of his protection.

She buried her face against his chest. "Yes. I do."

She let go and moved forward.

Time ceased to mean anything. They trod for hours. Days. No sleep, no hunger, no thirst could touch the ice casing that shielded her against madness, against flying into a million bits.

In her mind's eye, she could imagine them: Daddy with his arms around Mother and Betsey as they huddled together—the three who were left. For Victoria had died that day as surely as had David. Died to their hearts. To her own.

Sandor stopped and pointed. "There. I came with your mother once, after she told me."

That night. That awful night when Victoria destroyed them all. Ria became Victoria again, Victoria who dispensed trouble with a trowel, with a shovel…with a whole goddamn bulldozer.

She stood there, trembling, shaking as if a palsy crept along her nerve strands, ate greedily into her brain.

She took one step toward the path of repentance.

Toward the road to a forgiveness she would never deserve.

The ground tilted up to meet her, and Ria who was once Victoria gave up the fight.

CHAPTER TWELVE

SANDOR HAD WATCHED her go, wishing he could step beside her, hold her up, spirit her away. Her agony was palpable, her fear an aura wrapped around her so tightly he could hardly breathe himself.

Then, like a slow-motion replay, her slight frame folded in on itself with an eerie, heartrending grace.

He barely managed to catch her. Sank to his knees in the cool, damp grass. Pulled her close.

So pale. So still. So fragile.

In the moonlight, she could have been one of the statues, ethereal and lovely despite the chopped, crimson-tipped hair, the harsh modern clothing. Without her defenses, she appeared impossibly young, the lines of strain eased from her face, the sneer with which she protected herself vanished.

She was beautiful, he realized. Her mother's child, however little she would want to hear it.

She needed care more than anyone he had ever met. All her barbs and jabs served to shield a wounded, terrified heart. She pushed and slapped away attempts to help simply because she did not believe she deserved them.

He was ashamed of himself for taking the bait.

A messy coil, this mother and daughter, but the more he saw of Ria, the more he understood that she and Cleo were too much alike. For different reasons, neither trusted herself to be loved without limits and thus turned away exactly what they craved most.

I asked him to go, Cleo had said about Malcolm.

He's all I have, Ria believed of her child.

For the first time since Ria had reappeared in her mother's life, Sandor relaxed. The path between the two was littered with broken promises and sharp words, with misunderstandings and rejections. But perhaps he could repay Cleo after all by helping the two of them find their way back to each other.

So Sandor stood, clutching Ria in his arms. For a moment he looked toward her brother's resting place. "I believe she will return," he said to a young boy he'd never met. "And one day, perhaps she will understand that her punishment is at an end."

With a short nod, he carried Ria away.

HE DIDN'T DRIVE HER back to Cleo's. Instead, he took her home. Someone must be with her when she awoke, a person who could be calm and dispassionate with whatever reaction would grip her then.

He believed Cleo loved her daughter and would not be unkind, but the past was still too raw between them, and he had the sense that Ria could not endure much more without shattering.

She never stirred as he parked and opened the door,

when he carried her up the stairs. He didn't turn on the lights inside but let the moon's glow show the way to his bed.

There he placed her on the covers and removed her shoes. Started the air conditioner in the humid, still-warm night.

Then brought a straight-backed chair to the bedside.

And began his vigil.

CURLED ON HER SIDE, Ria awoke slowly, clinging to the feeling of safety. She snuggled into the pillow that carried the scent of comfort, of—

Sandor. She gasped. Opened her eyes.

To see his focused on her, gentle and concerned.

"Wha—" She frowned as memory teased at her.

Then she remembered.

Everything.

Betsey, despising. A stranger's greedy hands grabbing.

Sandor rescuing.

And the reality of her brother's grave. *He's buried there. He's really dead. I can't change the ending, no matter how I try.*

With a cry, she threw back the light cover and raced for the door.

Sandor caught her before she could escape.

"No, let me go—"

He didn't release her, and as much as she wanted to flee all that he knew about her, so she also craved to just give up, give in. Throw herself into his arms.

Beg.

But what she wished for from Sandor wasn't clear to her. Strength? Understanding? Kindness?

He'd granted her all that already, no matter how much she sensed his reluctance. Her mother was his first loyalty, not her.

Then she felt his body stir against her.

And understood two things in that moment. That he might not be pleased that he desired her, but he did.

And that she had no pride left. She could find the surcease she craved right here. Right now. And she could pretend, for a few minutes, that a man like him could care about her. He did, a little, she was nearly certain.

Just not in the manner she'd like.

But she was too desperate to wait for something that would never come, so she shifted in his arms and pressed herself along the front of him, standing on tiptoe to brush softness against hardness, ache against ache.

He went rigid and tried to shove her away. "No."

Ria held on and touched her lips to his, rocking her pelvis against him.

He didn't respond.

Sick with contempt for herself, she nearly gave up, but she'd already fallen too far. There was nothing left to lose. Misery prodded her, even as she knew it was wrong, that she risked tainting a good man with her blackened soul.

But that goodness was a pinpoint of light at the top of a very dark hole.

She crowded closer. Slicked her nails up his chest.

A shudder ran through his body.

She grazed her teeth over one strong cord in his neck.

And everything shifted.

Suddenly, his arms caged her. Crushed her. His mouth sealed to hers in a kiss that exploded into naked greed.

Ria lost herself in it, undulating against him, so hungry for what he had to offer that she lost all power of thought except a chant reverberating with every heartbeat, every pulse of blood.

More.

Abruptly, Sandor jerked away. Placed distance between them, his eyes dark with accusation, his chest rising and falling unevenly. “I will not let you do this.”

“Shut up.” She closed the gap and grappled for the moment so swiftly vanished. Her fingers slid into his hair as she stared into a cauldron of hunger and fear, longing and regret.

She could make him continue, she was certain. She glided down his body, falling onto her knees, already working at the fly of his jeans.

“No!” Sandor roared. “Get up. Now.” He jerked her to her feet.

“You desire me. You know you do.” She heard her own ragged breathing. Reached for him again.

He imprisoned her fingers in a painful grip. “Stop it, Ria. You do not want this.”

She tilted her chin. “You’re wrong. You’re hot for me, too. Don’t try to deny it.”

Then he surprised her. "That does not matter."

She fell back on a defense. "We're adults. It's no big deal. Just scratching an itch."

He was silent for so long that she was forced to look at him. She hated the sympathy she saw. "I'm outta here."

He slapped one palm against the door. "Ria." His voice was kind. Too kind.

She'd never felt more pathetic. "If you don't let me go, I'll scream until Billie wakes up and calls the cops." She'd go insane if she didn't get away, if he didn't quit looking at her as though she was some kind of misfit.

"I will take you home."

"Fine." She stood at the doorway, trembling, humiliation stinging her eyes.

But he didn't move. "Ria, you misunderstand."

"I can't talk anymore, Sandor. Just open the goddamn door or I'll—"

She snapped. Wheeled around. Threw herself at him, battering at his chest with impotent fists, sobbing against the shame and heartache.

He grasped her wrists and subdued her with his body against the door. Just when she thought maybe he'd relent and give her the oblivion she craved, he leaned back. Put space between them. "Listen to me," he ordered. "My body desires you, yes, but that is not enough."

She struggled to gather herself, convince him she didn't care, but he cut right through the pretense. "Silence. I do not wish to hear that tongue used as a weapon again."

She stared past his wide shoulders toward the window.

He muttered a curse. "I do this for you." When she snorted, he only shook his head sadly. "I will not be with you until you are whole. You will not use me to hide from yourself."

"Go to hell," she muttered, jerking her wrists against his grip. "I don't need you. I don't need anyone."

Instantly, he released her. His voice softened. "You crave love more than anyone I have ever met, yet with every breath, every cutting remark, you shove affection away because you believe you do not deserve it, when you are the one standing in the way."

She gaped at him, incredulous. Then drew herself into the thin shell of disdain. "It's not your life or your problem." With a jut of her chin, she nodded. "Now, open that door."

With a sigh, he twisted the knob and backed away. "Let's go."

"No, thanks."

"It was not a question."

He dogged her step all the way downstairs.

She was too exhausted to argue anymore. Silently, she climbed into his pickup and stared into the night.

With a muttered curse, he turned the key and pulled out of the driveway. The ride back to her mother's house was silent, yet the atmosphere inside the cab was crowded with unspoken questions and doubts, fears and accusations.

Ria rolled down the window because she couldn't breathe.

It didn't help. She clutched the frame as if it would keep her from flying apart, and every inch of the blocks between Sandor's place and her mother's felt like a mile.

When he came to a stop in front, Ria was out the door in seconds. Stumbled. Staggered like a drunk before she righted herself.

"Ria." Sandor's footsteps pounded after her. He grabbed her on the sidewalk. "I care about you, whether or not you believe that."

She focused on the ground, shivering with the need to escape from the concern in his voice.

Finally, he sighed, then stroked her hair and placed a chaste kiss on her forehead as if she were a child. "Get some sleep and we will talk…soon."

She didn't respond. They wouldn't talk, soon or ever. He considered her pathetic, and she would never forgive him for that. She'd made a fool of herself in front of him, and he hadn't even had the decency to hide how he really felt. She thought she had plumbed the depths of her capacity for self-loathing, but now she realized there was farther to fall.

All the way inside and up the stairs, she rubbed her forehead and scrambled for one clear idea of where to go next, what step to take, but her insides were a mess. She had no idea what else to do but try to get some sleep and hope if tomorrow—

"What are you doing to him?"

Ria jolted at her mother's voice. The next instant, lamplight flooded the room.

Her mother's face was taut with fury. "He's a good man, Ria. A kind one. If you have to play your games, do so with someone else."

Oh, great. Just great. Would her mother always presume her guilty first? She fought the urge to collapse on the ground and weep. "You're the only one who gets a boy toy, Mother?"

"Don't talk to me like that."

Rage flooded through her, and she roused herself to fight back. "At first I suspected that it was Sandor, but it's the coffee-shop hunk, right? He's years younger than you, Mother. Aren't you embarrassed? At least you can't get knocked up like Vanessa."

Every speck of color drained from her mother's face. "What?"

Rage fled, and shame slipped beneath her defiance. "Nothing."

"No, tell me what you said." Her mother sounded as devastated as Ria had been when Betsey had slapped her with the news.

How odd to feel that kinship. "I didn't—"

"Vanessa is pregnant?"

Ria recalled the yearning she'd seen flow between her parents.

How lovely the hope had been. "I—listen, Mother, I could be wrong. Betsey was mad and she threw it in my face. But maybe..."

"Betsey knows, too?" Her mother appeared near tears, but worst of all was seeing her proud, beautiful mother humiliated.

Ria understood exactly what that was like. "Mother, I'm—I'm sorry. I shouldn't have told you. I just—"

Cleo didn't appear to hear a word. Like a zombie, she walked to the door.

Ria grasped for anything to take that desolation off her face. She could handle her mother's anger but not her defeat. "Daddy loves you, I'm sure he does."

"It doesn't matter. Nothing…matters." As fragile and wounded as a survivor of a bomb blast, Cleo drew herself up so carefully that Ria was terrified she would shatter before her eyes. "I need to be in the shop early. Good night."

Ria took a step forward. "Mother—"

But as if she'd never heard a word, her mother slipped from the room like a wraith.

Ria started into the hall when her mother's door closed with a click.

We were doing fine until you showed up.

Ria leaned against the wall, too weary to move.

The night-light from Benjy's room spilled out into the hall, and Ria sought the comfort of her child's presence.

Tyrone blinked. Ria patted him, then turned to her son. She tucked the covers over his shoulders and soaked in his innocent slumber. Sank to her knees beside his bed and watched him breathe.

Struggled in the grip of paralyzing despair.

Leave him here…give him the life he deserves.

Was Betsey right?

What did she owe her mother? A child for a child?

No! Everything in her cried out at the thought crushing her chest. *I can't. It would kill me.*

"Mom?" A sleepy voice brought her head up.

"Shh, sweetie." She willed the terror from her voice. "Go back to sleep."

"I love you, Mom." His eyes drifted shut.

She pressed her lips to his forehead and brushed shaking fingers over his hair.

And died inside. "I love you, too, sweetheart." *Please, oh, please…don't ask this of me.*

Bowing her head with one fist beneath her forehead and the other clenched in his quilts, Ria sagged against her child's bed and prayed to a God who had surely forgotten her, begging for the strength to do what was best for the person she loved most in the world.

CHAPTER THIRTEEN

"MOM!" THE WHISPER was urgent enough to jar her awake, though she'd remained sleepless until nearly dawn.

Ria spotted lively brown eyes peering over the edge of the bed. Her smile was a long-familiar response to the sight of this beloved face. "Hey, there." She rolled to her side to get closer. "How did you sleep?"

"Fine. Mom, did you ever hear about s'mores? Nana says we can make some tonight for the slumber party. Grammy says you used to love them. I told her you always like chocolate, but I don't know about melting marshmallows, and..." He was off to the races, chattering nonstop in his excitement.

She extended her arms and dragged him up on the bed for a hug and a nuzzle to the neck.

He giggled and squirmed. "That tickles."

"I know." She waggled her eyebrows. "You're my prisoner, matey." She twirled an imaginary pirate's mustache, and Benjy giggled again. "But you can buy your freedom with a kiss."

Without the least trace of hesitation, Benjy threw his

arms around her neck and did as she asked, but instead of claiming his liberty, he laid his head on her shoulder.

Ria tightened her arms around him and fought the night's memories crowding this moment's exquisite pleasure.

"I love you, Mom."

She squeezed her eyes shut. *I can't, Bets. He's the one thing I've done right. If you could see us together, surely you'd agree.*

But at that moment, she caught a whiff of the bar smoke she thought she'd scrubbed out of her hair. Remembered coming on to Sandor. Devastating her mother.

The mountain of her sins seemed an unassailable peak. Where did she begin to reverse the damage? Why would anyone believe that she could?

"Mom, you're squishing me too hard."

"I'm sorry." With a shudder, she loosened her grip. Crawled from the swamp of regrets.

Found the safe shore of a smile. "So…what would you like to do today?"

"You don't have to go to work?"

Her mouth quirked in rueful acknowledgment. Sandor wasn't likely to want her within miles of him. She took a deep breath. "Nope. We've got the whole day to ourselves. What would Master Benjamin prefer?"

He cocked his head, and she could see the calculations whirring, but she didn't care what he asked—if it were humanly possible, she would figure out a way to grant his wish.

Everything came back to this child, this miracle she had never deserved.

Maybe she never would, but for today, she would banish those thoughts and focus only on the moment. Doing so would be good for Benjy, and if it was good for her, too, well...chalk up one more sin to her mountain.

"So...what's it gonna be?"

"Anything?"

"Unless I have to rob a bank to afford it."

Benjy grinned. Then began reciting his list.

SANDOR JERKED a bucket of nails from his truck and stalked into the restaurant, then dropped the bucket to the concrete with a bang that hurt his own ears.

He exhaled sharply, placed his hands on his hips and looked around.

She was everywhere, damn her.

Every time he'd awakened from a fitful sleep, he'd thought of her. Stewed over her. Replayed the night. The whirlwind of emotions.

Sympathy when Betsey devastated her. Impatience at her defeat.

Snarling, snapping fury at the sight of leering male faces and roving hands. At how careless she was with her survival.

The scars that demonstrated the depth of her despair. That sent a twist into his gut as he produced the thin barrier that kept her from trying again. Only her child stood between her and destruction, and now she was doubting her right to be with him.

The depth of her self-loathing scared the wits out of Sandor. She was unbearably fragile.

Yet she could be astonishingly brave. There was strength in her she didn't credit—to have made it this far, to have protected her son and brought him home to face her demons were not the acts of a coward.

If he lived to be a thousand, he doubted he would forget her terror over seeing her brother's grave site.

Or her courage at confronting it, however her body had betrayed her.

Or how his own had forsaken him.

To have responded like that was inexcusable, no matter how she had sought exactly that reaction. Battered at him until he thought he would lose his mind if he did not have her.

But why? After all the women with whom he had refused to go beyond the physical, why did this one tangle him up so? He could not manage to sort out his motives, and that disturbed him. He had loyalties to her mother that should make for an easy choice, yet the longer he knew Ria, the more she confused the clear boundaries. She baffled him, exasperated him. Worried him.

He felt sorry for her, though she asked for no compassion—slapped it away, in fact. And he admired her more than was comfortable, even…liked her.

But he did not like the effect she had on him. She touched something inside no one else ever had, and all his antennae were wriggling with warning.

He could not care for her. Could not begin to think about—

No. Love was not in the picture. He had plans, and they did not include a woman so precariously balanced on a shaky ledge. It was not time yet for him to become involved with anyone.

Certainly not Ria Channing.

"You gonna stand there, daydreaming, or we gonna work?"

Sandor whirled at Jerome's voice.

The boy frowned. "Hey…you don't look so hot. What's wrong?"

Sandor scrubbed his face. Shoved away his concerns. "Nothing." He inhaled sharply. "I am glad you are here."

"Hard to tell it."

"I have much on my mind, but that is not important." He turned away to figure out where to begin.

"Ria wouldn't be part of it, would she?"

Sandor frowned. "Why do you ask?"

Jerome shrugged. "She promised me she would be back if I was, too, but she didn't show yesterday and she ain't here today. I figure somethin's wrong, and it's probably between the two of you."

"You are only a boy. You cannot comprehend such things."

Jerome rolled his eyes. "I may be a kid, but I ain't blind. I see how you look at her. She gets under your skin, don't she? Got your interest."

"You are wrong. I do not desire her. She is too unsettled to be in a relationship."

"Whatever. You go right on trippin' that you ain't interested, my man. Me, I know what I saw between you." He grinned. "'Sides, I watched the woman take you on, and you ain't no pussycat. Seems to me she be stronger than you might think."

The situation was too complicated to explain to a boy. And too private. "We have work to do. Have you eaten?"

Jerome smirked. "We could get more done if you'd go after her, bring her back." At Sandor's glare, he held up his hands. "I'm just sayin'. But hey, you the boss. And yeah, I could eat." His grin was unrepentant.

Sandor would not chase Ria down. If she wanted to work, he would let her, but after last night, near him was the last place she would wish to be. That was just as well for him.

He put one arm around the boy's shoulders. "The breakfast wagon is down the block. Come along."

When Jerome didn't dodge the contact, Sandor felt rewarded and realized that perhaps time and distance would also be welcome to Ria, give her a chance to settle. Grant the same to him.

But he frowned once more, this time at himself, when it dawned on him that he did not intend to wait long to see her again.

JUST OUT OF THE SHOWER and newly dressed, hair still wet, Ria eagerly headed for the stairs to reclaim Benjy from Lola and get a start on their play day. When she heard their voices coming from Lola's room, she reversed her steps and paused outside her grandmother's door to watch through the opening.

"Benjamin darling, give me your hand," Lola said.

Benjy glanced up from his perch beside her vanity, where he had lined up bottles of lipstick and nail polish like little soldiers. "In just a minute, okay? I have to get these straight."

"Nonsense, doll. Nothing in life stays straight. The only interesting parts of life are curvy and unexpected."

"What does that mean, Grammy?"

"That the best things are often messy." She grasped his chin and shifted his head side to side. "Good bones. You'll photograph beautifully."

Benjy giggled again. "You're silly, Grammy."

She pressed a kiss to his nose. "And you, my love, are a heartbreaker in the making." Clasping his hand, she shook her head. "But not to worry. Grammy will teach you all about being good to women." She turned his hand over and studied his palm.

"I'm nice to my mom and Aunt Cammie and you and Nana Cleo..."

Ria heard his voice fall.

Lola had, too. "What, toots?"

He glanced up, his expression far too old and serious. "Aunt Betsey doesn't like me, does she?"

Ria ducked her head and hoped her grandmother had a better answer than she did.

Instead, Lola traced his lifeline lightly with one finger. Benjy's hand jerked and he giggled again. "That tickles."

Lola used all her fingers then, like miniature feet dancing on his palm. Benjy squealed and yanked his hand away, eyes going wide.

"Ah, a ticklish boy...hmm, what shall we do with him, my pretty? Eee-hee-hee-eeee," she trilled, in her best Wicked Witch of the West imitation.

Benjy backed up a step. Lola moved forward, fingers curled in claws, eyelashes fluttering.

His laughter was nervous, but his eyes sparkled. Then he ran.

Lola caught him about the waist, sat down and began to torment him. Benjy squirmed madly, screams becoming breathy giggles as they gyrated on the floor.

Her red wig flew off her head and slid across the polished wood.

Benjy went still, his mouth open. "Wow, your hair—" His gaze darted back and forth between her and the wig, his face screwing up in confusion. "You have two hairs."

Lola laughed, picked him and the wig up and stood in front of the vanity mirror, settling Benjy on the bench. "It's called a wig, darling." She plopped the hairpiece on his head, the profusion of red curls making him appear to be a pint-size clown. "See? What do you think? It's like playing dress-up."

At first, Benjy plucked it off his head and held it as he would a dead rat. Then he studied it with that serious little face, glancing between her, his reflection and the wig. He set it on his head backward, then rotated it but left it askew. "I never played dress-up."

Ria leaned her forehead against the doorjamb.

"Oh, doll, have you missed some fun. Why, we must indulge sometime."

"What do you do?"

"You pretend to be whomever you wish, and you dress the part."

"Who are you pretending to be?"

Lola laughed and batted his shoulder lightly. "Ah, a clever wit, too." She studied her own short white shag. "It varies from day to day." Perusing her closet, she reached inside. "Today, I think, calls for Ginger Rogers. Would you like to be Fred Astaire?"

Tiny dark eyebrows pulled together. "Who's that?"

Lola looked shocked to her marrow. "You're not familiar with Fred's work, doll-face? He's only the most divine dancer who ever lived." She grabbed Benjy and began twirling him around the room, holding one small arm out in proper dance position, his feet dangling far above her knees. "He and Ginger were poetry in motion." Her voice dropped lower. "He and I had a little dance of our own one splendid evening. Of course, we had to keep it all very hush-hush. Studio politics can be so brutal, you know."

A grin punched through Ria's pain. Lola had always regaled anyone within hearing distance with her purported mad and passionate affairs.

Benjy, of course, missed the point. Instead, he blinked at the ceiling, his smile widening. "It's all turning and turning, Grammy. I feel kinda whirly inside." Then he laughed from deep in his little belly. "I like playing Fred and Ginger."

He was having so much fun. Ria had tried, but she'd spent too much of his short life struggling to survive, to keep both Benjy and Dog Boy safe. Fun had been way down the list.

She prepared to go. She would let them play until he tired of the game.

Then she heard a thud and went racing back up the stairs and down the hall.

Benjy's voice. "I like playing Fred and Ginger—let's do it again!"

Ria's heart slowed. In the mirror, she saw Lola lying back on the bed, one hand on her forehead, eyes closed. "Maybe later, sweetheart. Grammy needs to rest now."

Just as Ria was coming through the door, she registered the sound of her child's voice again. Benjy was bent over Lola, hands cupping her face, dark eyes worried. "I can cover you up. I'll be quiet, like I am for Mom." The wig lost its purchase, falling from his head with a final plop on Lola's chest. "She gets tired sometimes, so I have to be a big boy."

Ria wanted to sink through the floor. Dear God. She hadn't realized how much of Benjy's childhood had been lost.

"I'm just fine, Benjamin. Just fine." Lola nuzzled her cheek against his hair as he snuggled closer. "And I don't want you to be quiet. You're here with us now, and you don't have to take care of anyone anymore. We're family, Benjy." Lola spotted her over Benjy's shoulder, and her eyes were filled with a sympathy that only emphasized Ria's shortcomings.

"Mom says families sometimes don't like each other. Aunt Betsey doesn't like me or my mom, does she? And Nana Cleo and Mom talk mean to each other. Except they sang together. Are they still mad?"

Ria backed away then, fighting the urge to run.

Lola caught her gaze with a shake of her head, as if she knew Ria's temptation. "They love each other, Benjy. At heart, they do. And no one is mad at you. None of this is your fault. Sometimes grown-ups just get mixed up. They fight and sometimes they forget how the fight started." She might have been talking to Benjy, but every word was aimed at Ria.

Benjy snorted. "That's dumb."

Lola smiled. "You're right. It is." Her glance flicked back to Ria.

"It's not so hard," Benjy continued. "You just say 'I love you.'"

Ria bowed her head, but she could still feel the weight of her grandmother's gaze. "Sometimes we make it too complicated and families lose their way."

"I love you, Grammy," Benjy said.

Ria glanced up as her grandmother's eyes filled with tears. "Oh, child, I love you, too." She pulled him close and kept rocking.

He'll have plenty of people to love him.

Ria retreated and left them together.

BUT SHE WAS GONE only long enough to gather her wits. Dash the tears away and resolutely shove the tangle of her thoughts into the deepest corner where she could hide them.

She'd made Benjy a promise, and she would keep it.

They hit the Children's Museum, rode the train in Zilker Park, had lunch at Chuy's, where Benjy delighted in velvet Elvis paintings, wooden fish hanging from the ceiling and hubcaps and tiny Volkswagen Beetles mounted on the walls, as well. They topped it off with a visit to a different Amy's from the one where her father had taken Benjy and the girls. Benjy's eyes were drooping by the time Ria reluctantly headed home so that he could nap in preparation for the night's big event. A part of her wanted to keep him all to herself, to simply drive on until they left everything behind. Her history. The pain and crippling doubts.

But it would be L.A. all over again. She still had no financial cushion; she would have to get a job and put Benjy in substandard day care because she couldn't earn enough to feed and clothe and house them on the hodgepodge of positions for which she was qualified—

So she took him home. Not home for her, but increasingly, a place of refuge for him.

While Benjy slept, she helped Aunt Cammie prepare potato salad and cake. Went to the store for paper goods. Swept off the deck and front porch, then searched for more tasks.

Anything to stave off the worries about facing her mother again. Or her sister.

By the time Cleo arrived, Benjy was awake and blissfully unaware that he was being used as an intermediary. Cleo was scrupulously polite to Ria, and Ria returned the favor. Both spoke to Benjy and Aunt Cammie and Lola but not to each other.

When Betsey arrived with the girls, Ria was outside with her son. As the girls raced to the backyard, she simply waved to her sister, who granted Ria a thoroughly Cleo wave back, then departed.

Ria supervised the children in the tree house while her mother remained inside, only venturing out long enough to check the coals in the stone barbecue grill Daddy had built years earlier.

While Ria tried to ignore her jitters over encountering her father.

When the children tired of the tree house and raced inside, it wasn't long before she heard the cheers and shouts. "Gramps, look at me." "Gramps, you know what?" "Gramps, come here and—"

She couldn't help smiling. Malcolm Channing was the best father in the world. None of the disaster named Victoria Channing had been because she hadn't felt loved by him. He'd tried harder than most parents would have to save her from the darkness swallowing her.

He was no less wonderful as a grandfather. Clearly, all three of them adored him.

"Gramps—" Benjy raced from Aunt Cammie to his grandfather, plastic bag of hot dog buns swinging from his hand. "Come on. Mom could use your help with the coat hangers."

As her parents entered the kitchen, though, Ria could see through the stiffness between them. When she noticed her father's yearning for her mother and her mother's studious attempts to block anything beyond politeness, Ria suffered a bitter shame. The fault for this lay squarely on her shoulders.

Her father dredged up a smile for her son. "Okay. Let's go."

When they reached the deck, Ria glanced up at him, but couldn't keep her gaze from skittering away.

"Hi, sweetheart." He moved to her side and clasped her shoulders, brushing a kiss across her hair.

"Hi, Daddy." Still she didn't look up, concentrating fiercely on straightening the coat hanger in her hand.

"You all right?" he whispered.

Guilt kept her silent.

She felt him studying her.

Malcolm plucked the wire from her hands and drew her a few short paces away. Out of the hearing of the others, he spoke softly. "What's wrong?"

"Nothing." She focused on the boards on the deck.

He tilted her chin upward. "It doesn't seem like nothing." His voice was so gentle and caring that she wanted to cry. "You heard about the baby. Am I right?"

She could only nod miserably.

"Your mother did, too?"

Stop being such a coward and face the music. Finally, she glanced up. "Oh, Daddy, I'm so sorry. I didn't mean to tell her. I was exhausted and angry." She sighed and pulled away. "There's no excuse. All I ever do is hurt people." Before he could speak, she gripped his arm. "Mother loves you. I'm sure she does. You still love her, too, don't you?"

Sorrow darkened his eyes. "If I did, it wouldn't change anything."

She ached to fix the damage. To take back her hasty words. He deserved so much better.

Before she could find the words to respond, Benjy called out, "Mom, come on. We're ready to roast the hot dogs. Gramps, I want you with me."

Ria started to turn and then stopped. "She's upset, but don't give up now. There's got to be a way." She ducked her head. "And I'm sorry I made things worse. I don't expect you to forgive me."

"Ria—"

He reached for her, but she dodged his comfort and joined her son, sick to her core for the good man she'd harmed.

THE HEART HAD GONE OUT of the evening, but Lola's gift for showmanship raced to the rescue. Though her parents and Ria were struggling to remain upbeat for the sake of the children, it was Lola who took over and got them all through the hours until it was time to put the kids to bed.

The s'mores were a hit, though there was as much chocolate and marshmallow on little faces and fingers as in their mouths. Her father gave endless horseback rides, and if her mother spent more time in the kitchen than anywhere else, Ria couldn't blame her. The air between her parents stung from the chill of unspoken words.

As for Ria, she held Benjy on her lap as often as he'd let her, quietly observing her nieces but not pressing them to interact; their uneasy glances made it obvious that they'd been warned about her.

Ria helped get the kids bathed and settled in their sleeping bags in Benjy's room. Cleo read them two stories. Lola and Cammie had long since gone to sleep.

Finally, only her parents and she remained downstairs. After a few miserable moments of straightening up the ravaged living room, Ria decided her best course was to leave her parents alone to talk. She hadn't been able to figure out any way to repair the damage by herself.

Her father gave her a hug she was certain he meant to be reassuring. Her mother said a careful good-night without touching her.

The awkwardness was painfully reminiscent of the past: Ria and her mother at odds, with Daddy stuck in the middle. Maybe nothing would ever be different as long as she was in the picture.

So Ria trudged up the stairs to her room. Showered and got into bed.

But despite almost no sleep the night before, she lay there awake, listening to the muffled, pained conversation drifting up the stairwell.

Finally, she threw back the covers. Frantically scoured her brain for options to fix the harm she'd caused. One hand on the edge of the door, she stepped into the hall and crossed to the top of the stairs.

"Snow, I wanted to be the one to tell you, but I didn't know how. I…the baby—"

"You don't owe me an explanation. You have your own life now. There's Vanessa, and soon, a child.

I'm...glad for you, Malcolm." A pause. "I hope you'll be very happy."

"Cleo, look at me."

"Don't. You should go, Malcolm. *Now.*"

"Not yet. You don't understand."

"You have no business here. Not anymore."

"I don't love Vanessa. I love you."

Ria's heart bumped up a notch.

"You bastard. How can you say that to me? How dare you, Malcolm?"

"I don't blame you. I can guess what you're thinking, but you're wrong. Vanessa doesn't want this baby. She doesn't love me, and I don't love her. Damn it, Cleo, listen to me. I need your help."

"Let me go, Malcolm."

"If I do, will you stay? Hear me out?" Then, "Stop squirming. You can't have forgotten how our fights always ended."

Ria's eyes widened at his husky tone, and she started to rise. This was too private.

She heard her mother's voice, almost a growl. "Don't you even consider it."

"Don't you think I realize how absurd this is? Please, Cleo. I won't touch you again. I just need you, as my friend. As the person who knows me best."

When he resumed, her father's voice was strained. "I'm aware that I don't deserve your compassion. I let you down in the worst way anyone who claimed to love someone ever could. I had no idea how to get us past the pain, but I should have been able to figure it out."

Oh, Daddy. It wasn't you.

"You didn't do it by yourself, Malcolm. It takes two people to give up on a marriage. I let my grief become more important than any of you. And I'm the one who asked you to go."

"I told myself you'd be better off without me. All we did was blame each other. The wounds wouldn't heal because we didn't talk, and when we attempted it, we kept ripping them open."

"I don't know where the blame belongs. We tried with Ria. So hard." Cleo's exhausted resignation twisted the knife blade into Ria's stomach. "It just—maybe there was never any way for us to reach her. And perhaps it was no one's fault. Just a terrible, cruel twist of fate."

They both fell silent. Then her father spoke again. "I'm in a hell of a mess, Snow."

"What do you mean?"

"Vanessa wants an abortion. Day after tomorrow is my deadline for figuring out an answer we can both live with. She never cared to have children, and she doesn't feel that she can interrupt her career right now, even if she did."

He laughed without mirth. "Pretty ironic. Remember me, the staunch defender of women's rights? Well, I'd have sworn I'd uphold any woman's privilege to decide for herself. I always have. But guess what? When it's my child in question, suddenly, all my principles fly out the window."

"Of course you feel that way. You love children. You'll be a wonderful father, just as before."

"I—it feels like a second chance, Cleo. A new child to…"

Oh, Daddy, no. Ria ached for her mother.

"You can't replace David." Cleo's voice was a sharp slap.

"Don't you think I realize that?" Ria could hear Malcolm's fury. "But I've been haunted for years over all I wish I'd done, the things I should have said. And not just with David. With the girls. With you."

"You can't undo the past, Malcolm. And every parent has regrets. Even with a new child, you'll make mistakes. You and Vanessa will struggle, just as we did."

"Vanessa won't be a part of this. She's already made that clear. I just have to come up with some way to convince her to bring the baby to term." He paused. "I sound like a fool now? Wait till you hear my other idea."

"What?"

"From the moment I learned of the child's existence, all I could think was what a great mother you are, how lucky this baby would be to have one like you."

Ria blinked in astonishment.

"Malcolm, you can't possibly suggest…unbelievable…" her mother sputtered. "You arrogant, selfish—That's the most—"

"I understand. I do, I swear. It's out of the question. Not even fair to ask. But I'd be lying if I said I didn't wish for it, Snow, because it's true. You have more love in one finger than Vanessa has in her whole body. You'd never punish a child for not being your own flesh."

"I have no clue what to say."

"How about 'You're a goddamn fool, Malcolm Channing, and get the hell out of my house.' It's the only smart response. And I wouldn't blame you. But you know me—nothing ventured, nothing gained. You'd be the best thing that ever happened to this baby. We're one whale of a team."

His faint laugh was tainted with rue. "Damn, I am some kind of dreamer, aren't I? Always was. But before you throw me out of your house, Cleo, *please* help me figure out what I can say to Vanessa to make her understand what she's giving up. I don't deserve your consideration, but this baby does. I'm begging you. I'm all out of ideas."

Her mother was silent for a long span. Ria was surprised by the humor in her tone when she finally spoke.

"We've had some bizarre conversations in our life together, Malcolm Channing, but I do believe this might take the cake."

"Ain't it the truth?" He fell serious again. "Cleo, I really have no clue how to handle her. I can't find the magic words."

"If you're ever to convince that woman, you need to be spending time with her, not with me, Malcolm. Maybe you don't love her now, but that doesn't mean affection could never grow between you. No woman is interested in being a broodmare for a man who doesn't love her. You've got to try to make it work, for that baby's sake.

Go back to her and tend whatever seeds of caring you have. Focus on what's good in her and build on that."

"But she's not the woman who holds my heart."

Even Ria could feel the pain swirling in the crowded silence.

"Damn it, it's not fair," her father said.

"Malcolm…" Her mother's voice was harsh with grief.

"This is killing me, Snow. How am I supposed to let you go again?" he whispered.

An anguished cry escaped Cleo. "Please. I can't… what we want doesn't matter. And who you love can change."

"You're wrong—" he shouted. "You're the only woman I've ever loved. Ever will. This can't be how it ends."

"It's been over for a long time, Malcolm." Her mother's voice shook. "What we had is gone."

"It's not, damn it. You didn't stop loving me, just as I never quit loving you. Is it that guy, that…kid you were with? If he wasn't in the picture—" His voice hollowed with horror. "Are you in love with him, Snow?"

"No. He thinks he is, but he's not the issue. The child is all that counts, Malcolm. Not us. Not the past."

The child is all that counts. Ria shuddered at the truth of her mother's words.

"Cleo." Her mother's name on his lips was part prayer, part anguish.

Ria's eyes filled with tears.

"Snow." His voice was raw with yearning. "Could I hold you? Just once?"

"No," her mother cried out with the desperation of a hunted animal. "Malcolm, *no*. We'd only make it worse."

An endless pause. Then a deep sigh. "I'm sorry. I'll go."

Ria heard her father's steps headed to the front door.

But he didn't open it yet. "I'd still like to see Benjy as often as possible, but I'll make sure you're not here."

The door closed, and only Ria heard her mother's broken murmur.

"Oh, Malcolm. Oh, my love."

Ria sat on the top step, frozen by the anguish in her mother's voice, the grief and loss. The finality of this parting.

Betsey hadn't been half harsh enough. Ria had cost her family more than anyone should be forced to bear.

At the sound of her mother's weeping, Ria started toward her, then halted. She was the last person her mother would want to see.

She rose like an old woman and crept back to her room. In the bed, she stared into the darkness and counted the cost of her transgressions as others counted sheep.

The tally was an ugly one, far worse than she had ever understood before. She'd been right when she told Sandor that there would never be forgiveness for her.

Even if her family could someday extend it, she would never be able to do the same for herself.

RIA COULDN'T SLEEP. Every time she closed her eyes, she saw her mother's devastation, her father's sorrow, despite the smiles they'd donned for the children's sake.

She'd tried to tell herself that her mother would have discovered the truth anyway, but unlike she had in her teenage years, Ria found it difficult to lie to herself anymore. Yes, Cleo would know, but perhaps her father would have broken the news in some way that would have eased the blow.

Instead of Ria delivering a dagger straight to her mother's heart.

She shoved back the covers. If she'd ever doubted her part in her parents' breakup, she didn't kid herself now. They still loved each other—it was written all over both of them. Theirs was a love that comes once in a lifetime, a passion few people ever experience.

But she'd been the source of the pressure that had broken them. She'd given them hell for years, and they'd weathered it, bending with the gale-force winds.

But when she'd cost them David, they'd finally snapped.

She could still see his grave, cast in moonlight. Sandor probably thought she was afraid to go nearer, but that wasn't it.

She couldn't go—hadn't earned the right.

Ria looked out toward the street, dark and quiet. She thought about heading to Joe's. It was no solution, but she was desperate to escape her thoughts. But Sandor might be there, and she didn't want to see anyone she knew.

So she considered going for a run. Once, Ria had

loved that better than almost anything in her life. She'd won the races on field day in grade school, outpacing even the boys. In junior high, she'd been the best miler, and her coach had predicted high-school wins and a college scholarship if she'd kept up the good work.

But she hadn't. By high school, she had shed that skin and become someone else.

After Benjy's birth, she had run on the beach or in the parks to get back in shape, rediscovering a place inside herself that had helped her stay strong. And until Dog Boy had gotten too sick to be left alone, she had done five miles almost every day.

On this mournful night, Ria needed the clarity that running brought. With quick movements, she dressed and slipped down the stairs, heading for the front door until she heard the murmur of voices.

Who could be up at this hour? She followed the noise to the den off the kitchen.

Lola had the sound low on the television, her gaze riveted to the screen.

"Lola? Can't sleep?"

Her grandmother turned and smiled, patting the cushions beside her. "The price of old age. But I can rest when I'm dead. Sit with me, doll, and watch my youth."

Ria's brow creased, but she complied, settling on the cushions of the old, comfy sofa. "Were you in this film? I don't remember that."

Lola shook her head. "No, but just look at him." She pointed to an actor Ria didn't recognize, a pleasant but perfectly ordinary man who had never become a star.

"Who is he?"

"Leo Markowitz. The biggest mistake of my life."

Ria cocked her head. "Why do you say that? Did he hurt you?"

"No. I hurt him. That dear, wonderful man wanted to marry me and adopt Cleo, but I knew he would never make it to the top, never get close." Lola turned to her, blue eyes glistening. "Doll, I always aimed for the stars. I had my eye set on bigger sights, and I couldn't see that Leo truly loved me. So I sent him packing, the best thing that ever came my way."

She sighed. "Cleo loved him. He was endlessly patient with her. If we'd had a dozen children, he would never have treated her as anything but his own."

She seemed so sad, so unlike the indomitable, effervescent Lola, that Ria reached out and clasped her grandmother's hand. "You and Mother did all right. She turned out just fine."

Lola shook her head. "If she grew up well, it was none of my doing. I should have provided her a stable home life, a place to grow roots. All she ever wanted was a family and place to call her own. That's why she clung to this house, even when she was alone in it. If I wasn't going to marry Leo and settle down, I should have sent her back to my parents in Kansas. She deserved a lot more than I ever provided her, with all my pipe dreams and endless quests."

Leave Benjy here. He's innocent and he deserves a better life than you've given him.

Betsey's words pounded in Ria's head. She squeezed Lola's hand, a little desperate. "Don't be so hard on yourself, Lola. Mother wouldn't be."

"That's just one more thing I have to live with. I believed I should keep her with me, but the truth is that I was afraid to live without her. Afraid of being alone. Oh, I cloaked my intention in the guise of mother love, but I didn't consider what Cleo needed. I thought too much of myself, and too little about my child."

Do you love him enough to give him the life he deserves?

Was Betsey right? Shaken to her depths, Ria rose. She couldn't listen anymore.

"Where are you going, doll?"

"Out for a run."

"Can't sleep?"

Ria tried for a smile. "Too much excitement tonight."

Lola laughed. "I think I'm about ready to return to bed now, but it was a good day. They had such fun, didn't they? Benjy has really taken to this family like a duck to water, hasn't he?"

Benjy needs family. Oh, Dog Boy, no. I can't.

Her head throbbed. "Yes," she said dully. "He really has."

He'll have plenty of people to love him.

Ria leaned down on shaky legs and kissed her grandmother's cheek, feeling the paper-thin skin that had once glowed with life. "Don't be so hard on yourself, Lola. We all love you, and the past is the past."

"Oh, child," sighed Lola, patting her cheek. "The past is with us forever."

Ria looked away from the love in her grandmother's eyes. No one knew better than she just how true that was.

When she made it to the living room, she stopped. Her focus trailed up the stairs to where her child lay sleeping, then shifted to the front door and back again.

More than anything, she wanted to collapse where she stood. Give up the fight. Let someone else decide what she should do. What was right.

Lola: *I thought I should keep her with me, but the truth is that I was afraid to live without her.*

Her mother: *The child is all that counts, Malcolm.*

Sandor: *Only you can answer the question of where he is better off.*

But she already knew the answer. She was poison, and sooner or later, she would damage the one person she loved more than anything in the world. She wouldn't mean to, but the past two days had been a vivid demonstration of her ability to wreak havoc, regardless. For every step forward, she fell two back.

And she owed her parents a debt she could only repay in one fashion.

By offering them another chance. Another son, as precious as the first.

Rebellion stirred. *I can't. No one can expect that of me.*

But all that counted was what was best for Benjy.

I cloaked it in the guise of mother love. I thought too much of myself and too little about my child.

Resignation balled in her stomach, heavy as granite.

Despair closed over her head like the last wave before drowning.

Then she felt the brush of a lifeline. A tiny voice whispering for her to keep fighting to rise.

Someday you might deserve him.

But it wasn't fair to Benjy to gamble with his life anymore. Not when she'd given no one a reason to believe she'd succeed. She'd tried to be a good mother; she really had.

But the risk of her failure was a price she could not ask him to bear. Another young boy who'd adored her had paid the ultimate toll, and Ria would rather die of loneliness than risk her son.

In a daze, she climbed the stairs and gathered her things, then sat on the edge of the bed and, with trembling fingers, wrote her parents a note.

Halfway through, she faltered. What would they tell him? How could she explain in a way a four-year-old would understand that she was leaving because she loved him more than her own life, that she didn't trust herself or fate to keep him safe?

Ria bent double and choked on the agony of what she was about to do. She couldn't breathe. The pen dropped from her fingers, and she fell to her knees, rocking and keening softly, racked by a pain that clawed at her with merciless talons.

Oh, God. Oh, God. I can't...I...oh, Benjy...

Her throat scoured by acid, her stomach cramping, her eyes blind with despair, somehow Ria got to her feet. For a moment, she considered leaving everything behind and walking away with the nothing that she truly deserved for all the suffering she'd cast into the lives of others.

But that tiny voice called to her, murmuring that there was a chance for her, that somewhere in the far-off, unseen future, maybe she could earn the right to return.

It was that one minuscule seed that sustained her as she walked into the hall. Made her way to Benjy's room, though she didn't know how she would ever find the courage if she saw him again.

At the doorway, she paused and realized that fate had played its hand. Benjy was nestled in his sleeping bag between his two cousins, and Tyrone lay, as usual, at his feet, obstructing any path for Ria to cross without waking all of them.

She attempted to swallow but couldn't. Dull resignation moved through her body as she drank in the sight of her child's face, his mouth curled in a small smile, even in his sleep.

He was happy here, more so than he'd been in a long time, maybe ever.

And safe. Everyone in this house would die to keep him that way.

She had to love him enough to leave.

"Don't miss me too much, sweetheart," she whispered. Her voice caught on a moan, and Benjy stirred.

She clapped one hand over her mouth, torn between sobbing and retching as grief suffocated her.

Blinded by tears, she forced herself to turn away and get out as fast as she could manage.

Leaving her heart behind.

CHAPTER FOURTEEN

SANDOR'S PHONE RANG before sunrise.

It was Cleo, breathless. "Sandor—thank goodness. I'm sorry to disturb you, but have you seen Ria?"

His stomach clenched. "What?"

"She's gone. We can't figure out where else to check." Her voice trembled.

He thought about the bar. The men. "Perhaps she is only late."

"No—she took her things. She left a note."

"Where is Benjy?"

"Still here—" Tears blurred her tone. "She wrote that he was better off without her. Sandor, I'm afraid she—" Cleo swallowed hard "—might hurt herself."

He wished he could set her mind at ease on that score, but all he could think of were the raised, jagged lines over tender blue veins. Her ravaged voice. *He's all I have.*

He paused too long.

"You've seen the scars on her wrists, haven't you? Sandor, I'm terrified for her."

"Have you been in touch with the police?"

"They can't do anything yet. Malcolm is contacting private investigators."

"He is there with you?"

"Yes." For the first time in the conversation, he heard hope. Joy tripping past nerves.

"Do you want me to come?"

"Thank you for asking, but I'll be fine."

And just like that, his place in her life slipped a notch. Regardless of Sandor's disapproval that Malcolm had ever left, he was back, the only man Cleo had ever loved.

Just as well. He himself was the last person who should be with her. He could not dodge his part in Ria's disappearance. Why had he not sought her out instead of waiting?

To avoid getting more deeply involved? Fool. She already has a hold on you.

"Sandor?"

He jerked himself back. "Yes?"

"I said I need to know what happened the other night. Where you found her."

He would give much to avoid telling her. "I am sorry to say that she was at Joe's Place."

"I'm aware that she was drunk. Did she mention anything to you that might help us figure out where she's headed?"

"Cleo, I would rather not—"

She didn't let him finish. "It doesn't matter how unpleasant the news is. We can't afford to overlook anything."

He exhaled. "I understand. This was not the first time I had found her there."

"Go on."

"Both times, she was having difficulties with…patrons."

"Sandor, stop protecting me. Exactly what was happening?"

"I was not sure the woman was her the first time. She was in the parking lot with a man who…" He paused. "I managed to intervene before it went too far, I believe."

"Dear God. What about the other night?"

"Suffice it to say that she brought her troubles upon herself. She was very inebriated and miserable, and she took…risks. I got her out of there immediately."

"And?"

"We argued. I do not like what she does to you, though that night I understood her pain. She had had a fight with Betsey, and Betsey had told her that if she loved her child, she would leave and let you have him. Ria was distraught."

"Dear God." Then muttered conversation. "Hold on." He could hear her relaying his comments to Malcolm and Malcolm's rumbling responses.

Then she returned. "Where could she have gone, Sandor?"

He'd been casting about in his mind for that very answer. Ria had told him so little about herself.

Then it hit him. "You might check David's grave."

"His…grave? But she doesn't—"

"She asked me to take her there, said that she had never seen it because she had been sedated until after the funeral."

"How did she react?"

He would never forget it. "She was terrified. She collapsed before she could make it all the way. I drove her home then." Should he complicate the issue by revealing that he had gone to his place first, much less what had transpired? "But something about her manner made me believe she might return."

"Oh, dear heaven," Cleo muttered. "Sandor, if you think of anything else—the slightest scrap that might help us, please call me."

"Shall I meet you there?"

"I—no. But thank you, Sandor."

He did not argue when she said goodbye and disconnected. Cleo and Malcolm were her parents, after all.

But Cleo's response would not stop him from seeking her out himself. He would find Jerome and alert him, call Hank as soon as the bar opened. Talk to Billie.

He let his head drop. Cursed himself for ever letting her out of his sight when he knew how upset she was.

He would look for her until every avenue was exhausted. But America was such a large country, so easy to get lost in. They might not ever find her.

And he would never forgive himself if they found her too late.

Ria—please. For your child's sake, live. He needs you. Your parents need you.

And he himself? He had no right to anything, not when he could have stopped her if he had not been so determined to avoid entanglement for the sake of his plans.

He headed for his truck, offering silent prayers all the way.

RIA HAD NO IDEA how she made it to the cemetery.

Or why she was there.

Her footsteps left prints in the early-morning dew, every step a little slower than the first. At the gravel path before the old oak tree, she stopped. Inside her chest, sorrow was a hot ache, spreading like poison.

Without Benjy, she couldn't find it in her to care.

At the edge of the grass, yards away, she hunkered down, knees shoved beneath her chin, arms gripping her legs. She swallowed once, hard, her throat tight.

She stared at the simple headstone until her eyes burned. Her head buzzed like a swarm of crazed bees.

I can't do it.

Make your peace. She could hear Dog Boy's voice, just barely.

There is none, my lost friend.

The buzzing became a clamor of twisting metal and screeching tires. Ria rocked from side to side, a wild keen slicing upward like jagged glass.

The profound hush crept in slowly to silence her. The weight of the dead pressed in...the air heavy with hearts broken by grief, loves ended too soon.

At last, in the stillness of early morning, she might

have been turned to stone, except that stone didn't throb like a raw wound. Didn't want to scream.

How could she face him, David?

How could she not? She'd already given up the dearest part of her heart. She was at the end of the jetty, looking out over boiling waves battering the rocks. If she didn't do this, she was finished, dashed to bits against all her failures, the shame of her past. If she ran away from David again, she would disappear even from herself.

And she would never deserve to get her child back.

She yearned to be strong enough, good enough to deserve him and his love. The faint voice of hope said she had to begin somewhere, however doomed the quest seemed.

She would start with this. She rose, but after a short distance, her legs wouldn't hold her, so she crawled. Every inch a mile, every foot a fortress wall. Her nails stained from grass, caked with mud, palms skinned by rocks, tender knees rubbed ruthlessly by the rough wet denim of her jeans. Still she crept forward, dragging air into her lungs to fuel the harsh sobbing of her breath.

But if she stopped, she would run away, and if she ran, she was lost. The last scrap of her worth would survive or die here.

The pale gray monument loomed before her, and Ria froze. But not for long.

At the foot of her brother's grave, Ria halted and tried to breathe. The words blurred, but she knew she would see them to her last days. *The Light Was Beautiful, But It Left Us Too Soon.*

Harsh truth seared what was left of her heart. *Oh, David. Oh, David.* And all the memories began to dance. To taunt.

Bouncing black hair. Too-soft brown eyes. Her shadow, always her shadow, dogging her every step. Loving her, despite everything. Admiring her, though God knows why.

Hey, cool. Yeah, I want to go with you to the party. Really? I can? His voice cracking as it stumbled across the chasm from boy to man.

And then later, not so thrilled. *Ria, I think we should go home. Let me help you outside.* The ferocity of his eyes as he leaped to her defense. *Get off my sister, you creep.* Again the voice cracked, but this time he landed as a man.

She could barely remember the trip home. *You sure you're all right to drive? I could call Dad. You know he'd come.*

Worried eyes. Sweet brown eyes, just like Benjy's.

Love. So much love.

Grief clawed its way through the long-barred door. Violently shaking her head, Ria bent to the stone, her arms stretched out to plead. "I'm sorry— I'm sorry— it should have been me, not you. I want to make it right, but it's too late and I'm so—"

She collapsed over her brother's resting place, digging her fingers into the cool grass. For endless moments, she sobbed out all the years she'd locked him away so she wouldn't have to think, to face what she'd done.

Finally, she fell silent, drained to her bones. Robbed of speech. Of thought.

And in the morning's soft light, a bird hopped up on the marker and began to sing.

The warbled tune reminded her of all the strays David had brought home and tried to heal, his concentration as fierce as his love. She rolled to her side and curled up, her hand pressing into the grass as though her brother could reach up and heal her, too.

When her tears slowed, Ria sifted her fingers over the damp blades, then wiped her wet cheeks with the edge of her palm. Pondered whether she had evened the scales by giving up one child to replace another.

And what she had to live for, now that it was done.

Her gaze caught on the scar threading one wrist.

From somewhere, Sandor's voice emerged. *You have the power to change everything, yet you fall into self-pity, instead.*

Ria sat up. Stared, unseeing. Wondered.

Was that whom she'd become? How long since she'd believed she had any power at all, since she'd done anything but merely survive?

Her shoulders sank. Too long to remember.

Go away, little girl. Run. Hide from growing up.

Damn you, Sandor. I can't do this.

"Oh, David. It's killing me to leave my child. I don't know what to do, where to go. I owe them so much. I hurt everyone so badly, but—"

Just then, she heard a car's motor on the closest road, and for a second, her heart stuttered with hope.

Maybe someone had come after her to tell her that there was no need to go. Her parents, perhaps, or Lola, guessing where she was. Ready with the answers she didn't possess. *You didn't have to leave, honey. We have it all worked out.*

Or Sandor, always so sure of himself and the right path.

But the car belonged to none of them. A woman not much older than her emerged, shoulders bowed with grief, and walked to a fresh, raw grave site nearby.

Ria couldn't talk aloud now to her brother, not when she hadn't a clue what to say. So she took out the small notebook on which she'd written the note to her parents, and she opened a new page.

And began to write:

David, I don't know how to make it up to anyone—Daddy or Mother or Betsey—and I can't bring you back, no matter how I wish I could take your place.

I tried to die once, but a friend saved me. I've thought about doing it again, but then I imagine how they'd feel, losing another one. About the kind of legacy I'd be leaving Benjy.

I have a son, Benjamin David, and he looks so much like you. He's good inside, just the way you were.

So I have to do what's right for him because he'd find out someday if I took the easy way out.

It's bad enough that he'll learn everything I've done anyway. I'm so scared of how he'll feel.

Before he died, my friend Dog Boy made me promise to square things with Mother and Daddy and Betsey. I tried to tell him it wouldn't work, but you can't renege on a deathbed promise. Besides, he saved me when I first ran away, and stuck with me when I got pregnant. If not for him, Benjy wouldn't be alive.

So I came back from California, but I was right and Dog Boy was wrong. Now I'm doing what Lola says she should have done for Mother, what Betsey told me was best for him, even though it feels like dying. I'm offering him a family who can provide the safety and security he deserves. I understand now just what I cost Daddy and Mother when my mistakes took their favorite child. Maybe by giving up mine to them, some of the pain I've brought will be healed.

Maybe someday, I can make something of myself and deserve Benjy again. If I do, I'll come back to see you, I promise.

I never knew why you loved me so much, Davey. I can only hope that wherever you are, you understand that I didn't deserve your love, but it meant everything to me.

Watch over my baby, please. Daddy and Mother and the others already cherish him, but everyone can use a guardian angel.

Ria

Once she finished, the stone lodged in her chest seemed to shrink a bit. She folded the paper, wrote "David" on the outside and tucked the paper under the empty vase in front of his stone.

And in the receptacle she placed the bundle of daisies she'd bought at an all-night grocery. They were her favorite flower, simple and sweet. Deceptively strong.

As she would need to be.

On impulse, she removed one bloom from the bunch.

"Oh, David…wish me luck." She pressed a kiss to her fingertips and transferred it to his stone.

But she would require more than luck to find her way now. She turned and began to walk, wondering, with every step, what to do with herself.

Without the little boy who had, for so long, been her only reason to go on.

BILLIE FACED Sandor on her front porch. "I was afraid of something like this. Her palm told me that a crucial fork in her journey lay not far ahead."

The conviction in her tone dried up any impulse to scoff.

"Her lifeline is faint at this juncture. She may not survive."

Her words sent a shiver down his spine. "I refuse to listen. She is stronger than she thinks. Than anyone knows."

Billie gripped his arm before he could turn. "It is you who will make the difference, Sandor."

He stared. "How? When I cannot even find her?"

Her eyes were sad. "That I can't say."

"What good is it to tell me this? I cannot—" He glared. "I do not believe you."

She shrugged. "That doesn't matter."

"There is no time for this foolishness." Furious, he tore out of her house and raced to his truck. Yanked open the door, then slammed it so hard the cab rocked.

He slapped his palms on the steering wheel as his pulse roared in his ears.

As he himself wanted to roar.

He could not seem to think straight since Cleo's call. Could not stem the fear that crawled up his throat. *Damn you, Ria, why do I care?* She was nothing but trouble, and he had built his new life on careful steps. Cautious plans that were only now beginning to bear fruit.

You can't seriously want to spend your time doing plumbing and painting walls when you are capable of beauty like this.

She did not understand him, nor did he comprehend what motivated her. She was a hurricane in the making, a pot always near boil, a woman who needed too much.

His shoulders sagged. That was unfair.

Ria only craved to be loved.

Believed she did not deserve it.

And understood him too well.

It is not practical, this carving. My efforts are directed toward building a business now.

Beauty doesn't have to be practical. That's not why people buy it.

It was also impractical to fall for Ria Channing.

But, he suspected, too late to change that. With the acknowledgment, the uproar within him departed. Fear took its seat on the bus.

It is you who will make the difference, Sandor.

Jaw set, he backed from the driveway to head for the next stop on his search.

A HUNDRED MILES back down the road she'd traveled so recently, terrified and fighting for hope, all Ria could hear was the echo of Benjy's voice from the backseat.

Pretend you're the princess, Mom, and you call for me to rescue you.

Maybe the princess should rescue the prince, instead.

No, silly. That's not how it works. The prince has to be brave.

You think girls can't be as brave as boys?

Not even a pause. *Well, you can, Mom. You're really brave for a girl.*

She couldn't see the road ahead. Shoved impatiently at the tears blurring her eyes. Was it courage to leave him behind? Or was she making the biggest mistake of her life?

Memories assaulted her. Benjy with her father, playing football, his face glowing with joy.

Laughing with her drenched but happy mother as he demonstrated diving like a whale.

Dancing with Lola. Cuddling with Tyrone.

He'll have plenty of people to love him.

But he doesn't have me—

Metal screamed as her car scraped against a guardrail. Ria grappled with the steering wheel. Fought to regain control. Spun on the pavement—

Shot across the yellow line as a horn blared and tires squealed.

No, I'm not ready. I have too much to—

Gravel flew, and the car fishtailed. A telephone pole loomed.

She gritted her teeth, yanked the wheel and jammed on the brake.

And prayed.

SANDOR DISCONNECTED his cell phone after speaking to the owner of the restaurant he was remodeling. To hope he would find Ria there had been foolish, but he had thought perhaps he would at least locate Jerome and enlist his aid.

He had left a message on the phone at Joe's Place. Now he searched for Jerome.

But his thoughts were consumed with Ria.

Where are you?

And earnest pleas.

Please. Keep her safe. Return her to her son.

But he did not intend to settle for simply that. Sensible or not, impractical as it was, he wanted more.

The first step was to find her. And bring her home.

AFTER THE CACOPHONY of terror, the silence was deafening.

Ria stared at the spot where her car had stopped,

scant inches from the pole. She pried cramped fingers from the steering wheel, only to discover that her hands were shaking too hard to open the door. She gripped them and took one steadying breath, then another. Then one more.

She savored the sweet taste of life after dancing so close to death.

And understood that after six years of wishing she'd been the one to die—

She was choosing to live.

CHAPTER FIFTEEN

HE HAD RUN out of places to search for her. With an oath, Sandor resisted, just barely, the urge to continue the futile loop, regardless. He had a job to complete, a business to build. And Ria Channing was her parents' problem, not his.

And if he repeated that to himself often enough, perhaps he would believe it.

He's all I have. I'm the one who owes a debt that will never go away. I'll wait until my dying day for forgiveness that won't come.

She believed it to her depths. Had seen no hope.

Go on, little girl. Run. Hide from growing up.

Had his been the push that sent her away?

Sandor scanned his surroundings. Cast about in his mind for another locale to try.

A glimpse of his watch told him that it was almost the afternoon window of time at the restaurant. Though his heart was not in it, the work was approaching completion. He had given the owner his assurance that he would finish on schedule, and when he gave his word, he kept it.

Elbow propped on the open window, he leaned his head on one hand and drove.

"WHAT YOU UP TO, boss man?"

Sandor nearly dropped the paintbrush at the sound of Jerome's voice.

He glanced over. "It would appear to be obvious."

"Ooh, like that, is it? I got the big guy p.o.'d?" Jerome strolled across the floor, his tone casual.

But when he stopped, Sandor could tell that the nonchalance was punctured by nerves. He checked the urge to lecture.

"Ria not show again today?" Jerome asked.

Sandor focused very hard on the touch-up. "Ria is gone."

"What you mean gone?"

"It is a simple word." Sandor choked down his frustration. His worry. "She has left town." He had relented and visited Cleo's house. Read the note they had found at David's grave. He was not certain he agreed with their interpretation of it, but the idea that Ria would not harm herself gave Cleo such relief that he would never express his own doubts.

Anyway, her opinion was the more comforting.

"Why you let her go, Sandor? You know you don't want her to."

Sandor's gaze snapped up. "You misunderstand."

Jerome rolled his eyes. "I see what I see. So she and her kid split, huh?"

"The boy is still here." And frightened. Sandor had

spent time playing with Benjy to distract him and give Cleo and Malcolm a break. From the first, the child's sweet nature had won him over.

And made him more determined to bring Benjy's mother back.

"No way." Jerome goggled. "Ria's crazy about that kid. She wouldn't leave him behind."

"There is much you do not know about her situation."

Jerome crossed his arms. "Then why don't you explain it?"

Because I cannot bear to think of my part in it any longer. "I have work to finish. Since you insist on calling your own tune, you may go or stay. It does not matter."

Jerome didn't respond.

Sandor did not look up. What business did he have, interfering in the lives of others? Telling them what was best for them when what he understood most was how to be alone?

But when Jerome picked up the bucket and began gathering trash, some of Sandor's torment subsided. "Have you eaten lunch?"

Jerome's face split in a wide, relieved grin. He had opened his mouth to speak when Sandor's phone rang. He stared at the displayed number with its unfamiliar area code, and despite his intentions, his heartbeat increased. "Hello?"

Only a faint crackling greeted him.

"Hello?" he repeated.

The silence pulsed, too full for a wrong number.

And somehow he was certain. "Ria?"

A tiny gasp.

"Ria, please talk to me. Are you all right?"

A long sigh. "I can't stand not knowing how Benjy is doing."

Sandor closed his eyes in thanksgiving. "He misses you. Everyone is worried. Where are you?" He itched to race out the door after her.

But it might make her run.

"Sandor, be honest." A catch in her voice. "Am I wrong for him? Is he better off without me?"

"No." He cursed himself for ever helping plant that doubt. "Your parents are searching everywhere for you."

"Mother should be thrilled. I gave up my child to replace hers." Her voice faltered. "It nearly killed me to walk away."

"Cleo is frantic with worry. She blames herself that you are gone. Your parents are doing their best to reassure Benjy that you are merely on a trip and will return. He is a brave boy, but he does not understand the sudden departure."

"I couldn't figure out how to explain." Her voice was tight. "God, I'm such a screwup. I want what's best for him."

"He needs you, Ria. As do your parents. Your sister."

And me?

"I'm so tired, Sandor. I—I nearly wrecked my car.

Again." A small laugh, a little hysterical. Then, barely a whisper. "But I didn't, this time. I only saved me, though. Not anyone important like David."

"You are important." Fear clawed up his throat. "Please, Ria. Where are you?"

"Sandor, your intentions are good, but..." A fractured sob. "What do I do? I don't want to run anymore."

"You do not have to. You are not alone."

"I feel that way." Her voice sounded so small. "You didn't like me at first. You still don't, really, but you've been kinder than I deserve. I'm not an easy person to be with."

Before he could formulate an answer, she pressed on. "I don't know why that is, Sandor. I wish I weren't."

"You are not so difficult, only...complicated."

A quick laugh, as if finding humor surprised her. "I think that might qualify as 'damned with faint praise.'"

"I did not mean—"

"It's okay." She was back to sad. "I appreciate that you're honest with me, even when I don't enjoy what I hear."

Would it help or harm her to hear that for the first time in memory, he couldn't keep up with the rapid shift of his emotions? "Ria—"

She cut him off. "But you know what, Sandor? I made an important decision when my car was skidding off the road, about to slam into a pole."

He forced his tone to neutral despite the rapid thump of his pulse. "What was it?"

"Letting go was so tempting. I'd left behind my

only reason to live." She paused. "But I didn't. There I was, finally with a real shot to finish what I started six years ago—only to discover, when it was too late, that I didn't want to die after all. That there still remained a little hope inside me that maybe I could get my act together and be good enough for my child." Her voice caught on a sob. "I was scared, Sandor. It was so close."

"But you survived." Thanksgiving raced through him like a cooling wind. "I am glad, Ria." He pinched the bridge of his nose. "Truly."

"The kick is that I haven't shown any talent for being good. I wouldn't bet on me, so why should anyone else?"

"I would."

He heard her quick inhalation. Then she continued as if he hadn't spoken. "Regardless, there's still the matter of my family. The damage I've caused. My parents were so in love…I can't stand thinking of them apart forever."

Sandor recalled the tenor of Cleo's voice every time she uttered Malcolm's name. "I do not believe love dies so easily."

"But the baby—"

He had not considered it his place to pass along her parents' news, but if it would bring her home, perhaps they would not mind. "That is no longer an issue. Vanessa terminated the pregnancy and moved out, leaving only a note for your father. She is gone for good."

"Oh, no—Daddy must be devastated. Benjy will be more crucial to him than ever."

"Surely you do not imagine that Benjy is more important to either of your parents than the daughter they have loved all these years."

"Maybe Daddy, but not Mother."

"Can you not see that Cleo has been trying to span the gap between you?" When she didn't answer, he went on. "Come home, or tell me where to find you. Your family needs you. Even Betsey is frightened."

"What about you?"

He hesitated. He had much to sort out.

"Never mind. I understand. Goodbye, Sandor."

"Wait—"

But too late. Ria was gone. And he could only wonder if he had helped or hurt the chances that she would return.

SHE STRUGGLED to remember Sandor's advice. His confidence that her mother was so worried she would welcome Ria home.

But all the way back, the confrontation loomed. If she and Cleo were ever to have a future, they could no longer skirt around David's death and its repercussions. They would have to wade through the muck and mire, the angry words and, even more so, the unspoken ones.

So how did you apologize to a woman whose life you'd made hell for years, when *sorry* was puerile and unworthy of the breath required to say it?

What words would ever be enough?

And how about what her mother had done to her?

Don't go there, Ria. She had to focus on smoothing over, not digging up—

But without warning, a fissure in her guilt split open, and long-buried pain spilled out like hot lava.

How could you turn away from me, Mother? I was your child, too. A mother's love should be unconditional.

The slap of tires hitting the side warning line jerked Ria out of the nightmare reverie.

Dear, sweet heaven. What a mess I am.

She realized, in that instant, that she was no more ready to deal with her mother than ever. She gripped the steering wheel and eyed the road for the best spot to make a U-turn and drive away.

No.

The running had to end.

Benjy was entitled to the best future she could provide him, and that did not include spiriting him away from the love that surrounded him here. She was deathly tired, but she had to press on.

Sandor's voice intruded. *I am volunteering to be your friend.*

Friendship might not be all that she was interested in, but the refuge he offered was a powerful lure.

She had to settle herself before she confronted her parents. She couldn't afford a misstep that would throw Benjy's life further into chaos.

Perhaps Sandor could help.

For her child's sake, she would swallow her pride and ask for it.

THE KNOCK BROUGHT Sandor bolting from the bed in which he was not sleeping. He grabbed a pair of jeans and slipped them on, then made his way into the living room. When he peered out of the peephole, his eyes widened. He yanked the door open.

"Hi." Ria, exhausted. Nervous.

He resisted the impulse to reach for her as relief surged through him. Instead, he merely nodded.

"I, uh—" Her hands fidgeted. Then she frowned. "Sorry. I guess I woke you."

"No."

She scanned his bare chest and feet.

He was abruptly conscious of being all but naked.

"Well." She tore her gaze away. "I should…go."

"Do you want to come in?" *Why are you here, Ria?*

She bit her lip. "You need to sleep. You have that job early in the—" Her hands fluttered. "I don't know why I'm…I'll go." She turned.

He snagged her arm.

And registered her trembling.

"Stay," he said, though it could not be a good idea to have her so near when the night was still and intimate. When he was rocked by too powerful an urge to gather her close.

"I'm desperate to be with Benjy, but…it's so late and they're all asleep." Her head was bent, her eyes fixed on the stairs.

"Come inside, Ria. You are exhausted."

"Yeah." But she did not stir.

He gambled that she would not leave, and released

her before he did something unwise. "Have you eaten?"

She shook her head. "I'm not really hungry."

"Then you must rest." He stepped back. "You can take my bed. I will use the sofa."

Still she did not move, staring out into the darkness.

"Ria?"

"Would you—" Her voice was faint. "Sandor, I know I'm a giant pain in the ass, but is it possible that, just for a minute, you would—" she cleared her throat "—hold me?"

If only she realized how badly he wanted to do so.

If he were certain he could stop there.

At last she confronted him, her eyes bleeding pain. "It's not fair to ask, but I'm—" She swallowed. "Scared to death. I don't want to give up Benjy. I'd like to be the mother he deserves. That means I have to face my parents and find some way to begin again, but..." She shrugged. "So much can go wrong. I thought maybe you could help."

He searched too long for a response.

"Never mind. Dumb idea. I'll be fine." She raked fingers through her hair and brushed past him. "I'll use the couch and be out of your way first thing in the—"

He grabbed her elbow. "You misunderstand."

She jerked from his grasp. "No, I didn't." Her eyes snapped. "And on second thought, my car will do just fine."

He planted himself in her path.

They were as close as a breath.

Then her head tilted; her eyes skimmed his body again. Caught. "Ah." She summoned a smile, ancient and weary. "I see. Well, hell, why didn't you say so?" She reached for the hem of her T-shirt and stripped it over her head. "Since neither of us is sleepy, good way to pass time."

She unsnapped her jeans. Her voice was casual, but her eyes screamed despair.

He gripped her hands. "No."

She slapped his away. Slipped two fingers beneath his waistband. "Oh, my. No underwear?" Licked her lips, her smile all bravado. "I'll have to be careful with the zipper, won't I?"

Standing there in a ragged lace bra, she broke his heart.

She sank to her knees and tugged at his snap.

"No." With a roar, he jerked her to her feet. Shook her. "Stop it, Ria."

She managed to slick her nails up his bare chest, then plastered her body to his. "You want me—don't deny it. We've been headed here since the day we met." She slid her fingers into his hair. "Kiss me, Sandor. Or better yet—"

Her lips sealed to his.

He fought for detachment even as his senses registered the soft texture of her skin, the moss-rose fragrance. The taste of her, sweet and ripe as sun-warmed melon. His control frayed.

"Please, Sandor…don't turn me away."

He could withstand the seduction, barely.

But her loneliness was his undoing.

He caught her to him. Abandoned the battle. His mouth grazed down her throat as he bent her over his arm, trailed unsteady fingers to the clasp of her bra. Bared her.

Then, ravenous, feasted.

Ria moaned. Panted as he nipped at her waist. Slicked his tongue over curved bone. Across the crease of her thigh—

She quivered, arched. Whimpered.

He lost it.

Lowered her to the floor, yanked open his fly. Clasped her hips—

And caught the contrast of his big hands on her fragile frame.

He could break her.

In more ways than one.

He swore viciously. Jerked from the brink. Shoved himself backward with his hands. Rose, stumbling like a drunk.

Ria opened stricken eyes. The air stung with thwarted passion, unanswered questions. And hurt.

She rolled to her side with a cry. Curled in a ball.

"Ria, it is not you—"

"Bullshit. You already rejected me once. Just—leave me alone. I feel so stupid. Oh, God, I—"

She fell apart.

There on his floor, naked but for a frayed strap still hanging from one arm, she huddled like some sea creature robbed of its shell. Exposed to the harsh sun and sharp rocks, to the predators who would devour her—

The tender, unguarded line of her nape shattered him.

Like a man gone blind, he groped for a throw on the sofa and covered her. Knelt beside her, shoulders bowed, clumsy as he patted her back.

Which only made her sob harder.

To let the call of her body rush him past good sense was wrong, was it not? “Ria, listen to me. I am trying to be fair to you.”

“Go away.” She yanked the throw over her head, exposing her feet, so slim and pretty. So vulnerable the sight of them made his chest ache.

The time to talk was not now. Feelings were running too high between them, and she would require strength and a clear head to deal with her parents. A small child’s happiness lay in the balance, and this unexpected powder keg between them was a distraction.

What was best for her now was his friendship, nothing more.

If she would still accept it, that is. She tended to slap away what she craved most. At the moment, he was not feeling much more rational, but for her sake, he must be.

So he scooped her up, blanket and all, and rose.

“Let go of me. Where are you…” She struggled in his arms for only a few seconds, then sagged into resignation.

He laid her on his bed gently. Fastened her bra and

covered her once more. Ignored his still-racing pulse and eager body. Bent and kissed her brow. “Sleep.”

Tears glistened. “I don’t get you.”

His lips curved with rue. “That makes two of us.”

She summoned enough energy to glare. “I hope you toss and turn all night.”

“I have no doubt your wish will be granted.”

She rolled over. Rounded her body. “You’re going to regret what you gave up,” she murmured as her eyes drifted shut.

“And you would regret it if I had not,” he whispered.

Then made himself close the door.

CHAPTER SIXTEEN

AS DAWN BEGAN to lighten the sky, Ria stared toward the living room and prayed Sandor was gone. Clutching the round metal knob, she twisted it by minute degrees, tensed for a squeak to betray her.

She should have known nothing in Sandor's world would be allowed to malfunction.

Or if it did, it was dealt with quickly. Repaired, straightened—tucked away, just as she'd been last night.

God, she wished she'd been drunk. Had any sort of haze to obscure her memories of every single, humiliating instant of throwing herself at him—

And being rejected. Again. Worse, put to bed like a child. With a kiss on the forehead, no less.

She hoped he'd been miserable. Surprisingly, she'd never slept better, cocooned in his sheets, lulled to slumber by the scent of him, the knowledge that he was near, watching over her.

Her clothes were neatly folded and stacked on the chest of drawers as if by an impersonal maid. Typical of him. He'd responded to her, damn it. He'd wanted her—at least, his body had.

His mind had not. Nor his formidable will.

The door opened without a sound.

Unfortunately, to the sight of him, asleep on the cramped sofa. He looked different in repose. Not so forbidding or overpowering.

Still gorgeous, though. Her fingers curled at the remembered feel of that hard, beautiful body. Of his touch, brutally restrained.

She'd snapped that control, though, hadn't she? For a few moments there, his discipline had abandoned him completely. She shivered inside at the memory of what had passed between them so briefly.

Then he'd recovered.

And she'd fallen apart.

She must have made a noise, because he stirred just then. She jerked herself from reverie and tiptoed slowly across the floor, barely daring to breathe. She kept her eyes on him until the last second.

Jubilant to escape before he awoke.

Resolved not to think of him again. She had other priorities now.

It was time to go home.

PARKED IN FRONT of her mother's house, Ria wrestled with what to say. How to begin.

It was early. They were probably still sleeping. Maybe she should leave and return later—

No. Her mother was a light sleeper, and she would not have rested much while she was concerned about Benjy. Whatever Ria's disagreements with Cleo, she could never doubt that her mother would set everything else aside to care for her grandson. The importance of family was an article of faith with Cleo Channing.

Seeing everything with new eyes, Ria understood just how great a part she had played in creating the divide between herself and her mother.

All she ever wanted was a family and place to call her own. Lola had pegged it. Nothing had ever been as important. Mother would not have opened the shop if the bomb named Ria hadn't destroyed Cleo's dream.

Now that Ria was a mother herself and had been granted the opportunity to see Cleo through the prism of that experience, shame suffused her. Once she had been Cleo's only child—if but for two years—and she knew how fierce and all-consuming was her own bond with Benjy.

Surely Cleo had loved her as much.

Hold on to that thought. Ria tried to still the rabbit-fast thump of her pulse. She stared at the front door, frozen in place by memory. By Betsey's accusations. Sandor's challenge to Ria to grow up.

Any chance of a future began here.

Or was forever lost.

She took an unsteady breath and grasped the door handle.

Then faltered. Leaned against the headrest.

Why would her mother remember two years of love when they'd been followed by twenty-five of turmoil? By the loss of a child so precious that the one at fault could barely be tolerated?

What would she herself do if she had a Ria in her own life—

And lost Benjy?

Ria buried her face in her hands. *How can she not hate me, Sandor? When I loathe myself?*

"Ria."

She jolted.

The car door opened. "Sweetheart."

Her mother.

Ria bit her lip as tears sprang to her eyes. Jaw clenched, she couldn't quite face her mother yet. The words tumbled out. "I understand why you despise me. You're right to do so. I don't know how to—"

Whatever she meant to say was swallowed up in her mother's embrace. "Oh, honey, you're wrong."

Cleo tightened her arms around her daughter and smoothed her hair, murmuring as she once had to a fretful little girl.

Ria broke down and sobbed. "Oh, God, I'm so sorry, Mother. I never, ever meant for it to happen. I loved David, and I wish it had been me, I swear I do."

"Shh, sweetheart. It's me who should apologize. Can you ever forgive me for being so blind? So selfish?"

Startled, Ria looked up, wondering if she had conjured this from her heart's deepest longings. Her mother's face was pale, her beautiful green eyes dark with misery.

"I was the selfish one. I resented him because he was everything good, and I was everything wrong," Ria said.

Cleo's shoulders bowed. She pressed her hand to her mouth and shook her head. "If I live a hundred years, I will never forgive myself for planting that seed in your mind."

But when she lifted her head, her eyes were fierce. Hot with shame. "You weren't an easy child, but I was the adult. I should have been able to make it right, to ensure that you felt loved."

Ria touched her mother's hand. "Sometimes I did, but I expected too much." She stared at their fingers, so alike, pale and slender. Why had she never noticed all they had in common? "I understand better now. I can't imagine having to divide my love for Benjy with another child. I love him so fiercely. I don't know if I have enough to share."

Her mother's gratitude showed in her eyes. "You'd find it. I felt the same about you, but somehow your heart expands with each one." Her voice cracked. "I always loved you, Ria. I'm sorry I failed to make you feel it." She paused. "Sweetheart, what you tried to do for Benjy—that was remarkable and courageous, but I can't take him."

Ria's breath stalled. "Why not?"

"You're his mother, not me. No one else can substitute."

She wanted to believe it so badly she didn't trust herself. "But what if I can't provide what he needs?"

"You already have. He's wonderful. Special and smart and sweet." Cleo squeezed her daughter's hand. "Stay," she urged. "If you don't want to live with us, please remain in town. We'd like to help you. Let's knit back our family again."

"Mother, I killed your child." A broken moan spilled from her throat. "How can you ever forget that?"

Cleo drew Ria into her arms. "We won't forget, any of us. It happened. We can't change that. But we go on." Cleo stroked her hair as if Ria were still a child. "His death was a tragedy, but it was an accident, Ria. You made a mistake, but so did I, lashing out at you in my pain when I should have been thinking of you. Caring for you. You were there. You...saw. You were screaming silently, craving comfort I could have given—" Her voice went hoarse. "I'll have to live with that forever, understanding what I've cost you."

Ria burrowed against her mother, holding tight as the sobs tore loose inside her chest. Even if her mother forgave her, how would she ever forgive herself? Harsh, acid tears burned her throat.

Then strong arms raised them to standing, enfolded both of them. She lifted her head and saw her father's eyes bright with moisture. "Daddy?" She didn't question why he was here, just grasped her mother tighter and leaned into her father's strength, her stomach churning with anguish. "Oh, Daddy...I hurt you both so much. Betsey, too. I hate myself for it."

"Shh," his deep voice soothed. "No more talk of hate. We've all dealt enough misery for a lifetime. Your mother's right—it's time to forgive and move on."

She lost track of how long they stood together, rocking slowly, letting years' worth of heartache seep away. Her tears scoured her clean, left her empty. She was dizzy, lost without the ballast of her guilt.

"Mom!"

Ria straightened at the sound of the voice she loved most in the world.

Benjy raced across the grass from where Betsey stood on the porch, her stance uncertain.

Ria ran to meet him. Fell to her knees as his arms went around her neck.

"Mom, I missed you. How was your 'cation?"

"Too long. I couldn't stay away. Oh, Benjy, I love you so much."

Her child leaned back. "Of course you do. You're my mom. You don't have to cry about it."

A strangled laugh escaped her, accompanied by her father's chuckle.

"Gramps, my mom is home. Can we show her the trick we taught Tyrone? Wanna see, Mom?"

She tried to get her breath. Steady herself. Slowly, like an old woman, she rose with him in her arms. "I sure do." The feel of him, the indescribable sweetness of his certainty that everything would be all right...

"Aunt Betsey and the girls spent the night, too. She says we can have a slumber party at her house next time. Doesn't that sound great?"

Ria caught her sister's eye over his shoulder and hesitated. "Aunt Betsey might not want to invite me."

Betsey's smile was as unsteady as Ria felt, but with measured steps, she narrowed the gap. "I was thinking—" Betsey clasped her hands together. "It might be an excellent way to get acquainted. Start over."

Ria let out the breath she'd been holding. "I'd like that very much, Bets."

They exchanged watery smiles.

Ria hugged Benjy close as she struggled to adjust to a new world. To hope.

Malcolm brushed at his eyes. He wrapped an arm around Betsey as he bent to kiss Ria's forehead, then traced one finger down Cleo's very red nose.

He cleared his throat. "I'm moving back into the house, and your mother promised to marry me again, once we found you." He cast Ria a glance. "So thanks for not making me wait any longer." The returning glimmer of mischief in his eyes warmed Ria's heart.

"We'd like it if you'd join us, at least until you feel the need for your own place. This old house is going to burst at the seams, but that's what your mother always longed for, to fill every nook and cranny with people she loves."

Benjy whooped. "Could we, Mom? I like it at Nana's."

There was nothing Ria wished for more, but first she turned to her sister. "What about it, Betsey? Are you okay with it?"

A woman who resembled the old Betsey smiled at her. "It's time for us to become a real family once more."

Family, Ria thought. She could belong again. Work to make things right where she'd done so much damage.

A shiver rippled through her, and in its wake, unaccustomed serenity spread. She couldn't quite take it in yet that the darkness was over, that she was free. Peace had a taste that slid sweet over the tongue.

"Sandor told me, but I didn't believe him," she murmured.

"Oh, dear. Sandor." Cleo straightened. "I have to tell him we've found you."

"He already knows."

Her parents exchanged startled glances.

"I, uh, got into town really late." She ducked her head. "I figured everyone was in bed here and—"

Her mother arched one eyebrow but didn't ask her. An awkward silence ensued.

"He would want to hear that everything is okay," Cleo said gently. "Why don't you phone him?"

"No." Ria squirmed. "That is, it would come better from you, unless you mind."

"Of course not, but shouldn't you—" Cleo shook her head and pressed one hand to Ria's cheek. "Sorry. Once a mother, always a mother. It's difficult to quit giving advice."

Ria wondered which one of them was more nervous. Then it hit her that she had the opportunity to steer them in a new direction if she dared. She covered her mother's hand with her own. "Actually, it's kind of nice to have someone care that much."

Cleo's glance was grateful. Her father squeezed her shoulder and smiled his approval.

She is more fragile than you recognize. Sandor's

voice echoed. *You have a second chance...the power to make the future different from the past.*

Did that extend to him? No, forget that. She couldn't imagine facing him again after last night's disaster.

"Come inside, sweetheart," her mother urged. "You must be weary. Let me fix you a good breakfast."

Ria was only too happy to abandon her thoughts. "One of your special breakfasts?"

"Great idea." Malcolm grinned. "We'll celebrate."

"We're having a party, Gramps?"

"We are, honey." Her mother's eyes glowed.

"What for?"

"Because we're a family again."

"That's good, isn't it, Mom?" Benjy turned to Ria for reassurance.

She nodded. "It's the best."

"Come on, sport. Let's show the ladies how manly animal pancakes are done." He lifted a giggling Benjy from her arms, settled him on his shoulders and led them all home.

CHAPTER SEVENTEEN

SANDOR PROWLED his new workshop in Billie's garage that night.

Ria was back for good, Cleo had said. Everyone was thrilled.

She had left without saying goodbye, damn her.

Why would she not, after what transpired? What else was she to understand but that you didn't want her?

He should be happy for all of them. Cleo and Malcolm were reunited. Ria had a home, Benjy had his mother. The suspense was over, the story had a happy ending.

While he had…nothing.

That was wrong. His plans were coming to fruition; just today, he had been contacted by a friend of the restaurant owner about renovating an entire building. Word was spreading that he was a reliable contractor. He had money in the bank, a new work space, a growing reputation—

It was not enough, and the knowledge of it dug into his heart with rusty spurs.

You can't seriously want to spend your time doing plumbing and painting walls when you are capable of beauty like this.

He cursed Ria's disembodied voice and stared at the block of wood on the workbench that stubbornly resisted revealing the shape inside.

She was wrong. Beauty was impractical. He had goals. Plans.

Curse her for making him doubt them.

For not caring enough to call him herself and tell him she was safely home.

Why should she? You never told her how deeply she moves you, how her courage is as powerful as her beauty—and you rejected her when she was at her most vulnerable.

Failure had a bitter flavor. He had been trying to protect her, but instead he had hurt her.

Hell. She must be aware that she was beautiful. It only required a look in the mirror.

You know better. You will have to say it. Show it.

His gaze caught on the wood again, and suddenly, its secrets emerged.

And like a man possessed, he could not pick up his tools fast enough.

RIA LOOKED in on her son one more time, smiling at Tyrone, who lay curled at his feet. She shut the door quietly and moved toward her own room, then decided to go downstairs first and tell her parents good-night.

But at the bottom of the staircase, she halted.

And smiled even as her eyes stung.

Her father and mother danced slowly, without music, not a micron of air between their bodies. How many times had their children rolled their eyes and snickered, certain that Cleo and Malcolm were too old to behave like a couple of besotted teens?

Kids can be so stupid, she thought. We took it for granted, derided it as foolish, had no idea how rare such love is. How exquisite and beautiful.

I want a love like that. Watching them was humbling, comforting…bittersweet and painful.

That devotion was the heart of their home, the foundation of every good thing she and Betsey and David had ever experienced.

Benjy had a right to as much.

But Benjy's mother had no idea how to provide it.

Inexorably, her thoughts turned to Sandor, but she shook them off. Not because he wasn't capable of such devotion.

Just not with her.

She couldn't erase the memory of his powerful body rising over hers, poised to make them one before he—

Oh, God. She wanted to curl up and hide. His rejection stung her.

But one unforgettable image overrode it: Sandor's kiss, full of heat, yes, and hunger, but…more. Because he'd pushed her away, refused to allow her to seduce him to satisfy her craving for oblivion, she'd managed to obliterate everything but the shame of it, when there had been such tenderness.

He'd tucked her into bed. Stepped back, just as he had once before when she'd kissed him.

You need love more than anyone I have ever met, yet

with every breath, every cutting remark, you shove affection away because you believe you do not deserve it, when you are the one standing in the way.

She didn't know what to think now. She'd been miserable and furious. Humiliated.

But now she saw the control he'd had to exert when his body had been primed for her. The way his chest had heaved and he'd been unsteady on his feet as he forced himself to give up what she'd so readily offered.

Because he understood that she'd been doing it for all the wrong reasons.

I will not be with you until you are whole. I am trying to be fair….

So what are you going to do about it? She could almost hear Dog Boy challenging her.

She must have made a sound, because her parents broke apart. Turned.

"Sorry, I, uh—"

Cleo crossed to her. "Are you okay?"

"Fine…I'm…" Her face warmed. "Fine."

"Want to sit and visit?" her father asked.

"No, I'm sorry I interrupted. I just…"

Her mother's cheeks were the ones flaring with color then. But she laughed and cupped one hand on Ria's jaw. "I guess kids are never too grown-up to be embarrassed by their parents."

"No. I'm not embarrassed. I mean, well, it's private, but…" She cleared her throat. "It's beautiful. Most people would give all they have for your kind of love."

"Oh, sweetheart." Her mother's eyes glittered. "You'll find your own." Her voice was fierce. "I want that for you so badly."

"Even if it never happens—" She caught her father's eyes, too. "I'm so glad you two have it and so sorry I—"

"No." Malcolm's tone was firm as he slipped an arm around her shoulders. "No more apologies, Ria. Today is a new beginning—for all of us. If a person likes where he is, he has to accept the road that brought him to that point."

She smiled at him, then at her mother. "Even if the journey was long and rough?"

"Even if." Her mother returned the smile. "You must be so exhausted. Want me to run you a bath? Make you some hot chocolate?"

"Actually—" She bit her lip. "I'd like to borrow the keys to your car, if you don't mind."

To her mother's credit, only a faint unease showed. "I'll get them," she said without further questions.

When Cleo returned, she still didn't pry.

But Ria wanted to answer. "I'm going to see Sandor, but I don't want you to worry that I'll, well—" The memory of her mother's fury, the night he had brought her home, the night when everything unraveled—

"I'm glad." Her mother surprised her. "He was very concerned when you disappeared. He tore the town apart, searching for you."

"He did?"

Her mother nodded.

"I don't know if..." She faltered. "It might be too late to go over. He gets up early, and he..."

Her father squeezed her shoulder. "No man minds being awakened by a beautiful woman."

"I doubt that's how he sees me." She cast a rueful grin. "Though he did say I'm not so much difficult as...complicated. Great compliment, huh?"

Her father laughed and winked at her mother. "Who needs a simple woman when you can have one who drives you crazy?"

Her mother gave him that flirty, smoldering look Ria hadn't seen in too many years to count. And the time-honored words: "You devil."

Then they only had eyes for each other.

Ria bade them good-night as she slipped out.

But she wasn't sure either of them heard a word.

WHEN SHE ARRIVED at Sandor's apartment, lights were on in the garage. She left the car on the street and closed the door softly so that she wouldn't awaken Billie or the neighbors.

As she walked up the driveway, every step seemed as loud as a gong. What was she doing? How would he react? What if he laughed and sent her home?

Oh, give it a rest, Ria. If he does, then so be it. He wasn't the right one. But at a minimum, she owed him gratitude for granting her the courage to come back where she belonged.

Belonged. What a lovely word.

When she reached the open side door, all her other words dried up at the sight of him.

The bright fluorescents were not on. Instead, most of his body stood in the shadows while his powerful forearms and hands were bathed in a golden pool of light.

His hands. Once again, they drew her as they caressed the lines emerging from a new block of rough wood. His fingers were long and strong and graceful, his palms wide, his arms a fascinating play of muscle.

She found it hard to breathe.

When she could tear her gaze loose from his hands, she studied the height and breadth of him, the burnished hair tied at his nape.

Detected the sorrow in umber shadings, the loneliness his strength of will obscured.

And wondered if, after all, she had something of her own to offer him.

So she took a step forward and entered his domain.

SANDOR WHIRLED at the noise.

And stilled, wondering if he was hallucinating.

"Hi," she said, sounding very real. "Am I bothering you?"

Oh, yes. But not the way you think. Aloud, he only said, "No."

"Good." She glanced around, wiping her palms on her jeans. "Last night, I didn't realize you had this all set up—" Appearing to reconsider opening the topic of the previous evening, she stopped.

But he could tell that she was remembering it, too. He had no idea how to begin to discuss it.

She has been through too much in recent days, he reminded himself. So he seized on a diversion. "How is your family?"

She grinned. "My parents were making out in the living room when I left."

"That is good, right?"

She nodded. "Absolutely." Then she chuckled. "Not even mortifying anymore."

"She loves Malcolm deeply."

"He adores her just as much. They never should have spent a single day apart." Her face drained of all but remorse. "If I hadn't—"

But just as he was about to advise her to let it go, she surprised him.

"I'm supposed to stop regretting my actions because they've forgiven me. Except that—" She splayed her hands outward.

"You have not forgiven yourself."

She frowned. "I'm not sure I like how easily you see into me."

A small tilt to her lips gave him hope. "Shall I apologize?"

The tilt widened. "You wouldn't mean it."

How he wanted to smile back, but beneath the humor lay a serious question. "Perhaps it is not so important that you be able to forgive yourself now, only that you begin the process."

"But David's still gone. There is no truly happy ending possible." Her eyes darkened. "And now that things are better, I miss him more than ever. God, I wasted so many good years."

"Keep David in your heart. Honor him by the way you live, and he will go on through you."

"How'd you get to be so wise?" She gnawed at her lower lip as she contemplated his words.

He did not feel very sage. He looked away before he yielded to the impulse to soothe that reddened lip.

"So what about you?"

Startled, he glanced back. "Me?"

She pointed to the wood. "Are you ready to take a few risks yourself?"

He stroked the rough edges.

Her eyes followed the path of his fingers.

Then she locked her gaze on his. Tensed. "Touch me, Sandor."

The image seared straight down his spine. He could not free himself from the grip of her eyes. "You are newly returned. Your emotions have been on a roller coaster."

An impatient shake. "That won't wash anymore. You were protecting me last night, weren't you? But now I'm okay, so what's your excuse this time?" She closed the distance between them and grabbed a fist-ful of his T-shirt. "Or is it you you're worried about?"

She released the fabric and stepped back, her expression accusing. "You told me to stop shoving love aside when I needed it so much. You said I was the only one standing in my way. Well, you were wrong, weren't you? I'm here asking, and it's you who's re-fusing me. Get it over with, then. Tell me you're only interested in being friends." She made an epithet of the word. "Don't pull your punches, Sandor. I may not be as whole as you think I should be, but I'm finding my path to it. If you don't want me, then say so."

Her eyes shone with tears but blazed with defiance. There was nothing of the victim in the woman before him, demanding that he display the same courage.

"I have plans—" he began.

She held herself painfully straight. "Fine. I get it. They don't include me." She whirled to go.

He grabbed her before she could escape. "Let me finish." He tried to turn her, but she resisted.

So he stood behind her and wrapped her close. "Most of my life, I survived by dreaming of a different existence, one where each day would not be filled with starvation and cold and despair that killed the soul. I swore I would find my way out, and when I was tempted to give up, I kept myself going by making plans." He lowered his forehead to her crown, feeling the odd softness of those red-tipped spikes.

"Nothing was in my control then. Even when I was an adult and there were no Soviets to prevent me, there was still loyalty to my grandmother to keep me from the life I wanted.

"Then one day, I was free to leave all of it, and I escaped the instant I could. I came to America to find the land of my father, yes, but also to discover who Sandor Wolfe could be, once he was no longer chained by the past."

She stiffened. "I'm not going to chain you."

He forced her around, though she remained rigid in

his arms. “What I did not realize was that I had only substituted that prison in the Old World for one I created myself.”

At last her eyes rose to his.

“I took a gamble in uprooting to America, yes, but most of my existence has been a battle for safe ground.” He smiled then. “And you insist upon jerking my feet from beneath me at every turn.”

Her lips curved. “That’s my best thing, creating havoc.”

Then she sobered. “You hurt me last night.”

“It was not my intent. I did what was right for you.”

She snorted. “Jerome warned me you always think you know what’s best.”

“Neither of you appears to have any difficulty ignoring me.”

“Maybe you need shaking up.”

“If so, you are the perfect candidate. You are a willful, maddening woman, Ria Channing.” When she would have escaped, he tightened his hold. Caught her chin and tilted her face up. “But I suppose a jailbreak requires upsetting order.” He lowered his head. “And wrecking plans.”

He brushed his lips over hers as she watched him, eyes wide and cautious.

More nervous than she would ever imagine, he trailed his mouth over her jaw, down the smooth white skin of her throat.

Her back arched. Her nails dug into his arm.

Satisfaction washed away nerves. “You asked me to touch you, did you not?”

Her lids fluttered. “Yeah.”

“I am considering a new plan.” His hand slid beneath her shirt.

She moaned softly. “Do we have to talk right now? I can’t think.”

“No problem.” He swept her up in his arms, mounting the stairs two at a time. “I can.”

Her eyes flew open. “Then I’m not doing this properly.” Abruptly, she shifted. Wiggled until she locked her legs around his waist. Gripped his hair and sealed her mouth to his.

After that, everything blurred. Sandor had no idea how he managed to get them both inside without crashing over the railing and breaking their necks.

He made it only to the sofa before they toppled.

Then Ria’s hands were everywhere, stripping his shirt and hers, grappling for the snap on his jeans—

Sandor grabbed her hands. Reversed their positions.

Straddled her as she glared and struggled.

Planted a slow, killing kiss on her mutinous lips.

“You drive me crazy,” she complained when she could get a breath.

“As do you.” He silenced her again the same way.

And emotion swamped him. He pressed his forehead to hers. “Ria, our first time should not be a race.”

“If you stop, it’s going to get ugly,” she warned.

He found that he could still laugh, though he had never experienced a moment that called more for reverence.

“You deserve to be cherished.” He laced their fingers together. Opened to her, held nothing back. “You stir me, Ria. I am unaccustomed to so much emotion. I have kept myself solitary for a long time."

"Why?"

"Because I had—"

"Don't tell me—plans." She grinned. Then she dropped her eyes. "I'm sorry. I shouldn't tease."

He squeezed their palms together. "I am a serious man, yes. I do not take this lightly, nor should you. Look at me, Ria." He didn't continue until she complied. "You have valued yourself too little in the past. I refuse to be a fling. I have resisted involvement for many years without being certain exactly why, but I begin to suspect that I was waiting for a maddening, complicated woman and her beautiful son."

"Benjy? You'd want—"

"He is a wonderful child. Any man would be proud to claim him."

"Of course he is, but—"

"You will not give your heart to anyone who cannot love him, too. I have it in mind that your heart will belong to me one day."

"You have it in mind," she echoed.

"We do not know each other well enough yet, but in time—"

He lost his train of thought when she burst into a blinding smile. He frowned. "What is so humorous?"

"You are an overbearing man, Sandor. In case no one ever said."

He shrugged. "Sometimes a polite request does not do the job."

"And you always complete the task, don't you? Regardless of what it takes."

"I am a thorough man."

One eyebrow arched. "Show me."

He leaned away. "First, you admit that this is more than sex."

She sat up suddenly; unbalanced, they fell to the floor. Lightning quick, she rose over him, then cracked her fingers like a virtuoso ready to play. "Too much talk. Let's get down to business."

"Ria—" He gripped her waist.

She smothered his protest with a blazing kiss. He exerted every bit of discipline he had not to respond.

"Damn it, Sandor." Then she sagged, and he saw both fear and resignation. "You're not going to give in, are you?"

He shook his head. "I will not. For your sake."

"You're tempted, though." She squirmed against the proof.

"I am, but we both deserve more. Trust me, Ria. Trust yourself."

She glanced down at their bodies, both sweating. Straining.

And sighed. "Okay, you win. It's more than sex."

"Thank God." He relaxed for the first time in days. "We both win." He bunched his muscles to reverse their positions.

She was smiling as he took her under.

EPILOGUE

Thanksgiving Day

CLEO'S CHERRY DINING TABLE groaned from the weight of the food. All the leaves had been inserted, and there was still barely enough space to set the places. Thirteen of them, Ria had counted. A far cry from her last Thanksgiving, with only Benjy and a failing Dog Boy to share a pathetic roast chicken.

The centerpiece she and Benjy had designed and executed with Marguerite and Elizabeth had been moved to the sideboard, except for the small paper turkeys they had spent hours decorating to put atop each plate.

"It's beautiful, honey." Cleo wrapped her arm around Ria's waist.

"A real Thanksgiving," Ria said. And sniffled.

Cleo retrieved one of her ever-present tissues from her pocket and tore it in half to share.

"Thanks."

"You're welcome." Each blew her nose.

"You two are going to be basket cases before we ever carve the turkey," Malcolm said, coming up behind them.

"I know. I couldn't be happier." Cleo turned into his embrace, then abruptly leaned back. "You're sweaty—what have you been doing?"

"Basketball. Heal the wounded warrior." He hauled her against him and planted another of the kisses they were forever sharing.

Newlyweds. Ria could only smile.

"Mom!"

She saw Sandor enter with a crowing Benjy on his shoulders. "Mom, me and Sandor slam-dunked Gramps and Elizabeth!"

"I'm thinking of suing Sandor for alienation of affection," Malcolm said.

"Oh, Daddy, you know Benjy loves you, it's just that—"

Malcolm burst out laughing and hugged her. "I'm only kidding, sweetheart. I already have the pleasure of being a father. Let Sandor enjoy it."

They watched as Marguerite climbed his legs and Elizabeth cast adoring glances at him while beside them, Jerome attempted to look bored.

"He's a natural." Betsey approached from Ria's side. "So when are you two going to quit dawdling?"

"Me? I'm not the person with the timetable set in stone. If I had my way, we'd be living together already."

"Mom—" Benjy raced to a halt before her. "Sandor wants you outside."

She glanced around and discovered he was no longer in the room. "Why?"

"It's a surprise. You gotta come." He tugged at her hand.

"But, Benjy, we're nearly ready to eat."

"Go ahead, sweetheart," her mother urged. "We still have a few minutes."

"Thanks, Nana." Benjy practically towed her out the back door, then raced to meet Sandor, who was standing beneath the tree house. "Here she is!" He flung himself at Sandor's legs.

"Thank you." Sandor bent and whispered in Benjy's ear.

Benjy's face split in a huge grin. "Yeah!" He turned and raced back to the house. "See you, Mom!"

"What's going on? Dinner's nearly ready. I need to—"

"Ria."

His face was so grave. "Is something wrong?"

He took her hand, drew her closer. Said nothing.

"Sandor?" What could put such a solemn expression on his face?

"You know you have turned my life upside down."

Her heart stuttered. Here it came. He'd had second thoughts. She was too much trouble.

"You unsettle me, Ria."

"Sandor, please…it's okay. You don't have to explain. Don't worry about it. I understand." She should never have let down her guard. All along, he'd been too good to be true. She'd handle this; there was no choice. Benjy needed her, and things were so much better with her parents and Betsey that—

"Ria."

She realized he was speaking. "What?"

"Slow down that busy head of yours." His smile was a thousand suns. "I am trying to thank you."

She blinked. "But I thought—" She paused. "Thank me for what?"

He drew her closer, the solemnity returning. "I will have my first show in March, all because you challenged me to gamble. A man should be grateful for such good fortune, and I am, but—"

But. She tensed.

"I want more."

"More?" She was still trying to catch up when he astonished her by sinking to one knee.

"Ria, would you do me the honor of becoming my wife?"

"Wife?"

"I do not believe you would qualify to be the husband." His words were teasing, but his eyes were serious, with a hint of nerves.

"You really want to marry me?" She stared at him through a shimmer of tears.

"I do."

She couldn't speak for a moment. "But— What about…" Joy came easier to her these days, but she couldn't say she trusted it wholly yet. "Your plans?" He'd had some invisible timetable worked out, with goals to meet before he could take the next step. She'd been surprised to discover security in his careful pace, after years of upheaval.

Not that she didn't do her part to throw him curves now and again. Her mouth quirked. "So you finally decided that I'm ready?"

"No."

"No?"

"There appears to be an echo out here." He smiled. "You will never be ready to be careful and measured in your steps. You will always add an element of chaos to my life." He drew a small, worn velvet pouch from his pocket. "If I am lucky, that is.

"The decision was more that I was a fool to be waiting when we could be sharing a life." He opened the fragile strings and shook out a slender golden ring into his palm. "This was my mother's wedding ring. It is not impressive, but it is dear to me."

"Oh, Sandor..." She sank down in front of him.

"If you wish for an engagement ring, I would like you to help me choose it." He touched her face. "Will you join your life with mine, Ria? Will you let me love you all my days?"

She studied the man who had given her strength when she was so terrified and alone, who'd helped her find the courage to seek out not only her family's absolution but grant it to herself. Without him, she would never have rejoined the magic circle of her parents' love.

In his eyes, she saw a look she recognized. It was the one that flowed between her father and mother every day.

"I do love you, Ria. I want to devote my life to making certain you feel cherished every second."

You shove affection away because you believe you do not deserve it.

Well, not this time, mister. She would grab tight with both hands and hang on. Give love back in full measure. "Yes, oh, Sandor, yes."

Sandor caught her to him and delivered a bone-melting kiss. Ria's heart soared even as her tears fell.

Not much later, Benjy skidded to a halt beside them. "I waited, Sandor, just like you asked. Did you tell her that I get to be your son? Mom, we can marry Sandor, right? He can be my dad?"

"Wait—you already knew?"

"I did good, didn't I? I kept the secret and everything."

Sandor laughed and released Ria just enough to include her child in their embrace. "You were wonderful. Thank you."

"So can we, Mom? Get married and live with Nana and Gramps and everybody forever and ever?"

"What would you say if we had our own house?" Sandor asked him. "I have an eye on one not far away."

"You do?" Of course he would already be planning the next step.

"If your mother agrees, of course." He winked at Ria.

She laughed.

"Our own place?" Benjy cocked his head. "Does it have a tree house?"

"Not at the moment. I thought perhaps you and I could build one."

"Wow. Like Mom did with Gramps." He turned to her. "Want to help us, Mom?"

"You bet, sweetie."

He was literally bouncing in place. "I gotta tell Gramps and Nana, okay?"

"You bet." She turned to Sandor. "Why am I not surprised you had a house picked out before you even asked me to marry you?"

He had the grace to blush. "Some things do not change so easily. If you do not like what I have found…"

Whatever he would have said was lost when she threw her arms around his neck and kissed him with abandon. His response was immediate and scorching.

At some point, Benjy was sent to retrieve them.

Ria remained plastered to Sandor's side, but he managed to lift Benjy into his arms for the journey into the house.

When at last they entered the dining room, applause and laughter erupted.

"'Bout time, boss man," Jerome said. "You sure don't get in a hurry, do you?"

"Some things are worth waiting for," Billie answered him. They shared the grin of conspirators. The two had formed an inexplicable but powerful bond.

"Everyone take their places, please," Aunt Cammie called out. "Malcolm, will you carry the turkey for me?"

"With pleasure. Excuse me, ladies." But he kissed Cleo before he departed.

Minutes later, they were all settled: Malcolm at one end of the table, ready to carve, Cleo at the other, beaming. Betsey holding hands with Peter, one daughter to each side. Jerome next to Billie, Aunt Cammie beside Lola, Benjy on one side of Sandor while Ria sat on the other.

Wreathed in candlelight, they joined hands while Malcolm gave the blessing.

When Malcolm finished, Sandor rose and lifted his glass. "I know you are hungry for this delicious food, but I would like to propose a toast."

Glasses were lifted.

"To Ria," he said. "Who, by coming home, has created a family."

Ria's jaw dropped. "But—"

His eyes were a warm gold. "For too long, you have believed the worst of yourself." He gestured at those gathered. "But your return reunited your parents, gave Betsey a sister and Benjy grandparents." He drew her to her feet and smiled tenderly. "And brought me more than even my ambitious dreams had dared to imagine. To Ria," he repeated.

"To Ria," they answered, and sipped.

She gazed at them all, this family she had lost and at last regained. "One more toast." She lifted her goblet. "To David." Her voice wobbled. "Much loved and much missed."

"To David," the assembled company chimed in.

More than one set of eyes was wet.

Ria dared a glance at her mother and saw there what

she once believed would never happen: true forgiveness. Sorrow but no bitterness. And love, so much love.

Ria blew a kiss to each of her parents, then rested her head on Sandor's shoulder, stroked her child's hair and conjured up dancing blue eyes and lively red curls.

And smiled through her tears.

Go ahead, Dog Boy. Say I told you so. Thank you for sending me home.

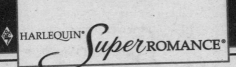

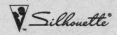